A CAB AT THE DOOR

A Cab at the Door

A MEMOIR
by

V. S. PRITCHETT

VINTAGE BOOKS
A DIVISION OF RANDOM HOUSE
NEW YORK

To Dorothy

A CAB AT THE DOOR

1

In our family, as far as we are concerned, we were born and what happened before that is myth. Go back two generations and the names and lives of our forebears vanish into the common grass. All we could get out of Mother was that her grandfather had once taken a horse to Dublin; and sometimes in my father's expansive histories, *his* grandfather had owned trawlers in Hull, but when an abashed regard for fact, uncommon in my father, touched him in his eighties, he told us that this ancestor, a decayed seaman, was last seen gutting herrings at a bench in the fish market of that city. The only certainty is that I come from a set of storytellers and moralists and that neither party cared much for the precise. The storytellers were forever changing the tale and the moralists tampering with it in order to put it in an edifying light. On my mother's side they were all pagans, and she a rootless London pagan, a fog worshiper, brought up on the folklore of the North London streets; on my father's side they were harsh, lonely, God-ridden sea or country people who had been settled along the Yorkshire coasts or among its moors and fells for hundreds of years. There is enough in the differences between North and South to explain the battles and uncertainties of a lifetime. "How I got into you lot, I don't know," my mother used to say on and off all her life, looking at us with fear, as if my father and not herself had given birth to us. She was there, she conveyed, because she had been captured. It made her unbelieving and sly.

A good many shots must have been fired during the courtship of my parents and many more when I was born in lodgings over a toy shop in the middle of Ipswich at the end of 1900. Why Ipswich? My parents had no connection with the town. The moment could not have been worse. Queen Victoria was dying and my mother, young and cheerful though she was, identified herself, as the decent London poor do, with all the females of the royal family, especially with their pregnancies and funerals. She was a natural Victorian; the past with all its sadness meant more to her than the hopes of the new century. I was to be called Victoria, but now surgery had to be done on the name, and quickly too, for my father's father, a Congregationalist minister in Repton, was pressing for me to be called Marcus Aurelius. The real trouble was more serious.

On my birth certificate my father's trade is written "Stationer (master)." An ambitious young man, he had given up his job as a shop assistant in Kentish Town and had opened a small newsagents and stationers in the Rushmere District of Ipswich. He did not know the city and had gone there because he thought he had a superb "opening." He did not know the trade but he had found "premises"—a word that was sacramental to him all his life. He spoke of "premises" as others speak of the New Jerusalem. He had no capital. He was only twenty-two; the venture was modest, almost pastoral; but he had smelled the Edwardian boom and it enlarged a flaw that had—I have been told—even then become noticeable in his character. One of nature's salesmen, he was even more one of nature's buyers. He looked at the measly little shop, stripped it and put in counters, cabinets and shelves ("You know your father, dear"). The suspicious Suffolk folk hated this modern splash and saw that he had spent so much on fittings that he had nothing left for stock. The bright little shop stood out as a warning to all in a crafty neighborhood. Few customers came. The new paint smelled of sin to them. At the age of twenty-two my young father was affronted and flabbergasted to find after a few months that he was bankrupt, or if not legally bankrupt, penniless and pursued.

There is a picture of him a year or two before this time. He is thin, jaunty, with thick oily black hair, a waxed mustache and eyes caught between a hard, brash stare and a twinkle. He would be quick to take a pencil out and snap down your order. He wears a watch and chain. Not for long: he will soon pawn them—as he had done before—and my mother's engagement ring too, escape from the premises, put her into those rooms over the toy shop. Once I am born, the young Micawber packs us off to his father's manse in Yorkshire, while he goes indignantly back to London to get a "berth." The fact that he has gone bust means nothing to him at all. He goes to the nearest Wesleyan church—for he has already left the Congregationalists—and sings his debts away in a few stentorian hymns. And so I, dressed in silk finery and wrapped in a white shawl, go screaming up to Yorkshire to meet my forebears.

Our journey to the Manse at Repton is miserable. Love in a nice little shop had been—and remained for life—my mother's ideal. Now, though a cheeky cockney girl, she was wretched, frightened and ashamed. ("We never owed a penny; us girls were brought up straight.") She was a slight and tiny fair-haired young woman with a sulky seductive look. In the train a sailor pulled out a jackknife and tossed it about: she called the guard. The sailor said he was only doing it to stop the kid crying.

The arrival at the Manse was awful. My grandmother was confirmed in her opinion—she had given it bluntly and within earshot when my father had first taken my mother there, wearing her London clothes—that her favorite son had been trapped and ruined by a common shopgirl of whom she said: "I lay she's nowt but a London harlot." She said she'd take the baby.

"She tried to snatch you away from me, Vic dear, and said she'd bring you up herself," my mother often told me.

Mary Helen, my father's mother, was a great one for coveting a dress, a brooch, a ring, a bag, even a baby from any woman. As for choice of words—this bonnie little white-haired woman with a smile that glistened sweetly like the icing of one of her fancy cakes, fed her mind on love stories in the religious weeklies and the language of fornication, adultery, harlotry and concubinage taken from the Bible, sharpened by the blunt talk of the Yorkshire villages. Harlots was her general name for the women of her husband's congregations who bought new hats. The old lady assumed that my mother, like any country girl, had come to leave me and would return next day to London to take up her profession again.

In the early years of my boyhood I spent long periods at the Manse. I have little memory of Repton, beyond the large stone pantry smelling of my grandmother's bread and the pans of milk; and of the grating over the cellar where my grandfather used to growl up at me from the damp, saying in his enormous and enjoyable voice: "I'm the grizzly bear."

My grandmother had always lived in small Yorkshire

towns or villages. Her maiden name was Sawdon and she came from a place of that name near the moors inland from Whitby; it is a purely Scandinavian part of England—and she was the youngest, prettiest and most exacting of three daughters of a tailor in Kirbymoorside, in the godly Pickering Valley nearby. My father was born there and spoke of seeing the old man sitting cross-legged and sewing on the table in the window of his shop. Grandma was vain of her clothes and her figure. She usually wore a dark-blue and white spotted dress. She had pale blue eyes deeply inset, a babyish and avid look, and the drooping little mouth of a spoiled child. Her passion for her husband and her two sons was absolute; she thought of nothing else, and me she pampered. With outsiders she was permanently "right vexed" or "disgoosted."

Her "Willyum," my grandfather, was let out of her sight as little as possible. The Minister had the hard Northern vanity also, but it differed from hers. He was a shortish, stout, hard-bellied and muscular man with a strong, frightening face, iron-gray hair and looked like a sergeant major who did not drink. He was a man of authority, with a deep, curt sarcastic voice used to command. When I was a child I had the impression that he was God and the Ten Commandments bound together by his dog collar. He was proud of his life story.

Gradually I learned that he was the youngest son of a fishing family in Hull—his father was a trawler seaman—and that all his brothers had been drowned between Hull and the Dogger Bank. His mother had picked him up and taken him inland to Bradford, away from ships, and had brought him up there in great poverty. He had known what it was to "clem"—to go hungry. He grew up and worked on the roads for a time, then ran off and joined the Army (this would have been in the sixties). And since only the hungry or the riffraff did this, he must have been in a poor way. He chose the Artillery. This led to an event of which he boasted.

There is a strain of truculence and insubordination running through our family: at any moment, all of us, though peaceable enough, are liable to stick our chins out and take our superiors down a peg or two if our pride is touched. We utter a sarcastic jibe, especially at the wrong moment, and are often tempted to cut off our noses to spite our faces, in a manner very satisfying to ourselves and very puzzling to amiable people. My grandfather was kindly enough, but one noticed that at certain moments he would raise one fine eyebrow dangerously, the eyes would widen into a fixed stare, the pupils would go small and look as hard as marbles, and the sharp arc of white would widen above them, as a horse's eye does when it is bolting. This is the moment of cold, flat contradiction, also the moment of wit. And there is a grin at the startled look of the listener.

This must have been the expression on my grandfather's face one day when his battery was stationed outside some seaside place, I believe, on the Mersey. They were at artillery target practice, firing out to sea, and the safety of passing vessels was regulated by a flag signal. It is quite in my grandfather's character that he fired his gun when the flag was up, contrary to orders, and sent what he used to tell me was a "cannon ball" through the mainsail of a passing pleasure yacht. There was a rasp of glee in his voice when he stressed the word "pleasure." He told me this story more than once when I was a child, sitting with him under a plum tree and eying the lovely Victoria plums in his garden at Sedbergh on the Fells—to which he moved after Repton. The yacht, of course, belonged to a rich man who made a fuss and my grandfather was arrested and court-martialed. He was dismissed from the Army. The moral was that you could never get a fair deal from the officer class; he could, he conveyed, have wiped the floor with any of them.

The tale would end with him getting a stick for me—I was about five at the time—and putting me through military drill. We had the movements of "Ready! Present! Fire!" and, more alarming, the "Prepare to Receive Cavalry." Down on one knee I went, in the manner of the first lines of the British squares, with the stick waiting to bayonet the impending charge of Lancers on their horses. He had a loud, resonant voice and, being a fairish actor, could evoke the gallop of horses and clash of swords instantly. The peaceful Minister concealed a very violent man, and religion had made him live well below his physical strength and natural vitality.

He then gave me a Victoria plum and moralized. He pointed out that war was wicked—on wickedness he was an expert—and that to become a soldier was the lowest thing in life, though he was proud of knowing what lowness was. And, he would add, that his wicked younger son—my father's brother —had brought sorrow on them all by running off to be a soldier in turn. The news had turned my grandmother's hair white—"in a night," of course. And, my grandfather said, they had got their savings together and gone off to York to buy the boy out at once for £25. I did not understand, at the time, but this episode was traumatic for them. My grandfather never earned more than £150 a year in his life and when he died all he left was £70 in Co-op tickets, which were kept in a tea caddy on the kitchen mantelpiece. That £25 must have drawn blood.

How and why did my grandfather, uneducated and living by manual labor, become a Congregationalist minister? In the middle of the nineteenth century, and especially in the industrial North where the wealth was made, the pessimism and anarchy of the early industrial times had passed. Even Manchester—the world's byword for poverty and revolutionary class hatred—was becoming respectable. The idea of self-improvement was being dinned into the industrious poor; ambition was put into their heads by the Dissenting churches; religion of this kind became a revolutionary force, for if it countered the political revolutionaries, it put a sense of moral cause into the hands of the ambitious. The teachings of Carlyle—the gospel of work—and later of Ruskin had their effect on hundreds of thousands of men like my grandfather. Snobbery and the Bible are dynamic in English life; respectability or—to be kinder—self-respect is the indispensable engine of British revolution or reform; revolutions occur not in times of poverty but when certain classes are getting just a little better off. As you rose socially so—see the novels of George Eliot—you rose in virtue. There is no doubt also that among Protestants the tendency to break up into sects comes from a nagging desire to be distinctive and superior, spiritually and socially, to one's neighbors.

After he was thrown out of the Army, my grandfather got a job as a bricklayer. It is a chancy and traveling trade and he went from town to town. He did most of his traveling on foot; thirty or forty miles a day was nothing to him. Eventually he appeared in Kirbymoorside. By this time religion must have been strong in him. It sounds as though the court-martial had given him a sense of injustice: he had been in the wrong; all the more reason to reverse the verdict and assert that by the higher law of God's justice he was in the right. The more wrong, the more right, the Old Testament offering its eloquent and ferocious aid.

It was easy to become a preacher in those days; gospel halls and missions were everywhere; the greater the number of sects, the greater the opportunities for argument. Soon he was at it in the evenings, after he had put down the hod. Yet to have got religion would not have been enough. I think that what impelled and gave him a rough distinction was his commanding manner and the knowledge that he had a fine voice.

He was a good singer, he loved the precise utterance of words. He loved language. All we ever knew was that a pious, spinster lady in Kirbymoorside heard him and was impressed by his militant looks, his strength and his voice. She got him off the builder's ladder and arranged for him to be sent to a theological college in Nottingham.

But the flesh—and ambition—were as strong as the spirit in Grandfather. He was courting the tailor's daughter and perhaps as a common workman he would not have got her. So at nineteen or twenty, on his prospects, he married her and went off with her to Nottingham as a student, and in a year was a father. He had only a small grant to live on. He got odd jobs. He told me he learned his Latin, Greek and Hebrew traveling on the Nottingham trams. He saved pennies, for it was part of the arrangement that he should pay back the cost of his education at so much a year in five years. My father had unhappy memories of a hungry childhood, and one of great severity. But once his training was over Grandfather triumphed. At twenty-two—the family legend is—he "filled the Free Trade Hall in Manchester" with his harsh, denouncing sermons.

Why was it, then, that after this success he was to be found in small chapels, first in Bradford and then—getting smaller and smaller—in the little towns of the moors and the Fells? It may have been that all his energy had been spent in getting out of the working class and becoming a middle-class man.

2

Perhaps Granda—as we always called him—was tired of hearing other women decried by his wife in the Manse; he was kind to my mother and liked her good sense and common London ways. She thought him a hard man, too God-fearing for her, but decent.

"I belong to the poor old Church of England, say what you like about it," she used to say to us.

When I was about seven, just before my youngest brother was born, I used to go up to her bedroom in the afternoons at a house we had in Ealing and worry her to let me go and work on the building site opposite our house. I had studied the builders and could tell her exactly how building was done. You dig a trench, you put the bricks in . . . "Go on, Mum. Why can't I? Let me," the perpetual song of small boys.

She told me bits about my grandfather. I stood fidgeting at her dressing table. Once I picked up a hand mirror with a crack in it. "Put that down." She snatched it—she was a fanatical snatcher—and said, "I don't want another seven years bad luck. I've had my troubles. Gran had her troubles too.

> Needles and pins,
> Needles and pins,
> When a man marries
> His trouble begins

Give me that brush."

She was brushing out her long straight hair and she looked like a funny witch with a narrow forehead. I hated—but with fascination—to see her dressing and undressing. Those bloomers! That corset!

She was always talking about her troubles. "Things you don't know about." Then she would laugh and sing a music-hall song:

> "At Trinity Church I met me doom
> Now we live in a top, back room
> Up to me eyes in debt for rent
> That's what he done for me."

"Go on, Mum."

"That's enough. Look at my hair. I can't do anything with it. You have a go, Vic."

So I brushed her hair.

"Your dad fell in love with my hair," she said. "But it's fine, thin; look at it. You can't do anything with it. My poor sister Fanny had such long hair she could sit on hers. So can Ada. Ada's is thick."

"Mum, can't I go out to the builders?"

At this time she did her fair hair on top in a teacake-like shape which was full of hairpins. She had salty, grayish-green eyes ("Green eyes, jealousy," she used to say. "That's me.

I'm a wicked girl"), a longish nose, a talkative, half-sulky mouth not quite straight and quick-tempered elbows, one with a large mole on it. She was lively, sexy and sharp-spoken in the London way and very changeable, moody, and in the long run, not to be trusted.

Mother had grown up in the London jungle, in the needy streets of Kentish Town, Finsbury Park and off the Seven Sisters' Road. Her father came from Bedfordshire. He had been a stableboy and gardener who went up to London to be coachman and gardener to a tea merchant who lived in Highgate. I never saw this grandfather; he died when my mother was a girl. From his picture he was a tall, noble-looking young fellow, with a beard that spread wide over his chest like a fine mist, fond of canaries, dogs, horses and chrysanthemums and tomatoes—said to be fatal to him because they gave him cancer ("It grew all over him like a tree, from those blessed pips"). He was a touchy servant. One day the tea merchant's lady said to her maid, "Put my jewelry away, the window cleaner's coming." Grandfather Martin said to the maid: "Take my watch, too, if there are dishonest people about." This was meant as a reproach to his mistress.

Death walked in and out of the Martin family in dramatic ways. My grandfather drove the carriage to the tea merchant's office to pick him up one evening and found his employer dead at his desk. He carried the body out to the carriage, propped it in a respectable attitude inside, and drove him home to his wife. Soon after, Grandfather died too.

The Martins were left without a penny. Gran, his widow, had been a pert little barmaid in an Oxford public house— she had relations in the fish business in Uxbridge—and now she was left with three daughters in North London. There was Fanny, the eldest and laughing girl, the "cure"; she was so funny as to be "chronic." There was Ada, funny, coquettish, but more genteel. These two girls were apprenticed to a well-known shop called Spiers and Pond when they were fourteen.

My mother, the youngest and the pet, was to be kept at home to work in the house, for Gran had taken in lodgers.

Fanny sickened; she was a gay consumptive. There was a cab rank opposite their house and Fanny trained the parrot to say "Walk up, walk up," at which the dozing cabbies would wake up, whip up their horses, because they thought the leading cab had been hired. Fanny, who read *Little Meg's Children* and *East Lynne* to her sisters, making them weep voluptuously, herself became a fading Victorian heroine. She died, saying as her last word, "Oh! Illuminations." She had entered heaven.

Ada worked in the china department at Spiers and Pond and eventually married another "cure," a young man called Frank Tilly who was in gents' tailoring at a shop called Daniels in Kentish Town. He had the waxen look of the young Chatterton and waving long dark hair. "Poor Frank" was a consumptive too; he married Ada and before the year was out he died. They had emigrated to South Africa, he collapsed in Cape Town, they took the next ship back, and he died at sea in the middle of "the worst storm for forty years." The Union Jack floated over his body at the burial, while Ada prayed in the storm, saying, "Oh God, let the ship go down." She was pregnant.

So Gran had seen three deaths and poverty too in a few years. Her relations helped her—the fishmonger at Uxbridge; Louie, her cousin, a poor dressmaker, a skeleton figure out of a Gissing novel; Cousin Emmy, a lady's maid; brother Gil, who whipped up the fish cart. Gran's grief had made her a savage little figure, terrifying to be with, for she had a prickly, bearded chin, and the sour smells of stout, port, cheese and onions were on her breath. She would sit in her bonnet, with the veil that covered her face raised to her wicked red nose, swallowing her quart of stout, and the crumbs of the bread catching on to her veil. She looked like a damp and injured beetle. Her temper was violent, for her knuckles were swollen with gout and rheumatism—she was embattled in pain. Worse was to happen to her in the end, years later, for Ada's gay little girl, Hilda Tilly, was to grow up and die also of consumption in her twenties.

But Gran had one fantastic stroke of luck and, in fact, it was a good deal responsible for my existence. One morning she traipsed off, grousing to herself as usual, to the butcher's. "I've got something for you, Mrs. Martin," said the butcher, pulling out a piece of bloodstained newspaper. It contained the Missing Money column. There the lawyers appealed for the relatives of a Mr. Hawes. Sure enough, it was Gran's brother who had died in Australia and Gran inherited a small sum of money. She was able to buy a house in Medina Road and take more lodgers. One of them was an actor, the other a young man who had lately become shopwalker in Daniels. He was to be my father.

It struck me a few years ago that I was born into a family of pets and favorites. Grandfather Pritchett, a youngest son, a pet, saved from the sea; Grandma Pritchett, the youngest, pet daughter of the tailor; Father, a pet also, for his brother showed early signs of being a distress; and Mother, the youngest pet of her sad family. It was ominous.

For at the age of seventeen, three years later than her sisters, my mother was sent as an apprentice to work in this large draper's shop. At Daniels, Mother was put into the millinery and there my father saw her. He saw her fair hair. She looked—he told me—like a goddess in her mutton-chop sleeves and so desirable with her tiny waist. ("Eighteen inches," she would put in.) She was so quick with the customers, he said, so clever with trimmings! She could put an ugly hat on a grumbling woman, give a twist, snatch a feather or a bunch of cherries and so dazzle the customer with chatter and her smiles.

As for my father, Mother was astonished by him.

"He was so clean, dear. You never saw anything so clean."

The poorly paid shop assistant fed in the basement, slept in the attics and went out to get drunk when the shop closed.

"Eight to eight, weekdays, eleven o'clock Saturday nights," Mother would say. "Old Daniels was a beast."

They worked in the cold drafts and the poisonous, head-aching smell of gaslight.

"He was high up in Masonry and a Wesleyan," my father would say, correcting my mother's temper.

"So clean," my mother would go on, "and so particular about his clothes—you know your father. Always the silk hat and spats. Countryfied though. I could tell that. Rosy cheeks. He might have got some bad girl if he hadn't had me."

She was in awe of him; he kept his nails perfect and there was a pleasant smell of Pears soap and cachous about him and his teeth were white. He cleaned them—as his mother did—with soot or salt.

At this period my father—who was eventually to become very fat indeed, going up to 252 pounds in his time—was a slender young man. He looked grave, his fine brown eyes seemed to burn, and he could change from the effusive to the canny hard look of the brisk young Yorkshireman out for the "brass." But there was sometimes a hollow-eyed and haunted look on his face. The fact is—and this is what he told my dumbstruck mother when they talked together—he had had a wretched childhood. My grandfather, so benevolent to me, had been a harsh, indeed a savage, father.

I had seen the Minister in his easy country days, idling with his small congregations of country folk, talking of Carlyle and Ruskin and English history. My father had known him as the disciplinarian not long out of the Army, living from hand to mouth in industrial towns, sending his children off to school hungry. They were forbidden to sit down at meals: it would make them soft. He made them stand rigid at the table in silence while they ate their food. His sons were in barracks.

My father and his brother were not allowed out of the house after six in the evening, not even when they were grown up. What schools they went to was never made clear to me by my father. He evaded the subject, either out of shame or because he hated being definite about anything. I know he had a French lesson, for he had learned by heart the phrase "*Trois hommes voyageaient en France.*" Education was expensive and my grandfather, who used to talk at large about the beauties of education, seems to have been able to give little to his two sons. He lived—as my father was to do—in a dream.

At fourteen my father had gone to work as a grocer's errandboy and then worked behind the counter. At sixteen or so, he seems to have had an interesting friendship with a young doctor in the village. This—in view of what I shall tell later about my father—was important. The boy was eager to become a doctor or surgeon, which would have been far beyond my grandfather's means. One evening he went to the doctor's surgery and watched him dress a man's poisoned thumb. The sight of pus and blood was too much: my father fainted. This led to delay in getting home. He arrived there after dark, just before eight in the evening, to find my grandfather waiting with a carriage whip in his hand. Whipping was common in the family, but now my father was nearly a man. My grandfather roared at him for disobeying orders, accused him of drinking or going after women—a scene which was to be reenacted by Father in his turn and for similar reasons, when my brother Cyril and I were in our late teens—and when Father answered back he was struck across the face and the back by the whip, two or three hard blows. That was enough: hatred had been growing for years. Father went up to his room and in the middle of the night climbed out of his bedroom window, hid in the railway station and went off to York next morning to stay with an uncle. Then he went to London. He had a cousin, Sawdon, in the rag trade: after short jobs in the drapery, Father arrived in glory in Kentish Town.

"I could tell," said my mother, feeling sorry for him as well as being in awe, "he had never met a girl before. And his mother standing there doing nothing, seeing her son horse-whipped—I could have limbed the old . . ."

Mother was an expert in leaving her sentences unfinished.

Daniels was a Wellsian establishment. It was a good "crib," or berth, and the workers were scared of losing it. From Mother's account of it, it was the leading humorous establishment in North London. "What us girls used to get up to. The nerve we had, dodging across the street, under the horses' heads, playing tricks on your poor father—he looked so stuck up till you got to know him—putting flypapers on old Daniels' chair . . . Oh, I was a young limb. One day I tipped a whole pile of hatboxes, the white cardboard ones, dear, on top of your dad. Us girls were always giggling round corners. Frank"—this was Ada's young man—"was a cruel mimic. Everything was in farthings in those days and poor Mr. Thomas could not pronounce his *th*'s. Frank used to go up to him and say, large as life, 'What's the price of this, Mr. Thomas? Frupence free farvings?' and old Thomas would go wild and say, 'I'll frupence free farvings you with a fump.' "

My mother's laugh was always near hysteria. She would sit on her chair by the fire with a long skirt pulled up over her knees to the elastic of her gray bloomers and rock back and forth as she talked. And when she came to the comic point she would spread her excited fingers over her face and stare through the gaps at us and go into fits until her untidy hair started to come down.

Frank's other gift was to say peoples' names backwards. This kept the shop "rocking." Ecirtaeb Nitram was my mother's name. My father's, which was difficult, became Retlaw Tetchirp.

"Dad didn't like it, you know he's proud."

Father was certainly easily offended. He soon told her something that alarmed her: he was not going to stay at Daniels at the end of the year. "My name's Walker," he said. He was going out "on the road." He was going to get a job with a "good comm. and A-one expenses." Mother cunningly persuaded him to come and lodge at her mother's house: he noticed that she was a flirt and playing him up with one of the other assistants, so he moved so as to keep possession of her.

He had a shock when he met Gran. There had been no drink at the Manse. At Medina Road someone was always going round to the off-license. And Gran was not very clean. She could not cook as well as his mother and he complained that London water was hard and did not get the dirt out of the pores of one's skin. He sent his shirts and underclothes back to Yorkshire to be washed and starched or ironed by his mother. Whatever you liked to say about his relations in Yorkshire, he pointed out, they were not servants, they didn't kowtow; they didn't keep pubs and they were all out to improve their position. The Martins were stagnant, and like all Southerners, they were all servile smiles and lies to your face. When he was in a rage with Mother in the years to come, I am sorry to say that he would shout: "I raised you from the gutter," and, with a glance of appeal to us, would say, "You can't make a silk purse out of a sow's ear."

These insults were no more than Yorkshire plain-speaking. All his relatives talked cheerfully like this to one another. As a cockney, Mother had a tongue too. She would mock Father's piety with phrases like "two-faced Wesleyans" and "Hallelujah, keep your hands off."

Gran Martin, of course, hated Father. She called him only by his surname for years. Father did not hide his feeling that the Martin family needed cleaning up. Morally, in particular; for he was soon taking my mother on Sundays to hear the famous preachers at the City Temple. Spurgeon and others.

He loved their dramatic manner. One of these preachers told how, when he was coming into the City Temple that morning, he heard two young sparks debating whether or not to go in. "Damn it, what odds," said one and went in. My father admired this remark. He quoted it for years. He wanted religion to smarten up and get snappy. He liked the evangelical singing and sang well, for he had been trained in one of the excellent Yorkshire choirs. But he sang mainly hymns, his favorite being "Tell Me the Old, Old Story," which came so richly from him that it brought us nearly to tears when we were young. He knew how much preachers were paid. "Big men," he would say. He liked "big men." It was the age when the Victorian Grand Old Man or Great Men were beginning to be succeeded by the Big, like Selfridge and the new race of great shopkeepers in London, Manchester and Chicago. He did not really distinguish between the big shopkeepers and the popular Nonconformist preachers, who had also broken with the theology of the Victorian age: for suddenly money was about, commerce was expanding, there was a chance for the lower middle class. They would have a slice of the money the middles had sat so obdurately on for so long. The difference between "goods" and "the good" was fading. My father took to smoking cigars, and my mother, hunching her pretty shoulders a little before his self-confident ambition, also sparkled and admired. He always ended by saying how hungry he was. Oysters—a poor man's food in those days—were pretty cheap. My father's later size was due to early hunger. He ate to make up for the craving of his childhood. He became cheerfully gluttonous. He talked for hours about food as much as he did about religion. Sixty years later when he died, his last coherent words were, "That woman meant well but she did not give me enough to eat." He was speaking of his landlady. It was untrue. The hunger of his boyhood grew and grew as he neared death.

Beatrice Martin's idea of pleasure was Hampstead Heath

Fair and the music halls. My father could not stand a dirty joke; and he mildly complained that in any music hall she was the first in the audience to see the joke and give her hysterical laugh, so that voices from the gallery shouted admiringly at her and egged her on.

So my father and mother courted in Finsbury Park and Parliament Hill, went boating out on the Thames, rioted with the mob on Mafeking Night, he carrying her on his shoulder round Trafalgar Square while she waved a Union Jack. He walked out, as he had promised, from Daniels and got another berth; then the Minister married them and they set off for Ipswich and bankruptcy, where Gran and Mother's sister Ada, lately widowed, appeared too. The battle between North and South was on.

Such was the family I was born into. There was this cock-sparrow, my father, now a commercial traveler, dressy and expansive with optimism, walking in and out of jobs with the bumptiousness of a god. And there was our sulky, moody mother, either laughing or in tears, playing "The Maiden's Prayer" on the piano—she could "cross hands" too—and also "The Mocking Bird," which was closer to her nature. She would sink into mournful tales of illnesses and funerals, brood on railway accidents and ships lost at sea. She loved a short cry, easily went pink on her cheekbones with jealousy or flew out into a fishwife's temper. She was a hard-working woman.

We were in a small villa of damp red brick in Woodford. I had a brother now, Cyril, eighteen months younger than

myself. My parents' bedroom contained a large lithograph
called "Wedded." A Roman-looking couple are walking
languorously along a city wall. The man had strong hairy
legs and, I believe, wore a tigerskin. I confused him with my
hairy father. In the twenties I met an Italian who had sat for
the legs of this figure, one more blow to my sense of the
uniqueness of our family. There was another lithograph
called "The Soul's Awakening," a girl with her nightgown
falling off in the wind as she was swept up to heaven. On the
washstand there was yellow chinaware which had a pattern
of Dutch girls and boys. Hidden behind the chamber pot in
the cupboard was a small copy of Aristotle's "masterpiece"
on gynecology, with startling pictures of the moronic fetus
in the womb. In another cupboard were my father's leather
top-hat boxes; already he was buying clothes for himself in
notable quantities. There were "words" if Mother had not
washed and ironed his underclothes or starched his cuffs and
collars as well as his mother had done.

In the small dining room there was red and blue linoleum
of floral pattern. There was a small palm in a pot. There were
ornaments with mottoes on them: "Dinna trouble trouble till
trouble troubles you," and "Don't Worry It May Never Happen." Also a picture which gave me my first lesson in the
"who" and "whom" difficulty. Two old men in red robes, with
their backs to each other, but looking with ancient grumpi-
ness over their shoulders, held an antique parchment in their
hands on which the following words were printed:

> In Men Whom Men Condemn as Ill
> I find so much of goodness still,
> In Men whom Men pronounce divine
> I find so much of sin and blot
> I hesitate to draw the line
> Between the two where God has not.

This poem was often bandied about and pointed at when
Granda Pritchett came down to London and denounced my

father's latest religion, for Father was continually going one better in the matter of faith. The other picture simply showed an envelope on which was written:

Messrs. Sell and Repent,
Prosperous Place,
The Earth.

This was the spirit of the early 1900's. Things, as Father said, were beginning to hum.

My parents rarely stayed in one house for as long as a year. After Woodford there is a dash to Derby where Father hoped to do well with a Canadian insurance company, and where, in North Country fashion, we had a pump beside the sink; in a month or so we are back. We had various London addresses: Woodford again, Palmers Green, Balham, Uxbridge, Acton, Ealing, Hammersmith, Camberwell are some of them; then back to Ipswich again, on to Dulwich and Bromley. By the time I was twelve, Mother was saying we had moved fourteen times and Father went fat in the face with offense and said she exaggerated. At this, she counted up on her fingers and said she now made it eighteen. We moved mainly to small red brick villas, the rents running from nine shillings and even to twelve shillings a week, once or twice to poor flats.

It seemed to us that Father had genius. By the time there were four children—three boys and a girl—Father seemed as sumptuous as a millionaire and my mother was worn down. It was like a marriage of the rich and the poor. She cooked, cleaned, made our clothes and her own, rarely had the money to pay for a girl to help her and went about a lot of the day with a coarse apron on, her blouse undone and her hair down her back. Patently genius was lacking in her. For it was he who came home in the evenings or at weekends from places like Glasgow, Bournemouth or Torquay, having stayed in hotels with names like Queens, Royal or Majestic, palaces of luxury. We learned to wait at the door and to open it for him when he came home, because he was affronted if he had to let himself in with his own key. We would often wait for an hour. When he got in he walked into the front room where we ate, sat down in an armchair, and without a word, put out his foot. Mother's duty was to kneel and unbutton his boots (until laced boots came in, when she unlaced them); eventually we squabbled for this honor. "Ease the sock," Father would say with regal self-pity. And he would tell her about the orders he had taken that week. His little order books were full of neat figures and smelled warmly of scent.

And then—the magic of the man!—without warning we would, as I say, get up one morning to find my mother in her fawn raincoat (her only coat) and hat, ourselves being pulled into coats too. A cabby and his horse would be coughing together outside the house and the next thing we knew we were driving to an underground station and to a new house in a new part of London, to the smell of new paint, new mice dirts, new cupboards, and to race out into a new garden to see if there were any trees and start in our fashion to wreck the garden and make it the byword of the neighborhood. The aggravating thing was that my mother was always crying in the cabs we took; and then my father would begin to sing in his moving bass voice:

> "*Oh dry those tears*
> *Oh calm those fears*
> *Life will be brighter tomorrow.*"

Or, if he was exasperated with her, it would be:

> "*Tell me the old, old story*
> *For I forget so soon.*"

I look back on these early years and chiefly remember how crowded and dark these houses were and that, after Uxbridge, there is always a nasty smell, generally of sour breadcrumbs at the edges of the seats of chairs, the disgusting smell of young children after my sister and youngest brother were born. And there was the continual talk of rudeness. It was rooted in our very name, for we soon learned that Pritchett was the same as Breeches for other children; one polite little boy called my mother Mrs. Trousers because he had gathered that "breeches" was rude. Mother—and especially her mother, Gran—were the sources of a mysterious prurience. Gran liked chamber-pot humor and was almost reverent about po's, mentioning that Aunt Short said that the best thing for the complexion was to wash one's face in "it"—and good for rheumatism too. The bottom was the most rude thing we had, and in consequence, the Double U. Rudeness became almost mystical if we caught Gran on the Double U when she left the door unlocked. Girls were rude because of their drawers; women, because of their long skirts, and more rude than men because they had so much more to cover. To crawl under a table and lift the hem of a skirt was convulsingly rude. At certain times Mother and Father were rude— not when she was in bed and her astonishing titty-bottles slipped out of her nightdress, like a pair of follies—but when she and Father went for a walk together and we walked behind them. We felt that it was rude to see a marriage walking about in front of the neighbors. Granda and Grandma Pritchett were never rude; Mother was rude in herself—she wore "bloomers" and often "showed" them—but Father, on his own, never. I was ashamed for years of a photograph of us children. The corner of my sister's silk dress had lodged on my knee as I sat next to her. *I* was rude.

One thing became noticeable in our removals. Very often my father and mother went to different destinations—she to the new house while my father and I would find ourselves at Euston Station in the middle of the night. I was off by the midnight train to my grandfather's in Repton and later to Sedbergh, to be away in the North for weeks or even months. My brother Cyril, it seemed, was off to Ipswich to stay with my mother's sister Ada. My sister and baby brother were at home. At one time I found myself sitting on the carrier of my father's bicycle traveling from Nottingham to Derby. Another time I remember traveling in a hansom to Paddington Station and yet again standing one winter's morning beside the driver of a horse tram going via Tower Bridge on a roundabout journey to King's Cross. So began my love of change, journeys and new places. As many London children do, I skillfully lost myself in the streets and was twice picked up by the police.

Most of these journeys which my father thoughtfully provided were, as I say, to the North. Repton I scarcely remember; but to Sedbergh, Kirbymoorside and Appleton-le-Moors I went again and again. We would get out of the night train, my father and I, at a junction near Kendal, at the gateway through the mountains to the Scottish border, cross the lines and take the little train to Sedbergh, that neat town of gray stone lying under the bald mountain I thought was called the Berg. The horse brake would take us up the main street, following a herd of cows. By the Manse and chapel, Granda was waiting. In the distance, on her whitened doorstep and close to a monkey-puzzle tree, stood Grandma in her starched white apron, her little pale iced-cake face and her glasses glittering. I remember an arrival when I was six. My grandmother would not let me into her clean house until she looked me over.

"Eeh Walter, for shame, t'lad's buttons are off his jersey, his breeches have a hole in them. I'm raight vexed with your Beatie, letting a son of her's come up with his stockings in holes and his shoes worn through. Eeh, he looks nowt but a poor little gutterboy. For shame, Walter. For shame, Victor. I lay you've been playing in the London muck. I dassn't show you to the neighbors. Nay, look at his breeches, Willyum."

"Mother made them." I stuck up for Mother, not for her sake but because of the astonishing material she used—

curtains from our house. Nothing covering a window, a table or a sofa was safe from my mother's scissors when the sewing fit was on her. "I'll get those old curtains down." She was an impatient woman.

My grandmother took me inside, undressed me in the hall and held the breeches up and looked at them. "Eeh Willyum, come here. They're not stitched. They're just tacked. T'lad'll be naked in t'street."

It was true. Mother's slapdash tacking often let us down.

On these visits, the Minister would be having a sarcastic argument with his son about the particular God of the moment, for Father had left the Congregationalists, the Baptists, the Wesleyans, the Methodists in turn, being less and less of a Jehovah man and pushing his way—it turned out—towards the Infinite. He was emerging from that pessimism which ate at his Victorian elders.

The afternoon bus came and he went. Up the back step of the station brake he skipped, to pick up a couple of hampers of traveler's samples in Manchester. I was glad to be rid of the family and scarcely thought of my mother or my brothers and sister for weeks. Here was what I was made for: new clothes, new shirts, new places, the new life, jam tarts, eccles cakes, seedcakes, apple puffs and Yorkshire pudding. My grandparents looked at each other and then at me with concern for my character. I did not know that almost every time we moved house Father had lost his job or was swinging dangerously between an old disaster and a new enterprise, that he was being pursued by people to whom he owed money, that furniture had "gone back" or new unpaid-for furniture had "come in." I did not know that my mother wept because of this, even as she slyly concealed, clenched in her fingers, a half sovereign that some kind neighbor had given her. And I remember now how many times, when my father left in the morning for his work, she barred his way at the door or screamed at him from the gate, "Walt, Walt, where's my money?" But I did see that here in Sedbergh there was domestic peace.

It is a small old town smelling of sheep and cows, with a pretty trout beck running through it under wooded banks. The Fells—cropped close by sheep, smelling of thyme and on sunny days played on by the shadows of the clouds—rise steeply behind the town, and from the top of them one sees the austere system of these lonely mountains running westward to the pikes of the Lake District and north to the border. One is almost in Westmorland and, not far off, one sees the sheepwalks of Scott's *The Two Drovers,* the shepherd's road to Scotland. The climate is wet and cold in winter; the town is not much sheltered and day after day there will be a light, fine drizzle blowing over from Westmorland and the Irish Sea. When it begins people say "Ay, it's dampening on." These people are dour but kindly.

Yorkshire is the most loved of all the many places of my childhood. I was sent to my first school, the village school at the top of the town, up the lane from the Manse garden—it is just as it was when I was a child sixty years ago. The school sat in two classes, and I suppose each class had about forty or fifty boys and girls, the girls in pinafores and long black or tan stockings. Douthwaite, Louthwaite, Thistlethwaite, Braithwaite, Branthwaite were the common surnames. The children spoke a dialect that was hard to understand. They came from farms and cottages, both sexes brisk and strenuous. We sat in three tiers in the classroom, the upper one for bigger children. While I was doing pothooks and capital *D*'s from a script, the others were taught sums. Being a London child with a strange accent I began to swank, particularly to the girls. One who sat with me in the front row offered to show me her belly if I lowered my own breeches. I did so, being anxious to show her my speciality—a blind navel, for the cord had been so cut that my navel was closed. In her opinion—and that of others—this was "wrong" and foretold an early death because no air could get inside me. This distinction made me swank more. She did not keep her part of the bargain; neither did any of the other girls in Sedbergh. She put up her hand and told teacher. This was the first of many painful lessons, for I instantly loved girls.

This incident was reported to the Manse. Also a scuffle or two in the schoolyard, being caught peeing over a wall to see how far we could go, with a lot of village lads, and a small burglary I got into with a village boy who persuaded me to slip into an old woman's cottage and steal some Halma pieces from her desk. My grandfather, waiting to catch me naked in the bathtub, gave me a spanking that stung for hours. I screamed at him and said that I hoped he would be run over by the London express at the level-crossing the next time he crossed the line at the junction. More spanking. I was removed from the school because the neighbors were talking. I was surprised, for I was a pious little boy, packed with the Ten Commandments and spotless on Sundays: the farmers' boys, the blacksmiths' sons and all the old wheelwrights, tree fellers, shepherds thought I was a townee and a softie. I would never be able to herd sheep, shoe or ride a horse, use a pickax or even work in a woolen mill. My secret was that I was going to be a preacher like my grandfather; he had begun teaching me Latin, pointing out the Latin words on a penny —*fidei defensor*. I was to be defender (with spears and guns if necessary) of the faith, "prepared to receive cavalry." For years I thought this and Calvary were the same thing.

The Manse at Sedbergh smelled of fruit and was as silent as church and even had churchy furniture in yellow oak, most of it made by country craftsmen who, in a fit of fancy, might carve, say, acorns or leaves all round the edge of a table. There was no sound but the ticktock of the grandfather clock. Everything was polished, still and clean. One slept in a soft feather bed and woke to see the mist low down on the waist of the Berg. On the old brick wall of the garden my grandfather grew his plums and pears, and in the flower beds his carnations, his stock, his roses and his sweet williams; and under the wall flowed a little stream from the mountains.

It was a kind, grave house. My grandparents were in their early fifties. For my grandmother cleanliness was the first passion. Whenever I stayed, in my first years with her, she bathed me in a zinc tub before the kitchen fire and was always scrubbing me. Once she tried to remove a mole from my nose, thinking it was a speck of tar. For two days, on and off, she worked at it with soap, soda, pumice and grit and hard brushes, exclaiming all the time like Lady Macbeth, while my grandfather growled, "Let it bide, you're spreading his nose all over his face." He had a genial sadistic touch, for he loved to point to a scar on the tip of my nose which seemed to shine like a lamp and make me ridiculous; and also to say that my nose was the nearest thing to an elephant's foot he had ever seen. He enjoyed making me angry. It was York-shire training.

Grandma always kept her white hair in curlers until a late hour in the afternoon, when she changed into one of her spotted-blue dresses. The only day on which she looked less than neat was Monday. On this terrible day she pinned a man's cloth cap to her hair, kirtled a rough skirt above her knees, put on a pair of wooden clogs and went out to the scullery to start the great weekly wash of sheets, pillow cases, towels, tablecloths and clothes. They were first boiled in a copper; then she moved out to a washtub by the pump in the cobbled yard and she turned the linen round and round with the three-legged wooden dolly—as tall as myself—every so often remarking for her neighbors to hear that her linen was of better quality, better washed, whiter and cleaner than the linen of any other woman in the town; that the sight of her washing hanging on the line—where my grandfather had to peg and prop it—would shame the rest of the world and the final ironing be a blow to all rivals. The house smelled of suds and ironing. Her clogs clattered in the yard. But, sharp at five o'clock she changed as usual and sat down to read the *British Weekly*.

On Tuesday she made her first baking of the week. This consisted of different kinds of bread and I watched it rise in the pans to its full beauty before the fire; on Thursday she made her second baking, concentrating less on bread than on pies, her madeira cake, her seedcake, her eccles cakes, her puffs, her lemon curd or jam tarts and tarts of egg "custard" —operations that lasted from seven in the morning until five in the afternoon once more. The "bake" included, of course, the scouring of pans and saucepans, which a rough village girl would help her with. At the end, the little creature showed no sign of being tired, and would "lay" there was no better cook in the town than herself and pitied the cooking of her sisters.

On Wednesdays she turned out the house. This cleaning was ferocious. The carpets were all taken up and hung on a line; my grandfather got out a heavy stick to beat them while she stood beside him saying things like "Eeh Willyum, I can't abide dirt." There was some nasty talk among the Congregationalists in Sedbergh about my grandfather's carpet-beating; they got their own back for the boasting of my grandma and some said out loud that he was obviously not the class of man to be teaching the word of God in that town. (Forty years later when I went back to the town after his death, one or two old people still spoke in a shocked way of their working-class minister who was under the thumb of his "stuck-up" wife. That came of a man's marrying above himself.)

After the carpets, the linoleum was taken up and Grandma was down on her knees scrubbing the floorboards. Then came hours of dusting and polishing.

"Woman," Granda often said on Wednesdays, standing very still and thundery and glaring at her, "lay not up your treasure on earth where moth and dust doth corrupt."

"Eeh Willyum," she would reply, "wipe your boots outside. Ah can't abide a dirty doormat. Mrs. So-and-so hasn't
whitened her step since Monday."

And once more she would settle down as pretty as a picture to an evening, making another rag rug or perhaps cro-
cheting more and more lace for her dresses, her table centers
and her doilies. By the time she was eighty years old she had
stored away several thousand of these doilies, chests full of
them; and of course they were superior to the work of any
other woman in the country. In old age, she sent boxes of
them to her younger son, who had emigrated to Canada,
thinking he might be "in want."

I remember a tea for Sunday School teachers at the Manse.
They came, excited young men and bouncing young women
who went out in the fields and trees along the beck to see who
could collect and name the largest number of different spe-
cies of wild flowers in an hour. An older woman won with 57
different kinds. We got back to my grandmother's parlor,
where the sun shone through the little square lights of her
windows, to see one of my grandmother's masterpieces, a
state tea laid on the table. The scones, the teacakes, eccles
cakes, jam tarts, iced tarts, her three or four different kinds
of cake—sultana, madeira, seed and jammed sponge—her
puffs and her turnovers were set out in all their yellows,
browns, pinks, and as usual, in her triumph, Grandmother
was making a pettish little mouth, "laying" that "nowt like it"
would be seen on any table in the town. The company stood
reverently by their chairs and then, to my disgust, they broke
out into a sung grace, conducted by the eldest of the teachers,
each taking parts, bass and tenor, soprano and contralto,
repeating their variations for what seemed to me a good
twenty minutes before setting to. To my wonder—for I had
been nicely brought up by my grandmother—the eldest
teacher, who was a very old man with the big hands of a
laborer, tipped his tea into his saucer, blew on it and drank.

"Look at the man," I shouted. "He's being rude."

There was a silence. The old man was angry. Grandma was vexed. There was a dispute about whether I should be told to leave the room. One of the girls saved me. But the old man kept coming back to it and it was the whole subject of the tea party, and for days the Minister and his wife had the matter over with me. If that was "London manners" the old man growled when he left, he didn't want owt of them. Such slights are never forgotten in the North; they go all round the town and add to its obdurate wars. The story was reported to my father in London and was brought up indignantly year after year. To think that a boy, a relation of the Minister's too, and already known to have exposed himself in school, should say a thing like that.

One experience I feared to tell them. That day of the flower hunt, I had found a beautiful white flower like a star growing near the river. I had never seen a white flower so silky and star-like in its petals and so exquisite. I picked it, smelled it and dropped it at once. It stank. The smell was not only rank, it suggested rottenness and a deep evil. It was sin itself. And I hurried away, frightened, from the river, not daring to mention it, and I never walked through that field again. For many years I thought of this deceit. I did not know this flower was the wild garlic, the most evocative of our aphrodisiacs, the female to the male musk.

The general portrait of the country people of Haworth which is given by Mrs. Gaskell in her *Life of Charlotte Brontë*, very closely fitted the character of my Yorkshire relations, if one allows for the taming effects of lower-middle-class gentility. Haworth-like tales were common among Grandma's people, the Sawdons. They were proud, violent, egotistical. They had—according to your view—either a strong belief in the plain virtues or a rock-like moral conceit. Everything was black or white to them. They were blunt to your face, practical and unimaginative, kind yet iron-minded, homely and very hospitable; but they suspected good manners, they flayed you with their hard and ironical eyes. They were also frugal, close and calculating about money— they were always talking about "brass"—and they looked on outsiders with scorn. They were monosyllabic talkers but their silences concealed strong passions that (as Mrs. Gaskell said) lasted for life, whether that passion was of love or hatred. Their friendship or their enmity was forever. To listen to their talk was like listening to a fire crackling. They had no heroes. They were cautious and their irony was laconic. I was in the city of York soon after it was bombed in the last war and I said to a railway worker: "Well, they didn't destroy the Minster."

"Ay, they say as how Hitler says he's going to be married there next May. But ah doan't know . . ."

With that last phrase drily uttered he gave me a look as hard as steel.

Year after year I went to Sedbergh to sit on the stool by my grandmother's fire, staring at the pots that hung simmering on their shining chains over the coals, smelling the green country bacon and the rising bread. One day a boy from the famous Public School at Sedbergh was called in to tell me how many years it would be before I reached the verb *sum* in Latin and could enter the school and go for their terrible fifteen-mile "runs" across the Fells, the toughest schoolboy run in England. I often saw the boys slogging along near the ravine. That was one of the many dream schools I never went to.

My grandfather's home life was laborious and thrifty. Coals were bargained for in the summer and sacked down, carefully counted piece by piece, in a heap near the stone shed. He would then grade the pieces in sizes and (reverting to his bricklaying days) would build them into a wall inside the shed. Each day he would collect, one by one, the various sizes of coal needed for an economical fire. They were small, slow-burning fires, often damped down in order to save, but in the winters of valley fog or snow we were thickly clad in Yorkshire wool and I remember no cold. After his work in the house he had work to do in his garden also. He had to dig all of it. There were his vegetables and his raspberries which, in the ripe season, he sold at twopence a cup to the town. Notices saying "Thou Shalt Not Steal" were placed on sticks on the wall by the school lane. He had little time or peace for his ministry, or opportunity for his secret vice: cigar smoking. The Congregationalists would not have tolerated tobacco smoking in their minister any more than they would have stood for drinking, but I've known him to drink a glass of strong home-brewed ale at an isolated farm, and as for the cigar, his habit was to sneak off to the petty, or earth closet, at the end of the garden, latch himself in with Bible and writing paper, light up, take his ease and write his sermon. My grandmother was always frantic when he was out of her sight for a minute—she did her best to stop him going on his parish visits, for she would "lay" the men would be out at work and he would have to see the women, which roused her instant jealousy—and on his cigar days her delicate nose would sometimes catch the smell coming out of the top of the petty door. She would run down the garden and beat on the door with a yardbroom, shouting: "Willyum, Willyum, come out of that, you dirty man."

Sunday was his day. On this day my grandmother respected him, and herself withdrew into a silent self-complacency as her Willyum prepared for the Christian rites. He had an early and a late service in the morning, another in the afternoon and one in the evening. He prepared for the day in soldierly way, as for battle. He shaved so closely that there was generally a spot of blood on his chin and his cheeks were pale. His surplice was a disappointing cotton affair, like a barber's sheet—poor quality I came to think, shop-shoddy—as he set off across the gravel path to the chapel which made one side of his garden cold and damp.

I was put into my Sunday best—sailor collar, vest that choked me, linen breeches that sawed at the crotch and cut me above the knees when I sat, legs dangling, swelling and aching in the pew; and my grandmother had on her best bonnet and costume. We smelled of new cloth, but she relieved this by soaking her handkerchief in lily of the valley and gave me a sniff of it. She also took smelling salts. Then comes the agony of sitting in those oaken pews and keeping my eyes fixed on Grandfather. What he says I never understand, but he goes on and on for a long time. So do the hymns. There is the cheerful break when the plate goes round, the happiness of putting in a penny; and then there is the moment which makes me giggle—and at times (when my brother was with me), the joke was too much. My grandfather would give out notices and announce the sum of last Sunday's collection, a sum like eight shillings and threepence halfpenny. (His living, by the way.) His voice is harsh, but what convulses me is his way of pronouncing the word halfpenny; he calls it, in curt Northern fashion, ha'penny, with the broad "a"—"hah-pny." I often tell my father of this later in London, who points out I have no call to complain when, in pure cockney, I talk of a boy who lives "dahn ahr wy."

I did not understand my grandfather's sermons. My mother, who had sat through many, told me his manner was hard and monotonous and that he was one to whom hatred and the love of truth were very much the same thing, his belief being that truth is afflicting and unpleasant. He argued people into hell, but not in the florid manner of the melodramatic hellfire preachers who set the flames dancing so that in the end they became like theater flames to the self-indulgent. My grandfather's method was to send people to hell rationally, contemptuously and intellectually. He

brusquely made hell unattractive; he even made it boring.
This was an error; later on his congregations dwindled, for
he offered no beanos of remorse, salvation or luxuriant ruin.
He could not see that sin is attractive and that therefore its
condemnation must be more voluptuous.

Frankly the congregations expected an artist and they
discovered instead a critic. They were puzzled. That enormous success in the Free Trade Hall at Manchester was not
repeated. Grandfather was essentially an intellectual and
some said—my parents among them—that his marriage to
a vain, house-proud and jealous girl who never read anything
in her life except the love serial in the *British Weekly* and
who upset the ladies of his many chapels by her envies and
boastings, was a disaster for an intellectual man. The Congregationalists invite their ministers and the news of her
character got round. But how can one judge the marriage
of others? There are families that are claustrophobic, that
live intensely for themselves and are indifferent to the existence of other people and are even painfully astonished by it.
Grandfather's truculence in the Army was a symptom of
solitary independence.

Back we go to cold beef, for it is wicked to cook anything
on Sundays—except Yorkshire pudding. This is sacred.
Light as an omelette yet crisp in the outer foliations of what
it would be indelicate to call crust, it has no resemblance
to any of that heavy, soggy, fatty stuff known all over England and America by the name. Into it is poured a little gravy
made of meat, and not from some packaged concoction. One
might be eating butterflies, so lightly does it float down;
it is my grandmother's form of poetry. Grandfather asks if I
would like "a small bortion more"—Nonconformists often
affected small changes of consonant, *p* becoming *b* and an *s*
becoming a *z;* the faithful always called themselves *uz,* the *z*
separating them from sinners—and then asks his wife what
she thought of the sermon. Her reply is to ask if he

noticed Mrs. Somebody's terrible new hat and to add that she didn't think owt to the material of the new coat Mrs. Somebody Else had dressed herself up in.

The afternoon is more serious. I had no toys or games at my grandfather's—nor did my father when he was a boy—and I did not miss them. There was enough in garden, country or the simple sight of things to keep me occupied, and, for years, in my parents' house the smell of toys seemed unpleasant and their disasters too distressing. One always thought of the money they cost. On Sunday afternoons at Sedbergh I was allowed into my grandfather's study. It was a small room with a few hundred books in it, almost all sermons, and he would read to me some pious tale about, perhaps, a homeless orphan, driven to sleep on straw in some shed in Manchester, surrounded by evildoers. The boy resists starvation, and after a long illness, is rescued by benevolent middle-class people.

When I tried to read these tales I found the words were too long and so I gazed out at the green Berg, watched the cloud shadows make gray or blue faces on the grass, and the sheep nibbling there. The quiet and loneliness were exquisite to me; and it was pleasant to smell the print of my grandfather's paper and hear him turn over the pages in such a silence. When I grew up the Christian God ceased to mean anything to me; I was sick of Him by the twenties; but if I think of a possible God, some image of the Berg comes at once to my mind now, or of certain stones I remember in the ravine. To such things the heathen in his wisdom always bowed.

The pious story of the Manchester orphan had one importance: for the first time I heard of the industrial revolution. This was real to the North Country people. We knew nothing about it in the commercial South. There were little mills in the valleys where my grandfather took me to see the mill girls at their machines. There were the tall chimneys of

Leeds and York. One spoke of people, not by who they were, but by what they did. Their work defined them. Men who met at street corners in Sedbergh knew of strikes and labor wars; and my grandfather told me of masters and men with war-like relish. These stories were not told in terms of rights and wrongs very much, though my grandfather was radical enough; Carlyle's *Past and Present* fitted his view. The stories were told with a pride in conflict itself. Hard masters were as much admired as recalcitrant workmen; the quarrel, the fight, was the thing. The fight was good because it was a fight. Granda's youth was speaking when he told of this.

The Ten Commandments, of course, came into my grandfather's stories, particularly the command to honor one's parents—though of mine he clearly had a poor opinion—because that led to obedience; then stealing—the old lady's Halma pieces, the allure of apples, raspberries and Victoria plums. Finally murder. About murder he was vehement. It attracted him; he seemed to be close to it. I felt I must be close to it too. I had a younger brother whose goodness (I jealously knew) was palpable. How easily I could become Cain. To the question "Cain, where is thy brother Abel?" how glad I was that I could honestly reply, "Uxbridge, near the canal," though I had once tried to push him into it. Granda kept on year after year about murder. When I was nine or ten and the famous Crippen cut up his wife and buried her in his cellar, Granda made me study the case thoroughly. He drew a plan of the house and the bloody cellar for me to reflect on. He had a dramatic mind.

In the summer my grandparents took a holiday, paying for it out of a few preaching engagements. We took the train across Yorkshire to the East Riding. For the first week we would stay with my great-uncle Arthur and his wife, Sarah, who was my grandmother's sister. After the placid small-town life of Sedbergh, York was a shock. We were in an aristocratic yet industrial city. The relations were working-class people. The daughters of the tailor in Kirbymoorside were expectant heiresses in a small way, but both had married beneath them. Very contentedly too: the difference cannot have been very great and was bridged by the relative classlessness of the North—relative, I mean, to life in the South.

We arrived at one of an ugly row of workers' houses, with their doors on the street, close to the gas works, with the industrial traffic grinding by. A child could see that the Minister and his wife thought themselves many cuts above their York relations. Great-uncle Arthur was a cabinetmaker in a furniture factory. The Minister glittered blandly at him and Uncle Arthur looked as though he was going to give a spit on the floor near the Minister with a manual worker's scorn.

Great-uncle Arthur was a stunted and bandy man, with a dark, sallow and strong-boned face. He looked very yellow. He had a heavy head of wiry hair as black as coals, ragged eyebrows and a horrible long black beard like a crinkled mat of pubic hair. A reek of tobacco, varnish and wood shavings came off him; he had large fingers with split unclean nails. The first thing he did when he got home from work was to put on a white apron, strap a pair of carpet kneepads to his trousers, pick up a hammer or screwdriver and start on odd jobs round the house. He was always hammering something and was often up a ladder. His great yellow teeth gave me the idea that he had a machine of some kind in his mouth, and that his teeth were fit to bite nails; in fact, he often pulled a nail or two out of his mouth. He seemed to chew them.

Uncle Arthur's wife was Grandma's eldest sister and in every way unlike her. Aunt Sarah was tall, big boned, very white-faced and hollow-eyed and had large, loose, laughing teeth like a horse's or a skeleton's, which have ever since seemed to me the signs of hilarious good nature in a woman. Though she looked ill—breathing those fumes of the gas works, which filled the house, cannot have been very good for her—she was jolly, hard-working and affectionate. She and Uncle Arthur were notorious (in the family) for the incredible folly of adoring each other. She doted on her dark, scowling, argumentative, hammering little gnome: it seemed that two extraordinary sets of teeth had fallen in love with each other.

For myself, Uncle Arthur's parlor, Aunt Sarah's kitchen and the small backyard were the attractions. The backyard was only a few feet square, but he grew calceolarias there. It gave on to an alley, one wall of which was part of the encircling wall of the city. Its "bars," or city gates, and its Minster are the grandest in England, and to Uncle Arthur, who knew every stone in the place, I owe my knowledge and love of it. One could go up the steps, only a few feet, and walk along the battlements and shoot imaginary arrows from the very spot where the Yorkists had shot them during the Wars of the Roses; and one could look down on the white roses of York in the gardens near the Minster and look up to those towers where the deep bells talked out their phenomenal words over the roofs of the city. They moved me then; they move me still.

Uncle Arthur's house had a stuffy smell—the smell of the gas works and the railway beyond it was mixed with the odor of camphor and camphor wax. The rooms were poorly lit by gas jets burning under grubby white globes; air did not move easily, for there were heavy curtains in the narrow passageway to the stairs. But the pinched little place contained Uncle's genius and the smell of camphor indicated it. The cabinetmaker was a naturalist—he used to speak of Nature as some loud fancy woman he went about with and whom his wife had got used to. On the walls of his kitchen hung pretty cases of butterflies and also of insects with hard little bubble bodies of vermilion and green—creatures he had caught, killed and mounted himself. In the lower half of the kitchen window he had fixed a large glass case of ferns in which he kept a pet toad. You put a worm on the toad's table—one of Uncle's collection of fossils—and the spotted creature came out and snapped it up.

The smell of camphor was strongest in the small front parlor. A lot of space in the window corner was taken up by another large glass case containing a stuffed swan. This enormous white bird, its neck a little crooked and sooty, was sitting on a nest of sticks and seemed to be alive, for every time a dray, a lorry or a distant train passed, it shook, and—by its stony eye—with indignation. In two other corners there were cabinets containing Uncle's collection of birds' eggs; and on the mantelpiece was a photograph of Uncle being let down by a rope from the cliffs of Whitby where he was collecting eggs under a cloud of screaming gulls.

Granda was the sedentary and believing man; Uncle was the skeptic and man of knowledge. He had been born very poor and had had next to no schooling. He told me he could not read or write until he was a grown man. A passion for education seized him. He took to learning for its own sake, and not in order to rise in the world. He belonged—I now see—to the dying race of craftsmen. So he looked for a book that was suited to his energetic, yet melancholy and quasi-scientific temperament. At last he found it: he taught himself to read by using Burton's *Anatomy of Melancholy*. This rambling and eccentric compendium of the illnesses of the brain and heart was exactly suited to his curious mind. He reveled in it. "Look it up in Burton, lad," he'd say when I was older. "What's old Burton say?" He would quote it all round the house. Burton came into every argument. And he would add, from his own experience, a favorite sentence: "Circumstances alters cases."

Burton was Uncle Arthur's emancipation: it set him free

of the tyranny of the Bible in chapel-going circles. There were all his relations—especially the Minister—shooting texts at one another while Uncle Arthur sat back, pulled a nail or two out of his mouth and put his relatives off target with bits of the *Anatomy*. He had had to pick up odds and ends of Latin and Greek because of the innumerable notes in those languages, and a look of devilry came into his eyes under their shaggy black brows. On top of this he was an antiquarian, a geologist, a bicyclist and an atheist. He claimed to have eaten sandwiches on the site of every ruined castle and abbey in Yorkshire. He worshiped the Minster and was a pest to curators of museums and to librarians.

In short, Uncle Arthur was a crank. When the Minister and he sat down in the parlor they looked each other over warily. The swan shook irritably in its glass case as they argued, and there they were: the man of God and the human- ist, the believer and the skeptic; the workman who had left his class and the workman who scorned to leave it. The Minister said Uncle Arthur was naïve and a joke; Uncle Arthur regarded the Minister as a snob, a manual worker who had gone soft and who was hardly more than his wife's domestic servant. The Minister was prone to petty gossip, as the clergy are apt to be. Uncle Arthur said, "Let's stop the tittle-tattle." He wanted a serious row. He puffed out his chest and grinned sarcastically at his brother-in-law; the Minister responded with a bland clerical snort. They were united in one thing: they had both subscribed to the saying, often heard in Yorkshire: "Don't tha' marry money, go where money is." They had married heiresses.

I fancy Uncle Arthur's atheism was weakening in those days and that he may already have been moving towards spiritualism, theosophy and the wisdom of the East—the philosopher's melancholy. There was a ruinous drift to reli- gion in these Northerners. I did not know that in this room there was to occur before very long an event that would have a calamitous influence on my family, but one that would play a part in starting my career as a writer. Uncle Arthur had two sons and a daughter. She was a brisk, jolly Yorkshire girl who was having a struggle with her parents. She was about to be married, and after coming home from work, her idea was to go round to the house she and her fiancé had found a few streets away. He would be painting and papering it and she would have things like fire irons or a coal bucket to take there. Uncle Arthur and Aunt Sarah thought this might lead to familiarities before marriage and would not allow her to go unless she had one of her brothers with her, but they were rarely at home.

The clever girl saw that I was the answer and petted me so that I was delighted to go with her. I was the seven-year-old chaperone and I fell in love with her. It piqued me that when we got to the house, her young man would spring out at her from the front door and start kissing and cuddling her. "Oh, give over," she cried out and said, "I'm going to marry him," pointing to me. I did not leave them alone for a minute. A bed had come to the house and the excited young man soon had us all bouncing up and down on it, rumpling my hair with one hand while he tickled her with the other, till she was as red as a berry. At last the wedding day came and I was sad. I longed to be with them and wanted to be their child and was sad that I was left out of it. Aunt Sarah teased me afterwards and said that since I was in the photograph of the wedding group, I was married too. This cured me of my passion. For at home in London we had a book, bought by my father, called *Marriage on Two Hundred a Year* which, like my mother's song "At Trinity Church I Met Me Doom," caused words between my father and mother. I was beginning to form a glum opinion about married life. Why did these tall adult animals go in for what—it seemed—was nothing but worry?

Uncle Arthur's eldest son was a tall, sad young man, with

puffy cheeks. Whenever I was in York and he was at home he took me out rowing on the Ouse. He was a hero to me, for he was a post-office sorter who worked on the night mail train to London. He had the superb job of putting out the mailbags into the pickup nets beside the line as the train screamed through at sixty miles an hour.

It was the other son, a lithographer whom I saw only once, who made the strongest and most disturbing impression on me. There are certain pictures that remain with one all one's life and feed disquieting thoughts. I was taken to a poorish house one evening in the winter, and there he sat, a pallid and ailing man with blue circles under his eyes, with medicine bottles beside him. Several young children were playing on the floor; the mother was giving the bottle to a new baby. There was, to me, the sickly smell of young children which I hated, for being the eldest in my family, I often had to look after my brothers and sister when they were tiny. This second cousin of mine was very ill; he had lost his job as a lithographer because of his illness, and looked as if he were dying. In fact, he was no more than a nervous, sickly dyspeptic, one of the victims of the Yorkshire diet of pastry, cakes and strong tea; and, my grandfather said with disapproval, he was an artist. One was shown a lot of people in Yorkshire who were "warnings": after the picture of Crippen the murderer in the papers, there was the town drunk of Sedbergh, the town fighter, the town gambler. This cousin of mine was the warning against the miseries of art, unwise marriage and failure. (When I was eighteen I wanted to be a painter and the sick smell, above all the sensation of defeat and apathy in that room, worried me.) Years passed. I must have been about eleven when Father brought home the news that the dying Cousin Dick had been suddenly and miraculously cured by Christian Science.

It was on one of these stays in York that my grandfather took me along the walls to the Minster and showed me the

Lincoln-green glass. I had already had many pernickety tours with Uncle Arthur, who pointed out bits of joinery and stone masonry and explained every historical detail. He was a connoisseur of carving and especially of tombs. His was a craftsman's attitude. It was a sight to see him standing, bandy, threatening and bearded in the aisle, with bicycle clips on his trousers—for he rarely took them off—and looking up to the vault of the aisles with an appraising eye. He often had a ruler sticking out of his jacket and on my first visit I really thought he was going to pull it out and start measuring up. He didn't go so far as to say he could have built the place himself, but once we got to the choir stalls and started on the hinges and dovetailing, he looked dangerously near getting to work on them. The choir stalls appealed to him because there are often potbellied and impish bits of lewd carving under a seat or on the curl of an arm, and he always gave me a pagan wink or nudge when he found one. Once he said, "That'd vex t'Minister." Uncle Arthur behaved as if he owned the place and would get into arguments with vergers and even bewilder a clergyman by a technical question.

My grandfather's attitude was different. The grandeur, height and spaciousness of the place moved him. He was enraptured by it. But, pointing down at the choir, he said that it was sad to know that this lovely place was in the possession of the rich and ungodly and a witness not to the Truth but to a corrupt and irrelevant theology.

The Minster was scarcely the house of God any more, but the house of a class. "And you cannot," he said severely, "worship God freely here. You have to pay for your pews." The clergy, he said, were like the Pharisees in the Bible.

We left the cathedral and went up the steps to the walls once more, at the point where the railway runs under an arch into the old York Station where Stephenson's Rocket stands; and we sat in one of the niches of the battlements and looked down on the shunting trains, the express to Edinburgh coming in, the Flying Scotsman moving out to London, under their boiling white smoke. And there Granda told me about the wrongs of England and of a great man like Carlyle and of another, John Ruskin, who had hated the railways.

"Great men," he said. "God-fearing men."

The granite walls, the overpowering weight of English history seemed to weigh on us. To choose to be a Great Man was necessary; but to be one, one must take on an enormous burden of labor and goodness. He seemed to convey that I would be a poor thing if I didn't set to work at once, and although the idea appealed to me, the labor of becoming one was too much. I wasn't born for it. How could I get out of it? In the South fortunately we were feebler and did not have to take on these tasks. I loved the North but I was nervous of its frown, and even of the kindly laughter I heard there.

After York we used to take the train to see the remaining sister of my grandmother, the third heiress. She lived up on the edge of the moors above Kirbymoorside where my grandmother came from, in a hamlet called Appleton. This was wild and lonely country. You drove up five or six miles in the carrier's gig; if it was raining, the passengers all sat under one enormous umbrella. There was a long climb to the common, with the horse snorting and puffing, and then you were in the wide single street of the hamlet, with wide grass verges on either side, and you were escorted in by platoons of the fine Appleton geese. You passed the half-dozen pumps where girls were getting water for their houses and arrived at a low flint cottage where my great-aunt Lax lived.

The frown went off Grandfather's face when he left his York relations. His preaching was over. He was free. He was back in his wife's country. Aunt Lax had a farm and land that she now let off. The industrial revolution, the grim days of Hull and Nottingham and Bradford were forgotten; we were in true country and had gone back a century, and Granda forgot his respectability and took off his clerical collar.

At first sight Aunt Lax looked severe. She was a tallish and skinny woman with iron-gray hair which she kept in curlers all the week except Sundays. She had a long thin nose, a startling pair of black eyebrows like charcoal marks, wore steel spectacles and was mustached and prickle-chinned like a man. Not only that, like a man she was always heaving things about—great pails of milk in her dairy—churning butter, clattering about on clogs, shouting across the street; and her skirts were half the time kirtled to her knees. Her arms were long and strong and bony. On a second look you saw that her lizard-like face had been beautiful; it was a dark Scandinavian beauty. But the amusing thing about this spinsterish creature—and perhaps it was what made her so gay and tolerant—was that she had been married three times. The rumor was that there had been a fourth. These marriages were a shock to the family, but Lax in name, Lax in nature, this indefatigable Wesleyan did well out of her weddings and funerals and had a long stocking.

When I was six I met the third Mr. Lax. He was a dumb giant who sat on a chair outside the cottage in the sun. He was very old and had a frightening glass eye. Since there were many ploughs, carts and traps and gigs in her farmyard, I came to think he was a moorland farmer, but this was not so. A few years ago, sitting in a pub at Lastingham nearby, I found an old shepherd who had known him well. "Nay, he was nobbut t'old watchman up at t'lead mine," he told me.

If Aunt Lax had done well out of her two previous husbands, the third was obviously a folly. And a strange one. The chimney of the lead mine—now abandoned—stands up like a gaunt warning finger in the middle of the heather that rolls away from Lastingham, and when she was a girl she was locked in the house, as all the village girls were, when the miners came down on Saturday nights to the village pub. North Country love is very sudden. There it was: a miner got her in the end.

Year after year I went to Appleton, sometimes alone, sometimes with Cyril, the brother who was a year or so younger than I. Aunt Lax had no children of her own, so that there was nothing possessive or spoiling in her affections. We hauled water for her at the pump, and for the rest, she let us run wild with the jolly daughters of the blacksmith and anyone we came across. We scarcely ever went to chapel. The smell of bacon woke us in the morning and we went down from our pretty room, which contained a chest of drawers made by Uncle Arthur, to the large kitchen where the pots hung on the chains over the fire and where she sometimes cooked on a spit. Her baking days were less fanatical than my grandma's and her washing days were pleasanter. Even the suds smelt better and there were always the big girls to chase round with us when the washing was brought in from the line or the hedges when the day was over.

When her third husband died, it was thought that amorous or calculating Great-aunt Lax would take a fourth. She had picked her second and third at the funeral feasts, at which dozens of local farmers could form a sound opinion of her as a caterer and housekeeper. They had a good look round at her stables when they came, knew her acres and her fame as the leading Wesleyan for miles around. Instead, she took in a female friend, a Miss Smith. She, too, died and on the very day my brother and I arrived at the cottage. We arrived in a storm and were taken at once to one of the outer sculleries where a village girl came in, stripped us, scrubbed off the London dirt and swore to us she'd let us see the body upstairs. We longed to see it, but the girl took us off to the blacksmith's where we had to stay. More promises were made but we never saw the corpse. But we were allowed to play in a barn and watch the country people coming to the funeral feast. We avenged ourselves by opening six or seven bales of rag strips which Aunt Lax used for her winter occupation: making rag hearth rugs. We threw them all over her orchard.

She was not very vexed. There was a lot of questioning of us afterwards in York and in London about who had come to the funeral, for Aunt Lax was supposed to have added to her wealth by Miss Smith's death and everyone was trying to guess if there would be a fourth or whether other relations were on the prowl. She grew to be rather witch-like.

The moorland life was eventless. Every so often Aunt Lax would dress up in a heavy gray tweed costume, put on her hat and go off to Kirbymoorside Market, sitting by the carrier. It was a state visit. She would go there to buy cloth, or pounds of flour and other things for her bins, and to see her lawyer. Once a week a peddler would come round or a man selling herrings from Whitby and she gossiped with them.

She understood boys. She told us of all the local crimes and knew the sites of one or two murders. She sent us down to the mill because a man had murdered his wife there years before. One year, when I was eight, I came up from London terrified with street tales about Jack the Ripper and I tried to get her to tell me he did not exist or had, at any rate, died long ago.

"Nay," she said. "He's still alive. He's been up here. I saw him myself at 'Utton-le-'Ole last market day." (None of our Sawdons "had an aitch to their names.").

This cured me of my terror of the Ripper: the fears of childhood are solitary and are lasting in the solitariness of cities. But in villages everyone knows everything that goes on, all the horrors, real or imaginary; people come back from prison and settle down comfortably again; known rapists drink their beer in the public house in the evenings; everyone knows the thieves. The knowledge melts peacefully into the general novel of village life.

But one alarming thing occurred when I was five or six, in Appleton. It had the Haworth touch and it showed the dour, dangerous, testing humor of the moorland people. We all set out one afternoon in a gig, my grandparents, Aunt Lax

and myself, to a farm, a lonely stone place with geese, ducks
and chickens fluttering in the yard. A few dark leafed trees,
bent by the gales, were standing close to it. We had tea in the
low-ceilinged kitchen and the farmer noticed that I was gazing at a gun which hung over the mantelpiece.

"T'lad is looking at yon gun of yours, Feyther," said his
wife.

"Ay," said the farmer. "Dost know what this is lad?"

"A gun. It shoots."

"Ay. And what does it shoot?"

"I don't know."

"Would 'ee like to see it?"

"Eeh. He'd be fair capped to touch it," said my grandmother. The farmer got the gun down and let me touch it,
then (helping me, for it was heavy), he let me hold it.

"Dost know how it works?"

I murmured.

The farmer broke the gun, showed me where the cartridges
went, closed it, clicked the safety catch and the trigger. He
gave it to me again and allowed me to do this. I was amazed.

"Would 'ee like to see the cartridges?"

"Yes."

"Yes *please*," said my grandmother.

"Please," I said.

He got a couple of cartridges from a drawer and loaded
the gun.

"There you are. It can shoot now. Hold it."

"Ready! Present! Fire!" said my grandfather. "You can
shoot a rabbit now."

The farmer steadied the gun which swayed in my small
hands.

"Ay," said the farmer. "Take off t'safety catch. Now if
you pull t'trigger it'll fire."

I trembled.

"Would it kill rabbits?" I asked.

"Ay," laughed the farmer. "And people. Come, Mother, come Grandma and Mrs. Lax, stand over against the wall, t'lad wants to shoot you."

"No," I said.

"Ay he does," said the excited farmer, waving them to the dresser, and there they stood laughing and the gun swung in my aching hand.

"Eeh, t'little lad wouldn't shoot his grandma as makes him those custard pies," Grandma said.

"Safety catch off. Now if you pull t'trigger—has 'e got his finger on it?—they'll all be dead."

"No," I said with tears in my eyes and nearly dropped the gun. The farmer caught it.

"Eeh well, it's a lesson," said the farmer, hanging the gun back on the wall.

"Old Tom likes a joke," they said, going home, but Aunt Lax said the kitchen was small and that was the way Mr. Robinson shot his wife "down 't Mill," no accident that was. But all the way my grandma moaned: "Eeh, who would have thought our Victor would want to shoot his grandma. Eeh. Eeh, well."

I sulked with misery, and after a couple of miles she said to me: "He's got a monkey on his back," a sentence that always roused my temper, for I felt at my back for the monkey and screamed, "I haven't. I haven't."

That was the night I told my grandfather again I hoped he'd be knocked down by a train at the Junction when he crossed the line, and I got my second spanking.

I came home from these Yorkshire visits sadly to whatever London house we were living in and would see in my mind's eye the white road going across the moors, like a path across a heaving sea, gray in most seasons but purple in the summer, rising and disappearing, a road that I longed to walk on, mile after mile. I was never to see one that moved me so strangely until, in my twenties, I saw another such in Castile.

It brought back my childhood and this was the cause of my walking across Spain. So, when one falls in love with a face, the reason may be that one saw such a face, perhaps of an old woman, that excited one in childhood. I always give a second look at any woman with Aunt Lax's eyebrows and her lizard-like face.

4

When I look back upon our history I see my grandfather as much an immigrant in a new country—for that is what his middle-class life was—as, say, an Italian is when he comes to settle in England or America. The process is exhausting; Grandfather retained the violence of his forebears. His son —my father—is the first emancipated generation, who, brought up in the early struggle and marked by it, is excited and able to take advantage of the new world and rapidly dramatizes and exaggerates his role in it. All the Yorkshire relations were as rooted, settled and certain of themselves as any of their ancestors had been since the time of the Danes: my father quickly rid himself of these traits; if emotionally he was still an obstinate boy from a small town in Yorkshire, his mind and speech soon became a Londoner's. Yet London was not a deeply known reality to him as it is to a real Londoner, to a real inhabitant of the big city; to him it was a fantasy and encouraged fantasy in himself. At no time did he seem to belong to the city, as my mother did, but rather to float and flutter about over it, even to regard it piratically as loot. Fantasy he had, but little imagination—my mother, as he continually complained, was the imaginative one—for imagination grows from indigenous roots; his energetic power of exclamatory self-renewal was really a weakness, a sign of superficiality.

Postcards came from hotels, north and south and west: "Big orders. Back Friday. Love to self and chicks. Walt." On Friday, Mother calms her fears of the railway system by having her weekly bath, and puts on a white silk blouse with a net front and a high lace collar. She won't let us come near her. She has a racy smell and is restless and disturbing. She now belongs to him and not to us. He arrives hours late; he is always late. We hear the cab horse blowing at the gate. Father has brought her a present—a Dover sole or a joint in a skewered basket. She says how worried she has been; he chases her round the house, almost falls over the sofa, and she screams with pleasure. "Don't, Walt, you'll kill me." The thin young man is now fat and bounces about like a ball.

There is a canal at Uxbridge, but for him it is not a canal. For him it is the Thames, the Ouse, the Severn, the Scottish salmon rivers. He buys himself a yachting cap, a blazer and cream trousers suitable for the Royal Yacht Squadron and Cowes and walks grandly among the old men fishing with worms off the towpath. Uxbridge is impressed by this young yacht owner, especially as he puts up a monocle, for a lark, from time to time. This getup is one of his incarnations. The fishermen put an idea into his head: he buys waders, a rod for perch and a rod for salmon, and even a gaff, and sets off to fill the family larder. The malicious anglers on the canal watch him hook himself to trees and even to passers-by.

At home he gets out his little notebooks in which he writes his orders. He reads the long list of items aloud. They are his poetry. So many gross of table runners, cushions, or tea cozies and so on, sold to the big drapers. Occasionally he does a sketch of the article he is selling. He is good at sketching, can draw better than most people. He has heard of Art Nouveau. This puts an idea into his head. He decides that my mother ought to be an artist and out he goes to buy an expensive box of oil paints, brushes, an easel, canvases. He sees her as a glamorous woman painter. She had been so clever in the millinery at Daniels. She might turn out a good line in the manner of "Wedded." There are two chocolate-colored prints of dreamy-bosomed ladies, their transparent gowns slipping off their shoulders, pale, large-eyed, languorous Guineveres, with their long waving hair falling over their shoulders; these are his notions of what my mother is like or ought to be like. They are excessively Woman, to my mind; embarrassing. Art has been put into his mind by a sideline of his: the new Art Pot fashion. There are a number of samples on the mantlepiece; he has gone into this line on his own and overbought, so there they are. Very expensive, he says. One enormous flower bowl has blue Chinese dragons on it and I spend hours of my childish years working out which dragon is chasing which.

Ideas, he says, are everything. What did Emerson say? Father's got it written down in his notebook. Something about the world carving a path through the woods to the door of the man who has an idea? The world is a wonderful place, he repeats, and buys stout shoes for shooting, pumps, high boots, low boots; button boots are going out. This leads him on to suits, overcoats, hats and shirts and pants. His underclothes are sacred. Everything underneath must be clean—and at this his jolly face goes pale and a look of disgust comes over him. He has a double chin now. Very often he goes off to wash his hands, runs his fingers along the edges of tables to see if there is dust.

"He's just like his mother," Mother says. "She'd scrub a goose inside and out with a scrubbing brush."

Their best friend at Uxbridge has a chemist shop and is about to start up in a new building estate at Gerrards Cross. We all drive out there in a horse charabanc to look at the new shop. We play with rolls of wallpaper and later get ourselves filthy among old tins in a rubbish dump among the gorse, while our parents are at the public house. We see a tramp asleep on the common and run away frightened; it is his sleep that has frightened us; perhaps he is dead. In the evening, we come home with the fast-trotting brake loaded with grownups who are singing "Daisy, Daisy," cuddling and occasionally throwing out a beer bottle. At home, my father toys with the economics of the pharmaceutical trade, but the idea drifts away, for obviously something better has turned up. Father points out that the chemist is a small-minded man, without ambition, and he has better things to do.

At Uxbridge, when we are naked after a bath in front of the fire, I snatch my glass slate from my brother and sit on it so that he cannot see what I have drawn. The slate smashes and cuts two large slices in my bottom. Mother rushes screaming with me to the surgery, is saved from wheeling me into the canal in the pitch-dark by a policeman. At the surgery I am given a sniff of chloroform and, coming to, see the doctor walking upside down on the ceiling. "Another inch," says the doctor "and he would have had them off." What? I get a fort, soldiers, a fire in my bedroom for this. It is worth it.

Suddenly we leave Uxbridge for the suburb of Ealing and another small but newly built villa, our first new one, with a small white balcony a foot wide and three feet long. "I'll have my breakfast on it," Father says, fancying himself on the Riviera. We can watch the trains go by from our bedroom window and have a maid called Edna who steals. We are prosperous. Father goes about humming airs from Wagner or a few hymns, subscribes to a business magazine called *System* which contains pictures of the loading yards of factories, grain elevators, the offices of large corporations and portraits of their owners. "A big man," he says, gazing at the glum, crop-haired businessman with admiration. "Poor Father," he says (reflecting on the Minister), "he did not realize his opportunities." Any moment now, our meaty magician announces, he is going off to the United States, first class on the *Mauretania,* all ex's paid—New York, Chicago, the city of the future. And this is no fancy: a cabin trunk, suits, shirts, pants, vests, socks, clothes of all kinds come into the house in larger quantities. Preparing for America, he has himself fitted out with horn-rimmed spectacles and false teeth—impresses the customers and looks more serious. We are awed by the flash of the new white teeth. He walks to mirrors, trying on grave expressions. He comes home one day and announces he has seen *Peter Pan*. He took a customer. We are told the plot.

"Do you believe in fairies?" the actor says, and a wonderful thing happens: all the children in the audience say Yes to stop a fairy called Tinker Bell from dying. This has moved Father so much that he has to wipe a tear from his eyes.

We, my mother, brother and I, are not envious or jealous. We have no desire to see things like the pantomime or *Peter Pan:* other children see such shows, but we prefer to send Father there on our behalf; it will be one more chapter of his fantastic life. For example, it is he who is asked to carve the joint in the commercial room of hotels; it is he who commands cabdrivers to carry his hampers of samples, tipping them a shilling. He knows Managers. Some of them are hostile and won't touch his stuff; but they soon find their mistake. They come crawling "on their hands and knees"— we see men in frock coats crawling down the street after him, begging now for what they foolishly refused. There are rival travelers, sinister, spying creatures, but they usually drink and lose their jobs or their trade and Father snaps it up. He threatens, in a crisis, to "knock them down." We see a number of men get a straight punch from our hero and lying flat on the floor. There are also a number of men at the top who think they are sitting pretty, but in fact, any moment, they will be down in the mud.

While we were away in Yorkshire my sister was born. My brother Cyril and I were silenced by this incomprehensible piece of news. Were our parents not satisfied with us? No sooner are we in Ealing than there is another baby, my youngest brother. Another betrayal. Why clutter up the place? It happens on my birthday too. It cannot be a good thing because Mother is always ill and talks about funerals and the illnesses of all her relations, and some woman comes in and cooks mutton stew which we refuse to eat. My little brother is called Gordon, after the General, and my sister, after one of father's trips to Dublin, is called Kathleen, after Mavourneen. My mother remembers her grandfather once took a horse to Dublin. Father sings "Kathleen Mavourneen" now. The horn of the hunter sounds in the amorous house.

With all our moving, school has been a nuisance. Father has no time to see about it. Education is very important, he says; we must not rush into it. Mother is opposed to education. All you want, she says, is schooling. Like she had. St. Anne's, Church of England; every morning the school bell sang out, she says, "To St. Anne's School, To St. Anne's School." We have had a few weeks at a penny-a-week school —we take the penny on Monday; we've been to rough schools, kept by Wesleyans. I am getting stuck in the chorus recital of the multiplication tables, also the capes and rivers of England. In history I am trapped by King Stephen and Matilda for several years. At last there is an emotional outbreak at home and we are rushed off—by Father—in the middle of term and arrive about eleven o'clock, when the children are painting irises. The paint runs. One day I throw my brother's cap onto a high hedge and we are just going into the garden to get it when we see an old lady looking out her window at us. We are terrified and run for our lives; we never came back from school by that street again and have to tell a few lies about the cap.

Then, very suddenly, that haunting cab is at the door. No trip to Yorkshire this time. We are heading for Hammersmith Broadway, Mother crying as usual, Father singing. We arrive at a shop close to the tube station in that rowdy, traffic-jammed neighborhood. Thousands of people ooze out of the tube station, the streets are crisscrossed by thousands of legs, the buses (motor buses now) stink and grind; radiators boil over. Dray horses fall down. Our bedroom looks out onto a London gin palace; our backyard is a few square feet behind a wall that looks down on the tube station. Half the night the trains whine, the porters shout out "Mahnd the dow-ers."

Something has gone wrong. The *Mauretania* has sailed without Father. The dozens of shirts are piled up on the bed, unworn, and my mother walks at a distance round the bed with a hostile look, as if looking at snakes. Father has opened up instead in the secondhand clothes business—society women's clothes resold. He also sells off his shirts. Mother serves in the shop. Left alone, my brother and I get out her oil paints, which she never used, and after squeezing out paint onto the curtains to see the effect, go to the yard, take our clothes off and paint each other all over.

One Sunday we all go off to a shop in Edgware Road to meet a woman called Mrs. Murdo who is an important figure in the old-clothes trade. We go through the suffocating smell of scores of coats and dresses and see a tall, stout woman robed in red velvet. She has glossy black hair, a plummy, booming way of talking and great breasts that look as though they are going to tumble out upon us. We wonder why she has not been fined for having breasts so large. She has a loving mouth and little eyes. She loves us and is going to be our greatest friend and we can't help noticing that Mother, wearing a brown felt hat with a feather in it and her old raincoat, makes a poor figure compared with this voluptuous woman. Later on Mrs. Murdo is not quite our best friend: some question of an invoice. Just as well, the noise and dirt and smoke of Edgware Road gave us headaches. Mother has them often now.

Usually there is no girl to help in the flat we live in above the shop, but one comes in sometimes and takes us to the Salvation Army. I begin to note that everyone drops his aitches here, like Mother, and has a sweaty smell. Going home through noisy streets, the girl tells us to hurry or the Fenians or anarchists will get us. They will throw bombs.

There is danger at Hammersmith. We can sniff it in the gassy, coal-gritty London air. Few customers come into the shop and Father amuses himself by ringing up the till; but sneak thieves, beggars and drunks have a go at our lives. One morning, a beautiful woman comes in, asks a fulsome question and falls full length, smiling, on the floor where she looks wide at the top and flat in the middle of the body, tapering like a parsnip. Mother drives us upstairs and we spy distantly a police barrow carrying the lady away, leaving a smell of whiskey behind her.

Another curious incident occurs at Hammersmith. I suddenly, without knowing it, become a writer and cause the first of a long line of serious questionings. Someone at the Wesleyan school has set us the task of writing a sentence containing the word "berth." Nothing easier in our family: Father and all his friends are always leaving one "guv'nor" for another and getting new "berths" or "cribs"; Father had even had a "berth" on the *Mauretania*. I reject this family obsession and write a confusing sentence. An evening or two later, after a report from the schoolteacher, I am questioned closely by my father and mother, who are in a hateful state.

Mother is pink in the cheeks—a bad sign with her—she has her sulky look of offended decency. This is absurd in a woman who goes about half-dressed, showing her breasts and leaving bloody things in the po. She sends angry signals to my father asking him to defend her from me. I have written on the paper: "Last night I went to see the berth of a child."

Now what (says my father, egged on by my angry mother) did I mean by "last night." Did I go out? Wasn't I at home? And then, who was the child and what did I see? Well, I saw a berth. Like a berth on a ship or a child being born? "How do you spell it?" says my father. "What does he mean he saw 'the berth' of a child?" says my mother with a small scream. "That's a funny thing for the boy to say." I see that something has gone wrong, but what? I begin to invent, or rather I describe how I have invented something. I was a doctor, I said, and I went along to see a child born. He brings a baby, I saw him bring it. "Now, keep quiet, Beat," says my father to my mother. "I want to say something to you, Victor. You are not a doctor. You made this up. You're not telling the truth."

"It's all the kid's imagination," says my mother indignantly.

"He gets it from you, old dear," grins my father.

"Not in front of his mother, I won't have it," says my mother. "Do something, Walt."

"Who gave you this idea?" says my father kindly.

"You said berth . . ." I say, beginning to cry. "I heard you."

"You'd better look after your spelling," says my father.

I perceive that my father and mother are in a nervously excited state.

"What I can't understand is where he gets his ideas from," says my mother, looking at me mistrustfully. "At eight I was helping Gran in the house."

"You ought to help your mother, you're the eldest," says my father.

I stop sniffling. The thing that worried me was the news

that I had "ideas." This sounded like a curse or an illness. Had this some connection with my closed navel? Perhaps I was going to die young like my mother's poor sister Fanny? The thought was voluptuously interesting.

Thank heaven, the cab was again at the door soon afterwards. Having attacked provincial towns, having tested the defenses of the London suburbs, Father now decided to strike boldly at the heart of this dirty city that became smokier as one got to the center of it. We arrived at Camberwell Green. In a street off Coldharbour Lane in which the smell of vinegar from a pickle factory hung low, a street of little houses, like Great-uncle Arthur's in York, and little shops that sent out such a reek of paraffin and packages that one's nostrils itched, we settled into one of our most original residences. It was, to our excitement, a flat. People lived above us. We could hear them trampling on the floor. Children raced up and down till the ceiling shook. We all got measles. A strange smell that had puzzled my parents soon showed its cause. Dry rot. We woke up one morning to find our bed was at a steep slope. The foot of the bed had gone through the floor. Father was equal to this, of course. He "got hold of the landlord" and said, "Confound you. For two pins I'd knock you down."

In a day we moved to an upper flat next-door. We were then able to see the beauty of our situation. A yard or two from our bedroom window, at the back, was one of the largest machine bakeries in London, and next to it the Camberwell roller-skating rink. I was enchanted by the lurid quality of industrial London. It all looked like something in a newspaper. The sound of these machines, their humming and clatter, was in our ears all day long; it became warm and assuring at night when the factory lights were on and we could see men in white coats and hats at the ovens and hear their shouts, and wake up after midnight and still see the show. In the small hours the delivery carts and vans woke us up. Competing with the noise of the bakery was the high,

rattling, swirling rumble of roller skates at the rink, and from
this came the screams of girls and the thump of a band. Life
had speeded up. Gentility, we appreciated, had gone. Something rank and urgently sordid was in the air. It scared me but
I liked it. Responsibility came to me. I had to look after my
brother Cyril and my sister and wheel the baby out. It was I
who had to shout "Mum, Mum, quick. He's done his business
in his trousers." Mother might send me out to get a basin of
pease pudding and a few slices of pickled pork, or a penny-
worth of pickles, or fish and chips in a newspaper; I bought
firewood and paraffin too.

The south of London has always been unfashionable and
its people have stuck to a village life of their own; they were
often poorish, but poverty, or rather not having much money
yet managing on it, has its divisions and subdivisions of
status. Respectability, the dominant trait of the English and
certainly of the two-faced London mind, prevailed. Camberwell had gone downhill since the days when the Ruskins kept
a carriage there or the Brownings thrived, and we were in
one of the reach-me-down parts of it, a place of street markets
and within call of the costers of the Walworth Road, known
for selling rabbits at fourpence. We were close also to
Loughborough Junction, noted for a dirty limerick; to go
"up the Junction" was one of our street trips. There was the
yelling and selling of the Brixton Arcades on Saturday nights.
Within a few weeks my brother and I were pissing happily off
the so-called roof garden of our flat into the yard below and
swinging on ropes hung round the lampposts outside. Soon
we would "bung a brick" through the lamps.

Instantly I knew I was, and always had been, a London
child and understood with pride my grandmother's word
about the gutter; not that we had lived in it, but to feel we
were close to it, cheered us. The school I was sent to—here
my mother, nearer in spirit to her own home ground, must
have made her sole gesture on behalf of my education—was

a rough Church of England school called St. Matthew's. (The church it was attached to, the school, and a lot of the neighborhood, including our flats, were destroyed by bombs between 1940 and 1944.) A couple of hundred boys from seven to fourteen were in this sooty, churchy building and sat in one great varnished hall. The teachers stood in a row with their canes before us unruly cattle; the headmaster, a little man with a long white beard, stood in the middle of the school on a dais. At a rap of his cane, we began with prayers and the school hymn:

> *"Loudly old Mathusians rally*
> *At the sound of the reveille."*

In shrill cockney voices we yelled it, kicking and giving punches to our neighbors as we finished off the scuffles of the schoolyard. Then a glass partition was drawn across the hall, the school was divided into two, and a couple of teachers got to work. In the middle of sums you would be distracted by the geography and history going on a yard or two away. My mind was a mixture of everything that was going on and brought to a standstill when, every now and then, a boy would be called out to be caned across the hand or, in bad cases, to be sent to the headmaster, whose cane was thicker. I was used to elementary schools and had been deadened by the turgid singsong of the Wesleyans' teaching by incantation; St. Matthew's was Dickensian. But there was one strange lesson —given, I suppose, because male shorthand writers were in demand at that time—Pitman's shorthand. Being bad at handwriting and spelling, I enjoyed the secrecy and elegance of those little signs and when I got home used to practice them. It was the beginning, for me, of the desire for other languages.

For the rest, small and alarmed by the violence of the bigger boys, I joined in the daily riot: the rabid games of marbles in the yard, with a fight every time a glass alley was hit. I learned to save mine to play with quieter boys along the gutter of Coldharbour Lane. There was often a shout of "Hump the knacker, one, two, three." In this game you leap-frogged over a row of lads, the leader having bent against the walls. Heavy boots, soled with hobnails, crushed one's shoulders. To complete the Victorian picture, the bearded headmaster suddenly died and we had a great funeral orgy. We had to walk round his coffin in the church next-door. According to the sermon, the headmaster had been a second Dr. Arnold.

At St. Matthew's the Health Inspector came round once a month to take the lice out of the heads of some of the older girls and boys. They came out in front of the class and as the inspector cracked the lice and dropped them into a basin of water beside him, the lads would wink or grin proudly at us and we would laugh back. There was a tall boy who worked in the market, whom we called Uncle because of his good nature.

"Cor, look at Uncle!" we said, admiring his distinction. One half wanted to find a louse oneself, but Mother was good at combing out the nits.

There was a hippodrome at Camberwell and on Saturday nights many of the bigger boys, the rowdy ones, used to get into the gallery. We soon found ourselves in the fashion. For ragtime had just come in and we picked up "Alexander's Ragtime Band," "Itchy Koo" and "Waiting for the Robert E. Lee" from the lads as they sang it going home in the streets. These we added to our mother's music-hall collection. More often now she sang:

> *"At Trinity Church I met me doom*
> *Now we live in a top, back room,"*

but would alleviate this by "A Bicycle Built for Two," "My Old Dutch" and "Only a Little Jappy Soldier." I loved this last, sad song.

That year I nearly won the 200 yards, and would have if my shorts hadn't fallen to my ankles only a few yards from the tape, while the crowd cheered. King Edward came to Camberwell and we waved our Union Jacks at that smiling man with the short legs and sloping stomach, his elegant Queen and his two solemn, sickly-looking children.

This was the peak; after that a decline. Everything went wrong. To start with, I set off to school and stopped to stare, unbelieving, at the posters all edged in deep-black. "King Dead," they said. "Death of the King." I ran back to tell my mother, who began to shake and say "Oh, poor Queen Alexandra." There was a picture of his bedroom in the papers and of his faithful white dog looking up at the empty bed. Mother cried and began on her long litany of royal troubles and funerals, which had a wide European range, moving from these to her dead dad, her poor sister Fanny, poor Frank buried under the Union Jack in the Atlantic, and then on to her dog Rover and a lovely little canary the cat got, which broke her heart. Somehow, one felt, they had all died for England and the Empire and I felt that year that my life was wrapped in patriotic flags and that my very body was stained red, white and blue every time I sang "Hurrah." My mother was adept at these tribal purgations.

Then a terror began to be whispered about our school. It was the terror about which I was to consult Aunt Lax at Appleton within the next twelve months. We would be standing, a row of us, in the stinking school jakes, happily seeing who could pee the highest, when the whisper would start: Jack the Ripper was about in Camberwell. What did he do? He took girls' bloomers down and slit them up the belly: better informed boys said "up the cunt." We left school in terror, and for me, with an agonized responsibility. I had the duty of collecting my five-year-old sister from a girls' school in the next street and Jack the Ripper was known to wait there. For weeks the boys talked of nothing else. I believed it, yet did not believe it. But one afternoon something sinister happened. It was in the winter and already a little dusk. I fetched my little sister and I walked, holding her hand, up Coldharbour Lane. Presently a shabby man with a feeble, knowing face came up beside us and said something like "Hullo, going home from school? Is that your little sister? Going down this way? I'll buy you a toy." And with this he took my hand. I was chilled with terror. The shop was just along the street, the way we were going, he said. I choked out "No" and sulkily said, "I don't want a toy." He kept on about the toy shop he knew, gripping my hand and stepping out with determination. " 'Ere y'are, in 'alf a mo'," he kept saying. Very soon we were outside the shop window, which was lit up and full of toys: talk of Satan taking Jesus up a high mountain and offering him the world. The story came naturally to my mind after staying in Yorkshire. " 'Ave this one. I'll give you sixpence." The philanthropist and child-lover looked ill, pale and seedy.

"No," I said.

"Come on, I'll give you a shilling—say what you want. 'Ere y'are, a shilling."

"No."

"I'll hold your sister's hand, you run in and get it."

Now there was no doubt: he was the Ripper.

By a stroke of what looks like genius to me now, in my agony I said, "That one," pointing to the biggest toy fort in the window. I could see it was the most expensive in the shop.

"I'll look after your sister," he said excitedly.

"You go and get it," I said.

"No," he said, and like a fool, he let go of my hand to put a shilling in it. It was my chance. I dropped the shilling and ran off with my sister as fast as I could. I was nearly scream-ing. We ran all the way home, past the shops, the long line of hoardings by the wasteland, the skating rink and the bread factory and hammered on the door of the flat. I made my

sister swear she would say nothing, as we went up the stairs.
And she didn't; she had noticed nothing strange and even
now does not remember the incident. I had been too
frightened to call for help in the crowded street and was too
frightened to tell my parents. When I was in my twenties I
told them at last, and they said I was making it all up.

"You have your mother's imagination," my father said.

London was dangerous. We had a girl to help my mother
for a few weeks and her mind, like the mind of the one at
Ealing, was brimming with crime. She took me to the Camberwell Bioscope to see a film of murder and explosions
called *The Anarchist's Son,* in which men with rifles in their
hands crawled up a hill and shot at each other. When the shed
which one of them was living in blew up, the film turned
soft blood-red, and the lady pianist in front of the
screen struck up a dramatic chord. In the bioscope men
walked about squirting the audience with a delicious scent
like hair lotion, that prickled our heads.

On the way to school we had to pass the hoardings, a
hundred yards of them. There were cryptic ones. There was
the huge portrait of an unshaven tramp, under which were
the words advertising Pears soap: "Ten years ago I used your
soap, since when I've used no other." There were the election
posters. Lloyd George was trying to get rid of the House of
Lords and there were comic pictures of dukes and earls with
coronets toppling off their heads. He was also introducing
health insurance and the words "Ninepence for Fourpence"
were printed in bold letters, a worry to me. But there were
two far less jolly posters. One showed the British working
man in moleskin trousers tied by string below the knee, the
general uniform of the laborer, sitting down to sausage and
mashed in his cozy kitchen with his wife and children. But
the kitchen door is open and a snarling wolf called Socialism
is coming in to rob the family of their dinner. Considering the
state of the London poor at this time—a dock laborer's wages

were about eleven shillings a week and the mass of English people had reached the lowest level of nutrition since 1760— as we know now from the researches of the Drummonds— this picture was a political crime on the part of the Tory party.

I did not understand these pictures, but they showed that London had the melodramatic spirit. There was another which I did in a way understand and which agitated my fancies. I must return first to the private life of our family to explain why.

As we ran about the streets during the day, as we swung on our rope from the lamppost, with the Catchpole brothers after school—they lived next-door, their father was a gas-meter inspector who came in to collect the sixpences from our slot machine—as we hung on to the tailboards of carts or lorries while the other kids shouted to the driver "Put your whip behind, guv'nor," the street cry of the period, we were aggressively happy. To show our mood—our Aunt Ada's daughter Hilda, aged seventeen, came down from Ipswich to stay with us, the one who went to "a boarding school for the daughters of gentlemen." This, as they say, killed us. She caught my brother and me at our occasional sport of peeing off the roof and was angry with us. I cheeked her back. She persisted, so I said: "I'll kick you up the arse hole. I'll bung up your lug." She said I was a nasty, common little boy, so I kicked her in the shins. She looked at me scornfully and went away.

We uneasily knew that we had become sordid and that the lives of our parents had, in some way, changed. My mother looked bedraggled. Her hair was always coming down, the coarse apron was round her waist. She plonked saucepans on the table full of rice boiled in water, or sago, and made stews full of fat which we could not easily eat. It turned out she was a bad cook. She had whitlows on her fingers and we had them too. At night, the soothing sound of the machines at the bakery was driven out by shouts and shrieks from the room next-door to us. My mother was shouting at my father, my father rumbled and then roared back. We had never heard them quarrel before, but these shouts went on for hours. We listened acutely for key words. The only one we could catch was ". . . That woman . . ." This was disturbing, for it had somehow got into my head that the word "woman" meant something wrong; my granda often addressed my grandma as "Woman" when he was rebuking her.

"Let's call for water," my brother said.

So we started up. "I wanta drinka water."

There was no answer. At last we got out of bed in our nightgowns. Our mother looked at us slyly and with derision. She got us the water and pushed us back to bed quickly and then continued with her tirade. Night after night this went on.

A few days after this, my father—looking very much the dandy—caught us swinging on the lamppost. He looked sick with anger and drove us inside. Mother turned on my brother and said he was round-shouldered, stupid and the image of my father's brother Edward, the weakling of that family; to me, she said, that I thought I was clever but I wasn't. She now sat by the fireguard muttering to herself. She pulled us about and punched us, and her appearance, the hair falling over her face, was savage. One evening, waiting for my father's return, she said she had toothache and called for brown paper and vinegar and made me warm it by the fire. Her face was swollen, she said, and when the paper was heated she held it to her face. Father got home, grave and dignified. Mother went to the oven, banged down a plate of chops on the table and said, "There it is. Eat it."

"What is the matter with your face, old dear?"

"You know what's the matter."

"She's got toothache," we said.

"Toothache?" said Father. "What is that? Now, Beat, you

know what I've been telling you. There is no such thing as toothache. You only think you've got it."

This interested us, for Father said this in the kindest and most rational of voices, and in fact, Mother had said nothing about toothache earlier in the day. We were anxious for the discussion to be continued but we were sent to bed, and then the nightly rumpus began again. It was still about "that woman." Who she was we could not find out and indeed did not find out for many years, but from this moment there was a shadow in our lives, often forgotten, but always there. The houses we went to live in, particularly the dining rooms and kitchens, seemed darker. I tried to wheedle the secret out of my mother, but she would give a steady, dishonest look, mocking, flirtatious and obstinate and sometimes say, very comfortably, "I'm a wicked girl."

Now on the hoardings in Coldharbour Lane there was for two or three weeks a poster that offered a confused solution to the mystery. There was something evil about all these gaudy posters, because through cracks in them you could see a piece of waste ground littered with tins and rubbish and rank weeds, and among them old men could often be seen loafing about, looking for things, men of the Jack the Ripper type. My key poster was the most sinister of all. It was a theater poster. It showed a bedroom. At the dressing table a woman, in rather naked evening dress, sits doing her hair—just as my mother did—and she is just about to give a stroke of the brush when she sees in the mirror that the bedroom door is opening. In the doorway stands a tall, dark man with a pointed black beard, startling eyes and wearing a cloak over his evening dress. There is an expression of horror on the girl's face. Above the picture is the title of the play—it is at the Hippodrome—the title is *The Bad Girl of the Family*.

Day after day I gazed at this picture when I passed. For some time I related the scene in the picture to another notice, stuck at the bottom of it: "Commit No Nuisance." People "committed suicide," "committed murder," were "committed for trial" and so on. "Committed" was an evil word. The man in the picture was clearly about to "commit a nuisance," whatever that was; but the phrase was repeated on other posters, so that Lloyd George, Pears soap, the House of Lords were engaged in the same monotonous crime. I gave up this theory and tried again. I began to suspect that the woman at the dressing table might be Mother—as I say, I was often with her when she did her hair; and although I knew she did not mean it, she often said she was a bad or wicked girl. Who was the man? I could think of no man for the part. Uncle Edward was wicked too, but I had seen him once and he was shuffling, lazy and fair-haired, not handsome like the man at the door. The only handsome man was my father and he certainly was not a villain. Yet (for my emotions were stirred) I had my first jealous sense that my father *just* could be the intruder in that room. And there was this curious underlying feeling that Woman had some side to her nature that it would be unlucky to know. It would be like falling into the canal and drowning. Even so, I knew—but in a child's way, without consciously knowing it—that the scene came out of a play about a girl being seduced by a villain. My mother's storytelling was always reckless and suggestive, because when she got to the sexy bit, she would stop short and not finish the sentence, but give a knowing nod. (This became a habit all her life, so that, by not finishing a simple sentence, she could make any innocent thing sound lewd.)

"So I said to the shopkeeper, 'I want a pair of . . .' and ran home and took off . . . and he said, 'Mrs. P, just hang them on the . . .' " or "So I sat down in the . . . and closed the . . ."

So, to return to the picture: it was a mixture of our life and a fiction. The bad girl was, in a poetic way, my mother, the man was my father; but who "that woman" of these new, violent rows was, was beyond me. There was no other woman but my mother, though you saw imitations in the street. My mother was Woman herself.

About these quarrels we were as indignant as little lords. By what right did these two grown-up animals have these consuming battles, put on these tremendous plays and not only keep us out of them, but in doing so, ignore us! It was intolerable. There was a growing feeling in my brother and myself that we ought to tell them so; and that they were selfish. This feeling was getting very strong in me.

Left out of the battle, I sulkily threw myself into the rough and tumble outside. I swapped my father's fishhooks for a skate and lost it in a fight on Denmark Hill. (Had he been alive, Ruskin might have seen an incident which has no parallel in *Et Praeterita*.) I fell in love with a girl who lived with the theatricals two doors down. I pinched, at last, a pound packet of haricot beans and threw them at the school-teacher and tore up my writing book. I got a couple on the hands for this and was made to stand on the bench in school after everyone had left. You could usually see three or four solemn figures doing this after school. Once a girl wetted her drawers and they swelled out like a white balloon. We had to wait for the teacher to release us. One by one the others were released, but my teacher did not appear. It was winter. The school darkened. I decided to escape. I got down and crept to the door and there I ran into the teacher. Now, I thought, I'm in trouble, but to my surprise, he said, "Good heavens, I forgot about you. Come home to tea. Then I'll take you home. I live near you."

There followed the most memorable tea of my life. The master and his wife gave me strawberry jam and cakes. Their room was full of books and had three armchairs. I sat in an armchair. We had only one in our flat. The teacher and his wife spoke to me as if I was their age, and soon, being always a talker, I told them all about my father and grandfather. Then the teacher took me home.

"I will speak to your father," he said. "I think you ought to go to a better school. You're good at shorthand."

What passed between my father and the master I do not know, but my father—and, surprisingly, my mother—were impressed by the shorthand. I was even congratulated and my father, instead of being simply good-natured, was almost respectful to me. I did not go to a better school, but the very next day my brother and I were sent off on the late train to Sedbergh. We had our classic arrival: torn jerseys, holes in breeches and stockings. It was our last visit for many years and after a month we were sent off from York, not to London, but to my birthplace, Ipswich. A new upheaval had occurred in my father's life—my grandfather had hinted as much and he, too, suggested there was a wicked woman concerned in it; for the moment, my grandparents supported my mother and said that except for cooking, housekeeping, sewing, etc., she was sensible. It appeared also that fortunately "certain people" did not know we had been living in Camberwell: we were there, it seems, in hiding. Father had gone bankrupt at Hammersmith and had started up again, somewhere else, in Mother's name.

5

In these sudden crises in our lives, when I went off with my father to Yorkshire, my mother sometimes took my brother Cyril to her sister's at Ipswich and left him there. When the two of us met again we would be astonished to see how long our legs had got and scarcely recognized each other's voices. Mine had the hard Yorkshire strain; he had the softer, politer voice of the South. Unlike myself, he was an affectionate boy and he observed more of the true situation in our home than I did. He was an easy victim and he early became a very bad stammerer. This vanished at our aunt's house, where he was the little gentleman, used to the drawing room, to servants and Edwardian niceties. When he came back to our rough and tumble, the sight of a table not properly laid and of rooms ill-furnished and knocked about by our life made him nervous and upset. He talked in a careful and elderly way at that time.

But now we were both leaving York for Ipswich on our own. The train ran through the empty landscape of the Fens lying under the wide skies that had moved the Norwich painters. We saw powerful Ely Cathedral on its hill in that flat land and were in sweetly rolling East Anglia, the country of large village churches, monastic buildings and pretty white pargeted and timbered houses, some of the loveliest things in England. This region had once been rich when England's great wealth was in wool and before the water power and steam engine of the North had captured the trade a century before. Strange names like Eye and March excited me. I had read *Hereward the Wake* and knew of fanes and that "silly Suffolk" meant holy Suffolk.

I saw the reason for my brother's distinction when we got out at Ipswich Station. We were met by a tall man of fifty who had a domed head like a very large pink egg, fluffy white hair and a short white beard. He looked like a pious ram. Perhaps those mild blue eyes and red wet lips were roguish—as my mother often blurted out in her cheery way—but he had a slow, considerate manner and the voice had the straying educated bleat. He was, I had heard, notorious for knowing everything and he had the most enlightened views. My plump cousin, Hilda, the girl whom I had threatened to kick up the arse hole, shook hands in a condescending way. She was his step-daughter. Instead of hiring a cab at the station, as bounders and commercial travelers did, we crossed Ipswich economically by tram, sitting on top under the sparks of the trolley. Our uncle—for so he was by marriage—pointed out the shipping on the river Orwell, mentioned the chief trades of the city, noted the birthplace of Cardinal Wolsey (a man, he said, ruined by ambition), and the ancient streets of the town, in a serious, prosing East Anglian singsong. Now and then my cousin firmly pointed to two or three houses belonging to her relations, houses that seemed like mansions to me and lying in luxurious grounds, protected by laurels, the most monied of English shrubs. She handed out lady-like social chitchat. We were wearing cloth caps and she asked, snobbishly I thought, where our school caps were. We hadn't got any, I said. She was put out. Obviously we who had come out of the depths were about to soar to the heights; but we had yet to know about family strategy. The tram set us down in a district of humble little villas on the outskirts of the city and there we found our house. Only Mother was there, waiting for us with the other children. Father had gone. He had left us. He lived seventy miles away in a flat in London and was to come very rarely during the next year for a day's visit. Our new uncle baa-ed some charitable words to my mother, as indeed he had done to the tram conductor and a couple of people on the tram who had deferred very markedly to him, and then went off. He was our aunt's second husband.

Our aunt Ada had brought off a coup. She was a cleverer, more independent and collected woman than my mother, and though she had my mother's chattering gaiety, was far more discreet in tongue and manner. Laughter with her had become a refined giggle. After she had buried poor Frank at sea and had given birth to her daughter, she had settled in Ipswich (after Father's abrupt departure in 1900), where houses were cheap; she lived with Gran, who kept lodgers. Gran Martin looked after Hilda while her mother went to work in a post office. For years, sitting behind the grill, Ada had sold stamps to this well-off and philanthropical gentleman who, hearing her story, proposed to her. He was much older than she was. They were married. It was a joke in both families.

Her Fred was the eldest and most solemn of thirteen children. His grandfather, I believe, had begun life as a cobbler in Norwich; in the next generation a small fortune was made out of leather; our new uncle retired young on his means, became the director of several waterworks and managed his property. He was a strong Presbyterian and active in Liberal politics and was, among other things, one of the trustees of the local Mechanics' Institute—one of those hundreds of libraries established privately all over England for the education of industrial workers. The high point of the family's social distinction was reached when Uncle let the house he had been brought up in to the German Kaiser on one of his visits to England. Among his brothers, sent to great Public Schools, was a barrister on the Eastern Circuit, famous at murder trials, an architect, an artist and one enormously successful businessman in the wholesale provision business, supposed to be worth half a million pounds and a partner of the famous Lipton. He had taken the house of a peer of the realm and—my mother said—drank champagne for breakfast. The only girl was one of the first women to go to Girton, and after looking after her mother half her life, married a well-off man who was in the trade. So it was respectfully reported to us; but they belonged to the sober generation of new wealth and were shocked by any sons or daughters who went in for high social pretensions. They were Presbyterians, public-spirited, bought pictures at the Academy, and were very respectable.

There was only one flaw in this family. This part of England had been settled in the early centuries of the Teutons and by the de Burghs, the family name indeed of the dukes of Norfolk, and although he made no absurd claims in the matter, my uncle was careful to recall that this was the origin of his name. But the English have always mumbled foreign language: my good uncle's name became Bugg. This he proudly stuck to, but many of his brothers couldn't stand it. They changed theirs to avoid low jokes. The news that dear Ada had married a Mr. Bugg sent my mother into fits; and Gran, who thought second marriages were wicked, grimly called her son-in-law plain Bugg for the rest of her life, and after a drink or two, would mutter about "the old bugger." It took the kind, patient man about twenty years to win her round.

The Buggs lived in the fashionable end of Ipswich and ourselves had been carefully placed at the other: there was no desire to make acquaintance. Even the two dear sisters scarcely communicated. We were that humiliating plague: poor relations. Far from ascending, we were sent off to a rough school in Cauldwell Hall Road. Not that that mattered to us: we were free, spending our spare time in the Suffolk countryside where at harvest time we were to see the rows of men cutting the corn with sickles in the fields. We brawled on the "Pansy," the name of a meadow near the school, and, as far as education went, I turned back to reciting the capes and rivers of England and Stephen and Matilda.

It was odd, considering my uncle's principles, that he was reluctant to see us; eventually, because he was a man of strong moral sense, he told us one of the reasons, and gossip between the sisters soon revealed the rest. One day, Mother said, putting on a mocking voice, "You are going to 'The Highlands.' High up—high in name, high in nature." It was the name of the house. We dressed in our best clothes and walked up the long hill to the house. The house seemed to us immense, but it was really an ample but unpretentious Victorian villa. There were far larger ones about it of the kind which are either pulled down or turned into flats nowadays. It was approached by a small drive, its two lawns were sheltered by pines, sycamores and a cedar. The dining room had its heavy furniture and heavy curtains. Two bronze gladiators gallivanted on the black marble mantelpiece, with a marble clock like a temple between them. On the walls were oil paintings, bought from the Academy, which looked like dark gravy mixed with cabbage. They were cribs from Morland and Constable. In the morning room, two thousand books were in their walnut cases—the works of Gibbon, Mill, Macaulay, Prescott, Motley, the *Life of Garibaldi*— indispensable to our uncle's generation—political, historical or philosophical volumes, and his classics as well. No fiction was allowed. After breakfast the three maids were called in for prayers. Our uncle, who was working his way chronologically through the Bible, had got once more to Kings and intoned a chapter in a voice of deep, rebuking melancholy; then all knelt down and listened to a long prayer.

After breakfast we walked round the garden as far as the conservatory, where our aunt talked in a fanciful way to the gardener, and then sat under a sycamore tree and my cousin Hilda brought out one or two improving books, for I was known to be a reader. I had read every line of several volumes of the *Home Magazine*—especially a grotesque serial called "The Wallypug of Why," an enjoyable fantasy about the plots of a cathedral gargoyle: also bits from the Children's Encyclopaedia, *Hereward the Wake,* comics and *Marriage on Two Hundred a Year,* one of the popular handbooks of the period. My cousin asked me what I thought of Montesquieu, who, it turned out, was French. That bowled me out, so she set about correcting my English. In the afternoon we walked with my aunt in the arboretum, where she paused at each unusual tree. She had gone in for carrying a lorgnette, as a lady-like thing, and raised it when she read out the botanical name. We returned then to her drawing room, done in the prettiest Edwardian fashion, and she got her lorgnette out once more as she took us on a tour of her collection of watercolors by a local artist called Barlow Woods. My aunt had a flirtatious manner: I decided, on the spot, to become a painter.

By now Uncle Bugg thought the time for seriousness had come. We were taken to a spare bedroom. There he unlocked a wardrobe door and from a shelf he took down five or six books bound in black cloth which had a cross and crown in gold monogram on them.

"I keep these books here, locked up, and for a special reason," he said. "In order," he said with a sly but forcible smile, "that no one shall ever read them. They belonged to one of my sisters whose life was ruined by them, and when she died, my first step was to go to her house and take them away. They are the works of a fraudulent American woman: Mary Baker Eddy. I am sorry to say that your father—who perhaps hasn't had the opportunities for education—has become a follower of that woman. I have told him that she is one of the false prophets the New Testament warns us against. It has already distressed your grandfather, and I am glad to say, your mother has understood the evil of this woman who has misled your father. His judgment in many things is weak. He has good qualities but he is easily carried away. I have explained to him that this is trash."

My uncle smiled gravely. He had a general vanity in knowing more about everything than anyone else, and his talk—as we got to know him—was a catalogue of moral and intellectual victories over everyone, from the Liberal party down to his servants.

This news meant only one thing to me. A mystery was solved. "That woman," who had rocked our nights at Camberwell, was an American prophetess. That was why my father was not with us. Instantly, but silently, we rallied to Father. It had gradually become clear to us that he was a natural follower. He followed all kinds of people. It struck us as rather fine. Just as he went to the theater, stayed at big hotels, went to smart restaurants, for our sake, as if we had sent him there in order to save ourselves the trouble of it, so we felt about his friendship with Mrs. Eddy. She would get a good deal out of it. We felt proud of him. He was far above us. It was not surprising that he had sailed into this high position and had left us.

Yet, once Uncle Bugg had locked the wardrobe door, I became uneasy. On our way home, Mother told us Father was coming to see us on Sunday. My brother, who adored him, was pleased; but I was not. I did not miss him. I did not think about him. He would spoil our Sunday. We would have to give up going to the camp in the peafield we had made with our gang of children in the street. We would not be able to sit up in the chestnut tree and smoke cigarettes for which some stoved window blinds served as tobacco. We would not be able to go off down the Orwell to watch the steamers. And—it now occurred to me—Uncle Bugg's story put a new meaning on that poster showing the scene from *The Bad Girl of the Family*. The handsome man in the opera cloak who looked in at the bedroom door and frightened the bad girl, would frighten me no more. He was my father for certain now and the Bad Girl was Mrs. Eddy. He had moved on to a prophetess.

I told Mother what Uncle Bugg had said, in order to find out more from her. But the moment I spoke, I could see her devious, watchful look coming on. I knew she would lead me on to find out what I knew and would then turn on me and laugh in my face. And then she would stop, looking shrewdly and keenly at me, and would look away up at the ceiling or out the window and go into thoughts of her own. Out of these she would speak and mysterious sentences would come.

"I dunno what to make of it," she said. "I told him not to do it."

"Who, Mum?"

"What are you talking about?"

"You said you didn't know what to make of it, told him not to do it."

"Did I? Well don't you do it either."

"I haven't done anything."

"Haven't you? Littering up Mrs. Bowser's hall with all

those notes you wrote to that girl—her mother came round
and said for you to stop it." Now, this was true. One of my
twenty-four-hour passions had blown up for the pretty little
daughter of Mrs. Bowser down the street, and I had been
delivering notes there at the rate of two or three an hour.
But I knew my mother. I knew she was escaping by turning
the tables on me.

Presently, having won her victory, she changed her mind.
"It all started with your uncle Arthur up at York. I don't
know how I got in with such a lot, but when you're young
you're thoughtless. It was your dad's cousin Dick."

And now one of her stories came out. That cousin of my
father's, the ill and miserable lithographer who couldn't
keep his food down and was out of work, had been cured by
this American woman, Baker something. The whole family
had been converted—except Uncle Arthur. He had stuck to
Burton and "circumstances alters cases" and fought back
angrily against them.

"Your father believes it," she said.

"Like Uncle Bugg said," I said.

She looked wary again.

"And there's been all this trouble," she said.

But at this she broke off and would not say what it was.

I could see there was a battle going on inside Mother's
mind, one which she was losing, but because of her tenacity,
never losing for good, and what it was about would come
out only in hints or in shouts in the next ten or fifteen years.
It tore my loyalties and my heart in two.

The "trouble" (gradually my mother and I put it together)
was this. Father's proposed journey to America had been
a device of his employer. The villain wanted to get Father
out of the country while he fiddled the books. A telegram
from the woman bookkeeper of the firm—she had come to
see us at Ealing—brought my father back from Liverpool
when he was embarking. He came back to London, and

hearing that the man had also been making advances to the unwilling girl, he had had a stand-up fight with him in his office in Aldersgate Street. It was a curious fight, for the man had locked himself in his office. My father, though short, was heavy and strong, and under his bland manner, had stores of violence: he charged at the door and broke it in, and of course, "knocked the man down." The sequel is vague. Undefeated, Father suddenly decided to go into the high-class secondhand-clothes business in Hammersmith, and having once been bankrupt in Ipswich, he opened up in Mother's name. That shop had failed too. He had fled to Camberwell and then, not to be crushed and having good connections in his trade, he started up again in the art needle-work trade in Newgate Street, opposite the Old Bailey. This new being, exalted by a new religion, heard of his sister-in-law's rich marriage and advanced hopefully upon Ipswich to get Uncle Bugg to put money up for his new firm. Father had placed us there as an outpost. Uncle Bugg considered my father's career and decided that he was too volatile an investment and also chaffy in his religious life. It was because of this and not entirely because we were poor relations that we were put at the other end of the town. Aunt Ada was not going to have her lucky marriage wrecked from the beginning by a bankrupt brother-in-law.

We knew nothing of this for years. Nor did we really know anything of my father's religion or even what it was called. George V was crowned that year—1911—and in Ipswich the affair was celebrated in the park by a mock attack on an Afghan Hill Fort which went up in smoke. Soldiers in red coats and pillbox hats walked about the streets. It was a fine summer. My cousin Hilda was kinder. Down to the Art Gallery we went and saw a huge picture of Lucrezia Borgia offering poison to a page, while the wicked Pope looked treacherously on. Hilda said she liked the Borgias.

They were not Presbyterians nor were they followers of a mealy-mouthed American prophetess.

Hilda hated her step-father and especially his religion. She was High Church and took me to see the ritual and smell the incense of that fashionable religion. I was bored.

There was trouble with my accent. I had given up Yorkshire speech and had quickly picked up the Suffolk singsong. At school we called each other "boa"—from the Teutonic *bauer*—and lilted to one another phrases like "Where y'now goin', boa?" And when we parted we always used the pretty Suffolk habit of saying "Farewell, boa," instead of "Goodbye." My brother and I spent hours in our chestnut tree smoking. We had moved to elderberry pipes now, but we went on with the window blinds. There were a dozen of these blinds to get through. They were made of stiff, dressed blue calico and were stored in the roof. Though scorching to the tongue, the blinds tasted better and burned better than chrysanthemum leaves. We finished all except two pairs that year. On April Fool's Day we got a lot of gents off their bikes by shouting out "Your tire's flat," and bawling "April Fool" at them. My mother sent us to the Congregational Sunday School, but it was a riot of thrown hymn books. She tried us with the Church of England, but not having heard of its theology or prayers, we were at a loss and were offended by the classy accents of the clergyman and congregation. It is odd, considering my father's religiosity: I was never baptized. Like the closed navel, it was a distinction I stuck to.

Then came the Saturday night when my father arrived and stayed until teatime on Sunday. Well-dressed and graver than I remembered him, he stood like an intruder among us. He surprised us by bringing us to order; he stopped us running out to the chestnut tree. He was in a temper about the blinds, the first temper I had ever seen him in. And he and my mother quarreled, my mother shouting about "that woman" again, and asking him what he thought we lived on, and of course the Bugg family was dragged in. These rows made me jealous and I stopped the quarrel by calling out: "Dad, Dad. Thou shalt not divorce thy wife. It says it in the Bible."

"There you are," said my mother. "Your own children know."

My father said sternly, "Little boys are to be seen and not heard."

"There you are," cried my mother passionately to me, and changing sides in a flash as she always did, "You dare talk to your father like that."

And then she started crying and said her dear sister Ada would take her in and Father said her "dear sister Ada" had scarcely spoken to her though she lived scarcely two miles away.

"And you know why," cried my mother.

At teatime a cab came for my father and we were glad to see him go; or at least I was. But Mother repented. She was a bad girl, she said, with a wicked tongue and Gran had a wicked tongue too. "Your father is doing everything for the best. He has got faith, remember that. He always had. When we were at Daniels," she went on, and she would soothe us and herself with the story of her life, looking nervously at the door when she did. For we noticed now that for a year or more—it had begun in Camberwell—she was frightened of doors, especially the front one. "Go and peep, don't let them see you. See who it is."

Once we heard her talking at the door to a man. "No one of the name of Pritchett here," she said. "Never heard of them. I'm the maid."

We stared at her. She gave us a threatening look, her greenish-gray and fretful eyes quick and full of lies. We felt we were either floating in the air or sinking through the earth.

6

We were off again, of course. The year's soft and lazy affair with my birthplace had passed. We had scarcely heard the word God at all for a twelvemonth in this pagan holiday. We had made two or three more visits to our Aunt Ada's. I see her, on one of them, duck-breasted, wearing a fanciful dress, and under a large Edwardian hat, raising her lorgnette to the one or two nudes in a local picture exhibition and te-he-he-ing in her bird-like way to me, telling me to come over and admire. Mother would have gone pink and pushed me out of the gallery. Uncle, a believer in practical education, sent my brother and me up the vertical ladder of one of the towers of his waterworks on Rushmere Common and instructed us in the digging of artesian wells and the economics of diesel power. There was an election that year and a crowd of us went into town, singing:

*"Vote, vote, vote for Mr. Churchman,
Kick old Goddard in the eye."*

At Felixstowe we saw the sea for the first time. It seemed like a wide-eyed face pressing against our faces and tingling in our hair. Mother talked of ships going down on the Goodwin sands and shouted from the shingle, "Don't go in deeper." A hotel caught fire.

In Yorkshire and in Suffolk there had been peace. No one spoke about money or the struggle for existence; there was none of our family talk about "getting on"; there was no anxiety. My brother and I had the freedom of country life; we need not "get on" at all. These influences slowly made me feel that although I was not as clever as many boys at school, I was clever enough and egotistical enough to be able to do what I liked with my life, and that my mind was already deciding what this should be. Money would have nothing to do with it. Just as I could feel myself grow and urge myself to grow more, so I felt that the important thing was to be alone—alone in the street, in the Fells or on the Suffolk commons. And always walking and moving away.

My aunt's pictures gave me a hint of how this would be possible: not her gravy-colored Academy landscapes, but the watercolors of Barlow Woods. This gentleman was alive. He was also young. He was witty, my aunt said. He sat down alone in a field by the Orwell and painted the trees by the water, the tide ebbing from the silvered mudbanks. I liked painting and I wondered, when I walked to the lane where Gainsborough had painted his elms, whether some of that influence would fall upon me. The thought of being a writer had not occurred to me. I did feel that I could choose some studious kind of life, but the barriers to knowledge seemed to me far too great. I would not have to read or know, to be a painter. A picture took one instantly through a door into another world, one like our own, but silent. There were no

raised voices. There were no rows. And there, alive, was
Barlow Woods creating these scenes. I never saw him.
Whether he was a good painter or a poor one, I do not know.
But, unlike ours at home, his pictures were done in real
paint. In Ipswich, in that peaceful interregnum of my boyhood, the idea of being a painter began to dawdle in my
mind.

But we left.

There is a short tunnel on the south side of Ipswich Station
and we all came out of it in a cloud of smoke and steam,
with the solemn knowledge that we were now heading for
London's aching skies. We had one glimpse of the blue
spear of sea in the Stour estuary and at the sailing boats of
Manningtree: except for days at Felixstowe and Torquay we
were sea-starved children and went into moans of self-pity
because of this. We had said our last Suffolk "Farewell, boa"
to the lazy and forgotten country of slow-talking Suffolk
people who had been stunned by the east wind. We got two
shillings each and some cultural advice from Uncle: not bad.

We arrived on a dull May day, in London, at the pleasant
suburb of Dulwich. The center of Dulwich is still a Georgian
village of fine houses and stately trees. There was the College
and the old college chapel; and near it the small and famous
art gallery. Everywhere one saw notice boards reading
"Alleyn's College of God's Gift." College boys in their blue-
striped caps were in the streets. Ruskin, always dogging me,
had often visited the gallery; Browning had walked in the
woods that overhung the village; and the Crystal Palace,
built for the Exhibition of 1851 and moved to Sydenham
Hill, dominated all with its strange glass towers and its lollop-
ing glass dome, like a sad and empty conservatory. From the
Parade, at the top, one could see the dome of St. Paul's only a
few miles away, and a distant slit of the Thames.

We noticed that the family fortunes had gone up a little
when we got to Dulwich. Our destination was not the sedate

part of the district, but on the outskirts at the Norwood end. We found ourselves in a rather taller villa than usual, in a street where dozens of houses were to let, for this was the period of the Edwardian housing slump. Father was indignant at the rent: sixteen shillings a week. He was often in arrears with it. The house had one distinctive feature— he proudly pointed out—dark-blue fireproof paper in its front room.

But the London air was mottled with worry. We had come back to a father who had changed his character. The merry, bouncing fellow with the waxed mustache and the cigar, the genial carver of the commercial rooms, the singer of bits of Kathleen Mavourneen had shaved off his mustache and had been replaced by a man whose naked face was stern. In the past year he also had experienced freedom—freedom from us. He had been living in a comfortable furnished flat and had had leisure to remake his own life. He had found another self. We had come back and this new self was trapped in a situation he could not get out of. He stared at us and the corners of his mouth drooped: he saw the ineluctable. When I was eighteen he once said bitterly, "I'm warning you. Don't make my mistake. I married too young, before I knew my own mind." I hated him then, and even more for saying this. At Dulwich it was plain that he had passed through some crisis, and not a simple one. The idea of righteousness was very powerful in him, despite his unreliability; it was this idea, I believe, that began to corrupt him. An emotional struggle—I would guess —and then righteousness killed his heart. His gaiety vanished. Self-punished, he slowly drifted into punishing us. How else to account for his black moods?

But his losses had their gains—perhaps, after all, the will meant more than the heart to him. One short-term gain for him was his new religion which, since Mother rejected it, he kept to himself. We knew nothing about it, but we knew it existed. He was determined to keep *that,* a false romantic compensation and counselor which corrupted him very quickly. Or, perhaps he corrupted it. He once told me more about his conversion. Mother was wrong in saying that Cousin Dick's peculiar recovery from chronic dyspepsia was the main cause. The decisive thing—and the decisive would always be personal for him—was the death of a friend of Cousin Dick's. This man was dying of tuberculosis but believed that he could be cured by Christian Science treatment. The worse he got, the more he believed; and just before he died he declared that he knew it was "the Truth" and made my father swear to stick to it. It was this tragic failure, arriving at a moment when (I think) Father himself felt he was in a desperate situation, that converted my father.

The second gain was remarkable. He had refused to give in to bad luck in his business and now he had at last succeeded. In that year while he was alone in Dulwich, and with the help of the clever woman who had got him back from Liverpool in the nick of time, he at last realized his dream. And this time it was no deception. He had got out of the despised retail trade; he had left the jaunty and vulgar world of the commercial traveler and out of that came one remarkable change, one that separated us from him, as if there had been a real divorce. His name had changed. Until now he had been Walter S. Pritchett; now the Walter was dropped. His second name appeared. He was Sawdon Pritchett, a name so sonorous, so official, so like a public meeting that we went off into corners and sniggered at it. He would, all the same, lower his eyes with his touching modesty when he said it. He pulled out a card to establish his new name with us. There it was:

> *Sawdon Pritchett Ltd.*
> *Art Needlework Manufacturers*
> *Offices and Showrooms Newgate Street*

"Opposite the Old Bailey," he pointed out.

> *"When will you pay me*
> *Said the Bells of Old Bailey,*
> *When I grow rich*
> *Said the bells of Shoreditch,"*

Mother sang. Ominously too.

He took us to his office. Pigeons laid their eggs on the dirty balcony of his floor of the building. The crowds queued outside the Courts for the murder trials and down below, on the wood-blocked streets, scavenger boys in white coats dashed in and out of the traffic with brushes and wide pans to sweep up the horse manure. My brother and I envied their dangerous and busy life and their wide-brimmed hats.

Father's elevation and dignity had a silencing effect on our home. The words Managing Director put him in a trance. He told us that we now had many privileges; first, we were the children of a Managing Director, living in a refined neighborhood among neighbors who would study our manners. We also had the privilege of living within a couple of hundred yards of a remarkable family and an even more remarkable woman, the secretary to the company, whose brother, high in financial circles, played tennis at a most exclusive club. My father doubted if this family would feel able to know us immediately, but if by some generous condescension they did, we would remember to have our hands and shoes clean, brush our hair, raise our caps and never sit down until told to do so. Father's face had lost its roundness. It had become square, naked and authoritative. It also looked pained, as if he were feeling a strange, imposed constraint.

Mother supported him vigorously; in fact, as we soon saw, with unnatural vigor. It was irony on her part. Our debt to this family and to this lady was total, she said. The lady appeared almost before Father finished speaking, which took my father and mother aback, my mother's hair (as usual) being not quite in a state for receiving another woman. And we were taken aback too. We had expected perhaps another operatic Mrs. Murdo in red velvet; instead a tall, beautiful young woman with burning brown eyes and black hair came in. Her eyelashes fluttered. She had alluring lips and, on the upper lip, a few black hairs at the corners which, before the fashion changed, made women sensually disturbing. Her voice was a shade mannish, low and practical, she was slender and wore a business-like coat and skirt with a white blouse. She struck us as elegant, even fashionable. To our delight she teasingly addressed our father as "Father," which made him blush. She even called him "Sawdon"; it was as if she had called him Lord. She put us so much at our ease that we loved her at once and got boisterous; my father deferred to her and so did my mother, who also blushed.

One of her first questions to me was, when was I going to sit for a scholarship to the College? This was startling to me and I looked for help to my father.

"When he is ready," said my father. "I do not want him to imagine that just because his father has his own business he has only to sit about waiting for everything to fall into his lap."

"Which school are you going to send him to?" She turned to my mother.

"I really don't know," said my mother.

"We are considering the matter," said my father in his board-room manner. "It may be this or that. It may be the College, though we shouldn't limit ourselves to that. There may be other, better schools, than the College."

My father's evasions stopped. Certainty appeared and a look of polite but firm rebuke came to his face. He liked the gaiety of the lady, but he was not going to allow her to lead the way in his family or anywhere else. The matter was raised to a graver, higher and crushing tribunal.

"He will go where the Divine Mind wishes him to go, for he is a reflection of the Divine Mind, as Mrs. Eddy says."

This puzzling remark lifted me into a region I had never

heard of before; my head seemed to stretch painfully. I thought someone had put on me a hat that came down over my ears.

My mother looked appealingly and mistrustfully at the lady. "Are you in this too?" she seemed to signal anxiously, but what she said was: "I never had much education myself."

"We were brought up very poor but my parents were careful. We had to earn our livings early, my brother and I. We worked hard and went to evening classes. Father made us get our diplomas," said the refined lady in her precise way. "My brother qualified as an accountant."

My spirits fell. After the gaieties of Ipswich we were once more caught by the doctrine of hard work and bleak merit. Mother's neck wobbled in a pained way, as if she had been shot but was too lady-like to mention it.

"If I may offer a thought there," said my father, for he had not quite lost touch with the charms of an easy life, "what these boys need, what we all need, is the Truth."

"Stick to the point," said my mother, desperately blinking at him.

"I'm sure you've been too busy to think about it yet," said the lady tactfully, but Mother did not take it as tact, and gave her one of her looks.

"Why don't you do something about it, making a fool of me in front of that woman?" my mother shouted at my father when the lady went. "And why don't you get those boys to a school?"

Father pointed out that now my mother had a friend and we all had a friend and that soon our general tone would be raised by this fortunate contact. This did not happen. In the years to come my mother kept herself apart from this family.

"Who was her father? Only a man on the railway and the mother takes lodgers. Why are we beholden to her?" Mother said. For many years the lady was known to us as "Miss H."

There was my father sitting in that office with "that

woman" all the week, Mother said: why didn't he stay with her if she was so wonderful. We know she put up the money. How did she get it? Cheese paring. My mother was not going to cheapen herself by visiting them. She might not be educated but she knew the difference between sixpence and a shilling and had been brought up straight. We were shocked. Mother was jealous. There were two women: Mrs. Eddy and this lady, Miss H.

And why had we got to be so polite to her? The Business, that's what it was, Mother said. The Business. Our father had ceased to be our father. He now became "the Business." It was a shadow in our fireproof room.

And then this woman, Miss H, was a woman, and women are woman-like, Mother said. Not that she had any doubts about Father, for she knew he was true, but if women don't get one thing, they go for another. They don't let go.

As for Father being true, this is as certain as anything can be. He really hated women. He despised them. They existed to be his servants, for his mother—as my mother said—had waited on him hand and foot. Of course he charmed women; they liked talking to him, he appealed to their masochism. If they fought back or showed any signs of taking charge of him, his face went cold. His favorite gesture was to hold up his hand, palm outwards, and wag it insultingly up and down, silently telling them to shut up. Their role was to listen to him, and he had a lot to say. But once let them discuss, differ or suggest another idea, and the hand went up, playfully at first, but if they persisted, he was blunt with them. He described these incidents to us often. His phrase was, "I put her in her place." It was unlucky that he had not met Mrs. Eddy. She was dead. It was unlucky also that in his trade most of the workers were women. It must be said that several of these, who admired his vitality, loved him all their lives. Perhaps Miss H, the bookkeeper, did; Mother scornfully thought so.

At Dulwich the question of schools became grandiose for

my brother and me. We were the sons of a Managing Director: our value rose. Prospectuses came in from half the great Public Schools of England. Eton and Harrow were dismissed easily; it was astonishing how many boys from such schools passed false checks in the course of a decade and got into the papers. We saw ourselves at Dulwich College, swaggering arm in arm like the college prefects in their tasseled hats. We walked behind them, listening with awe to their astonishing man-of-the-world talk about girls. We caught drawling hints of musical plays and lavish disputes about whether the Indian Civil Service or the Army was to be preferred. One day we heard a youth pity another whose father was in a Line regiment. These snobberies had—I now see—the effect of gin upon our unaccustomed fancies. We began to live double lives. I read the prospectuses eagerly. At these schools one was away from home, and that I longed for. But I saw the fatal difficulty: I knew no Latin. For twopence cadged off my mother I bought a secondhand Latin primer. I decided to teach myself and enter paradise.

I was defeated on the very first page. There was a sentence that ran, "Inflection is a change in the form of a word." There was no dictionary in the house. Mother had never heard of the word "inflection" nor had Father. But I had heard of "form." But how could a word have form? It wasn't a thing like a table or a vase. I drew a pencil line, carefully following the shapes of the letters round a word or two; that led nowhere. I skipped to *mensa,* but what on earth did "by, with or from a table" mean? I'd never heard anyone say it. Mother hadn't either. As for the verb *sum,* mentioned idolatrously by my grandfather when I was five or six, I couldn't find it in the book.

One morning there was a click at the letterbox and Mother said in a panic, "What was that?"

"Someone at the door," we said, but all stood still, knowing that this was a dangerous moment.

"Stay here," said my mother. "Vic, open the kitchen door and peep up the hall." I peeped. No person stood beyond the colored glass of the front door, which threw a sad and bloody light on the passage, but a letter was on the linoleum.

"A letter," I said.

"Wait," she said, drying her hands on her apron; then all advanced towards the letter. My mother stopped about a yard away, looking cautiously at it. Then she made a dart at it and picked it up. It was only a circular.

"It give me a turn," said Mother, whose English had deteriorated in the last year.

It was a circular begging on behalf of Treloar's Home for Crippled Children and contained pictures of the schoolrooms, the workshops, the dormitories, the playgrounds by the sea in the south of England where these children lived. I envied them. How lucky to be a cripple. If only, in some game of football in the park, I could get my leg broken, go on crutches, and helped onto a train, go to this place. The thought was luxurious. For an hour or two I tried limping.

Then, with the suddenness with which everything happened to us, Father having gone off at seven to be at his workroom before the "hands" got there to see they did not cheat him of his time, Mother put the two youngest children with the next-door neighbor and marched my brother and me for a mile and a half, muttering to herself, to Rosendale Road School, near Herne Hill.

"I've brought these two boys," she said, giving us a push, to a dapper little man in a tail coat and who looked like a frosted pen nib. His name was Timms.

What Mr. Timms said I don't know, but I was aware of what I looked like. Mother had a hard time making both ends meet, and on a day like this, wanted us to be dressed in something respectable. The day before, she put the sewing machine on the dining-room table, took out a paper pattern and set about making me some trousers. She made many of her own dresses and a lot of our clothes; indeed, if she was making a dress for herself or my sister, I was often the model. I had to stand up while she pinned patterns all over me. She was often puzzled by the strips of pattern that were left over. If only she had her cousin Emmy or better still Cousin Louie, the dressmaker, she would say; for it was a fate with her often to cut out, say, two left sleeves, or to be short a quarter of a yard on the length. She knitted our stockings and never learned how to turn a heel, so that a double heel often hung over the backs of our boots: jerseys for us she never finished; but for herself—for she did not want to make victims of *us* —she would knit recklessly on while I read the instructions to her, and turn out narrow tubes of wool that she would stretch, laughing till she cried, to her knees. She had to pay for the material for her dressmaking out of the housekeeping money and she would raid any free material in sight. I have described her attacks on our curtains. Her own bloomers were a byword, for in gay moments she would haul up her long skirts above her knees and show my father—who was always shocked—what could be done with a chair cover or some-thing robust of that kind. "You want me in the Business instead of 'that woman,'" she'd say.

For she had a vengeful streak in her, and looking at our father, the impressive Managing Director, and counting his suits and knowing how she couldn't get a penny out of him for our clothes, she attacked his wardrobe. She found a pair of striped trousers of the kind worn with morning dress. Just the thing for me. Out came the scissors. Slicing the enormous trousers roughly at the knees she saw that my brother and I could get into them both at once. She was upset by our laugh-ter. She now slashed at the trousers again and narrowed them to my size. The insoluble difficulty was the fly buttons; these were pulled round to the side of one leg; cutting and then tacking her way up the middle while they were on me at the final try-on, she sewed me up totally in front.

"I won't be able to *go*, Mum," I said.

She was flabbergasted, but in her careless way, she snipped a couple of stitches in her tacking.

These were the trousers I was wearing as I stood before Mr. Timms, very pleased by Father's fashionable stripes and willing to show any boy who was interested the original touch of having Savile Row fly buttons down the side of one leg. What I feared was happening: the hole was lengthening in front. I could feel an alarming draft. I dared not look down. I hoped Mr. Timms would not look down, as my mother chatted on and on about our family. Nothing happened. I went to my classroom; at playtime I dared not run, for fear the tacking would go. When I pulled the thread to tighten it I was left with a length of thread hanging down from the vulnerable part. When I went home after school the thread went altogether and I had to cover myself with my hand.

So my first day at Rosendale Road School began. Wearing my father's classy cutdowns I knew the distinctiveness of our family and its awkward difference from the families of all the other children. No one else had a Managing Director's trousers on. No one else had (I was sure) our dark adventures. We were a race apart: abnormal but proud of our stripes, longing for the normality we saw around us.

I was eleven. Between the age of ten and fourteen a boy reaches a first maturity and wholeness as a person; it is broken up by adolescence and not remade until many years later. That eager period between ten and fourteen is the one in which one can learn anything. Even in the times when most children had no schooling at all, they could be experts in a trade: the children who went up chimneys, worked in cotton mills, pushed coster barrows may have been sick, exhausted and ill-fed, but they were at a temporary height of their intelligence and powers. This is the delightful phase of boyhood—all curiosity, energy and spirit.

I was ready for a decisive experience, if it came. It did come. At Rosendale Road School I decided to become a writer. The decision did not drop out of the sky and was not the result of intellectual effort. It began in the classroom and was settled in the school lavatory. It came, of course, because of a personal influence: the influence of a schoolmaster called Bartlett. There were and are good and bad elementary schools in London. They are nearly as much created by their districts and their children as by their teachers. The children at Rosendale Road, which was a large school, were a mixture of working class and lower middles, with a few foreigners and colonials—Germans, Portuguese, Australians, French and one or two Indians. It was a mixed school. We sat next to girls in class and the class was fifty or sixty strong. We had overgrown louts from such slums as Peabody's Buildings and little titches; the sons of coalmen, teachers, railwaymen, factory workers, sailors, soldiers, draftsmen, printers, policemen, shop assistants and clerks and salesmen. The Germans were the children of people in the pharmaceutical trades; they had been better educated than we were and had more pocket money. One dark, satanically handsome boy owned a phonograph and claimed to be a direct descendant of Sir Francis Drake and did romantic pictures of galleons. At fourteen the girls would leave school, work in offices, in factories like my father's, or become waitresses or domestic servants.

In most schools such a crowd was kept in order by the cane. Girls got it as much as the boys and sniveled afterwards. To talk in class was a crime; to leave one's desk, inconceivable. Discipline was meant to encourage subservience and to squash rebellion—very undesirable in children who would grow up to obey orders from their betters. No child here would enter the ruling classes unless he was very gifted and won scholarship after scholarship. A great many boys from these schools did so and did rise to high places; but they had to slave and crush part of their lives, to machine themselves so that they became brain alone. They ground away at their lessons, and for all their boyhood and youth and perhaps all their lives, they were in the ingenious torture chamber of the examination halls. They were brilliant, of course, but some when they grew up tended to be obsequious to the ruling class and ruthless to the rest, if they were not tired out. Among them were many who were emotionally infantile.

A reaction against this fierce system of education had set in at the turn of the century. Socialism and the scientific revolution—as H. G. Wells has described—had moved many people. New private schools for the well-off were beginning to break with the traditions of the nineteenth century and a little of the happy influence seeped down to ourselves. Mr. Bartlett represented it. The Education Officer had instructed Mr. Timms to give Mr. Bartlett a free hand for a year or so and to introduce something like the Dalton or tutorial system into our class. The other teachers hated him and it; we either made so much noise that the rest of the school could hardly get on with their work, or were so silent that teachers would peep over the frosted glass of the door to see if we had gone off for a holiday.

Mr. Bartlett was a stumpy, heavy-shouldered young man with a broad, swarthy face, large brown eyes and a lock of black hair wagging romantically over his forehead. He looked like a boxer, lazy in his movements, and his right arm hung back as he walked to the blackboard, as though he was going to swing a blow at it. He wore a loose tweed jacket with baggy pockets in which he stuck books, chalks and pencils, and by some magnetism he could silence a class almost without a word. He never used the cane. Since we could make as much noise as we liked, he got silence easily when he wanted it. Manners scarcely existed among us except as a scraping and a sniveling; he introduced us to refinements we had never heard of and his one punishment took the form of an addi-

tional and excruciating lesson in this subject. He would make
us write a formal letter of apology. We would make a dozen
attempts before he was satisfied. And when, at last, we
thought it was done, he would point out that it was still
incomplete. It must be put in an envelope, properly addressed: not to Mr. Bartlett, not to Mr. W. W. Bartlett, not
as I did, to Mr. W. W. Bartlett Esquire, but to the esquire
without the mister. It often took us a whole day and giving
up all the pleasant lessons the rest were doing, to work out
the phrasing of these letters of shame.

At Rosendale Road I said goodbye to Stephen and Matilda
and the capes and rivers of England, the dreary singsong. We
were no longer foredoomed servants but found out freedom.
Mr. Bartlett's methods were spacious. A history lesson might
go on for days; if it was about early Britain and old down-
land encampments he would bring us wild flowers from the
Wiltshire tumuli. He set up his easel and his Whatman boards
and painted pictures to illustrate his lesson. Sometimes he
changed to pastels. And we could go out and watch him and
talk about what he was doing. He made us illustrate our work
and we were soon turning out "Bartletts" by the dozen. He
set us tasks in three's or four's; we were allowed to talk to
one another, to wander about for consultations; we acted
short scenes from books at a sudden order.

For myself the lessons on literature, and especially poetry,
were the revelation. No textbooks. Our first lessons were
from Ford Madox Ford's *English Review,* which was pub-
lishing some of the best young writers of the time. We discussed Bridges and Masefield. Children who seemed stupid
were suddenly able to detect a fine image or line and disen-
tangle it from the ordinary. A sea poem of Davidson's, a
forgotten Georgian, remains in my mind to this day: the
evocation of the sea rolling on the shingle on the coast between Romney and Hythe:

The beach with all its organ stops
Pealing again prolongs the roar

Bartlett dug out one of James Russell Lowell's poems, *The Vision of Sir Launfal*—though why he chose that dim poem I do not know—we went on to Tennyson, never learning by heart. Bartlett must have been formed in the late days of Pre-Raphaelitism, for he introduced us to a form of writing then called half-print. He scrapped the school pens, made us use broad nibs and turn out stories written as near to the medieval script as possible. (This and German script, four years later, ruined my handwriting forever.) We had a magazine and a newspaper.

Many of Bartlett's methods are now commonplace in English schools; in 1911 they were revolutionary. For myself, the sugar-bag blue cover of the *English Review* was decisive. One had thought literature was in books written by dead people who had been oppressively overeducated. Here was writing by people who were alive and probably writing at this moment. They were as alive as Barlow Woods. The author was not remote; he was almost with us. He lived as we did; he was often poor.

And there was another aspect; in Ipswich I had been drawn to painting and now in poems and stories I saw pictures growing out of the print. Bartlett's picture of the *Hispaniola* lying beached in the Caribbean, on the clean swept sand, its poop, round house, mainsails and foretop easily identified, had grown out of the flat, printed words of *Treasure Island*. Bartlett was a good painter in watercolor. When we read *Kidnapped* he made us paint the Scottish moors. We laughed over *Tom Sawyer* and *Huckleberry Finn*. The art of writing became a manual craft as attractive—to a boy—as the making of elderberry pipes or carpentering. My imagination woke up. I now saw my grandfather's talk of Great Men in a new light. They were not a lot of dead Jehovahs far away; they were not even "Great"; they were men. I went up to the dirty secondhand bookshop in Norwood where I had found the Latin grammar; now, as often as I could cadge a penny off my mother, I went there, and out of the dusty boxes I bought paperbacks called *The Penny Poets*. One could have a complete edition of *Paradise Regained* (but not, for some reason, *Paradise Lost*), or Wordsworth's *Prelude,* the *Thanatopsis* (but what on earth was that?) of William Cullen Bryant, the poems of Cowper and Coleridge. To encourage my mother to open her purse, or to reward her with a present, I bought penny sheets of secondhand music for her. I was piqued by her laughter.

"This old stuff," she said, sitting down at the piano. " 'The Seventh Royal Fusiliers'."

"The gallant Fusiliers, they march their way to glory," I sang out.

"You're flat," she said. "Where did you get it?"

I had found a collection of the worst patriotic songs of the Crimean War, full of soldierly pathos. The music sheets were very dirty and they smelled of hair oil, tea and stale rooms.

That I understood very little of what I read did not really matter to me. (Washington Irving's *Life of Columbus* was as awful as the dictionary because of the long words.) I was caught by the passion for print as an alcoholic is caught by the bottle. There was a small case of books at home, usually kept in the back room which was called my father's study. Why he had to have a study we could not see. There was an armchair, a gate-legged table, a small rug, piles of business magazines usually left in their wrappers; the floorboards were still bare as indeed were our stairs; Father had temporarily suppressed his weakness for buying on credit. I had not dared often to look much at his books. It is true I had read *Marriage on Two Hundred a Year,* because after all the quarrels in our house, marriage was a subject on which I had special knowledge. From the age of seven I often offered my parents bits of advice on how to live. I knew what the rent was and what housekeeping cost. I had also read *Paper Bag Cookery*—one of Father's fads—because I wanted to try it. Now I saw *The Meditations of Marcus Aurelius* in leather: it defeated me. Wordsworth and Milton at least wrote in short lines with wide margins. I moved on to a book by Hall Caine called *The Bondman*. It appeared to be about a marriage and I noticed that the men and women talked in the dangerous adult language which I associated with *The Bad Girl of the Family*. *The Bondman* also suggested a doom—the sort of doom my mother sang about which was connected with Trinity Church and owing the rent.

Hall Caine was too thundery for me. I moved to Marie Corelli and there I found a book of newspaper articles called *Free Opinions*. The type was large. The words were easy, rather contemptibly so. I read and then stopped in anger. Marie Corelli had insulted me. She was against popular education, against schools, against public libraries and said that common people like us made the books dirty because we never washed, and that we infected them with disease. I had never been inside a public library but I now decided to go to one. Mr. Bartlett had advised us to get notebooks to write down any thoughts we had about what we read. I got out mine and I wrote my first lines of English prose: hard thoughts about Marie Corelli.

This exhausted me and the rest of the notebook was slowly filled with copied extracts from my authors. I had a look at *In Tune with the Infinite*. I moved on to my father's single volume, India-paper edition of Shakespeare's Complete Works and started at the beginning with the *Rape of Lucrece* and the sonnets and continued slowly through the plays during the coming year. For relief I took up Marie Corelli's *Master Christian,* which I found more moving than Shakespeare and more intelligible than *Thanatopsis.*

On the lowest shelf of my father's bookcase were several

new ornate and large volumes of a series called *The International Library of Famous Literature*. They were bound in
red and had gold lettering. They had never been opened and
we were forbidden to touch them. I think Father must have
had the job of selling the series, on commission, at one time.
I started to look at them. There were photographs of busts
of Sophocles and Shakespeare. There were photographs of
Dickens, Thomas Hardy, of Sir James Barrie and Sir Edmond
Gosse in deep, starched wing collars, of Kipling rooting like
a dog at his desk and of G. K. Chesterton with his walking
stick. There was Tolstoy behind his beard. The volumes contained long extracts from the works of these writers. I found
at once a chapter from Hardy's *Under the Greenwood Tree,*
and discovered a lasting taste for the wry and ironical. I
moved on to Longinus' *Of the Sublime* and could not understand it. I was gripped by Tolstoy and a chapter from *Don
Quixote.* In the next two or three years I read the whole of
The International Library on the quiet. These volumes converted me to prose. I had never really enjoyed poetry, for it
was concerned with inner experience and I was very much an
extrovert and I fancy I have remained so; the moodiness and
melancholy which fell on me in Dulwich and have been with
me ever since must have come from the disappointments of
an active and romantic nature; the forms of Protestantism
among which I was brought up taught one to think of life
rigidly in terms of right and wrong, and that is not likely to
fertilize the sensibilities or the poetic imagination. The poet,
above all, abandons the will; people like ourselves who were
nearly all will, burned up the inner life, had no sense of its
daring serenity and were either rapt by our active dramas or
tormented by them; but in prose I found the common experience and the solid worlds where judgments were made and in
which one could firmly tread.

An extract from *Oliver Twist* made me ask for a copy for
Christmas. I put it in our one green armchair and knelt there

reading it in a state of hot terror. It seized me because it was about London and the fears of the London streets. There were big boys at school who could grow up to be the Artful Dodger; many of us could have been Oliver; but the decisive thing must have been that Dickens had the excited mind, the terrors, the comic sense of a boy and one who can never have grown emotionally older than a boy is at the age of ten. One saw people going about the streets of London who could have been any of his characters; and right and wrong were meat to him. In all of Dickens, as I went on from book to book, I saw myself and my life in London. In Thackeray I found the gentler life of better-off people and the irony I now loved. To have been the young man in *The Virginians,* to have traveled as he did and to find oneself among affectionate, genial and cultivated families who enjoyed their fortunes, instead of struggling for them, must be heaven. And I had seen enough in our family to be on the way to acquiring a taste for disillusion.

My mother's tales about her childhood made the world seem like a novel to me, and with her I looked back and rather feared or despised the present. The present was a chaos and a dissipation and it was humiliating to see that the boys who lived for the minute and for the latest craze or adventure were the most intelligent and clearheaded. Their families were not claustrophobic, the sons were not prigs, as I was. There was a boy with a Japanese look to him—he had eyes like apple pips—who had introduced me to Wells's *Time Machine.* He went a step further and offered me his greatest treasures: dozens of tattered numbers of those famous stories of school life, *The Gem* and *The Magnet.* The crude illustrations, the dirty condition of the papers indicated that they were pulp and sin. One page and I was entranced. I gobbled these stories as if I were eating pie or stuffing. To hell with poor self-pitying fellows like Oliver Twist; here were the cheerful rich. I craved for Greyfriars, that absurd Public

School, as I craved for pudding. There the boys wore top hats and tail coats—Arthur Augustus D'Arcy, the toff, wore a monocle—they had feasts in their "studies"; they sent a pie containing a boot to "the bounder of the Remove"; they rioted; they never did a stroke of work. They "strolled" round "the Quad" and rich uncles tipped them a "fivah" which they spent on more food. Sometimes a shady foreign-language master was seen to be in touch with a German spy. Very rarely did a girl appear in these tales.

The Japanese-looking boy was called Nott. He had a friend called Howard, the son of a compositor. *The Gem* and *The Magnet* united us. We called ourselves by Greyfriars names and jumped about shouting words like "Garoo." We punned on our names. When anything went wrong we said, in chorus: "How—'ard! Is it Nott?" and doubled with laughter dozens of times a day and as we "strolled" arm in arm on the way home from school.

I knew this reading was sin and I counteracted it by reading a short life of the poet Wordsworth. There was a rustic summer house at the end of our back garden. It had stained-glass windows. Driving my brothers and sister out, I claimed it as my retreat and cell. When they kicked up too much noise I sat up on the thatched roof of the house where, when life at Grasmere bored me, I had a good view of what other boys were doing in their gardens. I forgot about prose and said I was going to be a poet and "Dirty Poet" became the family name for me. Sedbergh is not far from the Lake Country: destiny pointed to my connection with Wordsworth. We had a common experience of lakes and fells. His lyrical poems seemed too simple and girlish to me: I saw myself writing a new *Prelude* or *Excursion*. Also the line

Getting and spending, we lay waste our powers

struck home at our family. I read that Wordsworth had been poet laureate: this was the ideal. To my usual nightly prayers that the house should not catch fire and that no burglar should break in, I added a line urging God to make me poet laureate "before I am twenty-one." This prayer lasted until I was sixteen.

One day Mr. Bartlett made this possibility seem nearer. He got us to put together a literary magazine. Nott and Howard efficiently produced a pair of thrillers, one set among the opium dens of Hong Kong. I got to work on a long poem. Finding—to my surprise—that Wordsworth was not a stirring model, I moved to Coleridge's *Cristabel*. My first line thrilled me. It ran: "Diana, goddess of the spectre moon." I turned in fifty or sixty lines of coagulated romantic imagery in this manner and waited for the startled applause, especially from Mr. Bartlett. There was silence. There was embarrassment. Nott and Howard were stunned by the poem. Ginger Reed, a little red-haired cockney flea, skinny, ill and lively, who skipped around cheeking me in the streets and clattering the hobnails of his brother's boots that were too heavy for his thin legs—Ginger Reed tore the poem to bits line by line: why call a "bird" Diana? Why "spectre"—was the "bird" dead? Metaphor and simile, I said. Stale, he said. I was very small, but he was smaller and people in Herne Hill might have been surprised to know that two urchins, one pestering the other at a street corner, were on the point of fighting about a poem, while a pale child with owlish glasses called Donald stood there as a kind of doleful referee. The thing to do was to wait for Bartlett, but he would not speak. At last I was driven to ask his opinion as he walked in the schoolyard.

"Too many long words," he said. And no more.

I was wretched. A gulf opened between myself and Coleridge.

To me, my "Diana" was a burst of genius. I have never had the sensation since.

I went home and, sitting in our attic on a tin trunk which

I called my desk study, I finally gave up poetry for prose once again and started on my first novel. My father had sensibly given us the Children's Encyclopaedia and in that I had found some more Washington Irving, simplified and abridged from his book about the legends of the Alhambra. The thought of that ethereal Moorish girl rising from the fountain entranced me. Here was a subject: the story of that girl who rises and is caught in the wars of the Moors and the Spaniards. There was more than a boyish interest in war in this choice of subject. Nasty wars had been boiling up in Edwardian Europe. We had had an illustrated history of the Boer War at home; and in the illustrated papers there had been dramatic pictures of contemporary wars in Greece and the Balkans, pictures of destroyed, muddy towns and fleeing people. The Balkan wars seeped into my novel. When I was short of invention—I could never make the Moorish girl do anything except wave her languorous arms—I put in a battle scene, usually a tragic defeat, ending with my stock device: a lament by the Moorish women looking on the battlefield for their dead. Laments had an intimate appeal; my mother lamented often in these days. Day after day I wrote, until my novel reached about 130 pages, and I showed some of it to my friends.

"How-'ard is it Nott?" they said, tactfully advising me to cut out the laments. I kept the manuscript from Ginger Reed. He was spiteful in these months. He always came top in arithmetic and was leaving school to become a vanboy: stunted, he was older than the rest of us, we discovered. He was over fourteen and he jeered bitterly at us. We were rich, he said. We had opportunities, he jeered, as he ate his bread and dripping (his breakfast), as he danced about us in the schoolyard.

Then two bad things happened and their effect was to poison my life and was lasting. It took me many years to recover from them. Father discovered I was reading *The*

Gem and *The Magnet*. To think that a son of a Managing Director of a Limited Company which had just paid off its debentures, a son who was always putting on the airs of a professor, and always full of "Mr. Bartlett This" and "Mr. Bartlett That": who had been brought up in the shadow of his grandfather's utterances about John Ruskin—and possibly even deceived himself that he was John Ruskin—should bring such muck into the house.

We were sitting at tea. It was Sunday. The family looked at the criminal and not without pleasure. I had tried to force books on them. I had cornered them and made them listen to my poem and my novel. I had read *Thanatopsis* at them. I had made them play schools, which they hated. I had hit out at the words Dirty Poet and had allowed no one near the tin trunk and in fact, had put an onion in a jar of water on it, as a piece of nature study, to mark the intellectual claims on the spot. Naturally they couldn't help being a little pleased. My mother, always capricious, liable to treachery, and perhaps glad not to be the center of a quarrel herself for once, betrayed me also.

"He reads them all day. Dozens of them. Dirty things."

"Where are they? Bring them down," said my father. I went upstairs and came back with about twenty or thirty grubby *Gems* and *Magnets*.

"Good godfathers," said my father, not touching the pile, for he hated dust and dirt. "I give you your Saturday penny and this is what you're doing with it. Wasting the money I earn. I suppose you think you're so superior because you have a father who has his own business and you spend right and left on muck like this."

"I borrowed them. A boy lent them to me."

"A man is known by the company he keeps," said my father. And getting up, his face greenish with disgust, he threw the lot in the fireplace and set fire to them.

"Walt, Walt, you'll have the soot down," screamed my mother. "You know we haven't had the sweep."

But father liked a blaze. What could I say to Howard and Nott?

"Why do you read that muck when you could be reading John Ruskin?"

"We haven't got any of Ruskin's books."

"He writes poetry. He wants to be a poet," said my brother Cyril.

"He's writing a book, all over the table, instead of his homework," said my mother.

"No, upstairs."

"Don't contradict your mother. What's this? So you are writing a book? I hope it will improve us. What is it? Where is it?"

"Upstairs," the traitors chimed. "Shall we go and get it?"

"No," I shouted.

"Go and get it."

"Oh, if he doesn't want us to see it . . ." my mother began.

"I suppose a boy would want his own father to see it," said my father.

Anger put me on the point of tears. Very easily I cried when Father reprimanded me.

I brought the manuscript and gave it to my father.

"The Alhambra—remember we used to go to the Alhambra, Beat?" he said.

"It's the Alhambra in Spain," I said scornfully.

"Oh, superior!" said my father. "Let's have a look at it."

And, to my misery, he began reading aloud. He had scarcely read ten lines before he came across the following line: "She adjusted her robe with ostentatious care. She omited to wear a cloak."

"Ostentatious," exclaimed my father. "That's a big word —what does it mean?"

"I don't know," I sulked.

"You wrote a word and you don't know what it means?"

"It means sort of proud, showing off . . ." I could not go on. The tears broke out and I sobbed helplessly. I had got the word from Marie Corelli.

"Ostentatious," said my father. "I never heard of it. And what's this? 'Omited.' I thought they taught you to spell."

"Omitted," I sobbed.

"Don't bully the boy," said my mother.

I tried to rescue myself in the Howard-Nott manner. "O mite I have done better," I blubbered.

"O-mite, omit—it's a pun," I said and sent up a howl.

It ended, as trouble usually did in our house, with a monologue from Father saying that he had always dreamed, for a father always dreams that having founded a business, he might have a son who—if he were worthy of it—might conceivably be invited to come into it, a privilege hundreds of young men less fortunately placed would give their eyes for. Only this week he had had an applicant. A young man who thought just because he was his father's son (his father being something big in the trade and making two or three thousand pounds a year), he could just walk into anything. A matter on which Father instantly put him right, for he might have been to Eton and Harrow, but that meant nothing. For my father's business was God's business. Unlike other businesses, it was directed by the Divine Mind. "And by the way," Father said, "I always look at a man's boots when he applies for a job." My father's voice became warmer and more benign as he expanded on the subject of the Divine Mind, who was his manager, and we drifted into other fields. My mother's mind, less divine, wandered.

I took my novel back. I put it inside the tin trunk. Blackened by hatred, I did not touch it again. I hated my father. And one morning in the winter the hatred became intense, or rather I decided I could never talk to him again about what went on in my mind.

It was an early morning of London fog. The room was dark and we had lit the gas. I was reading Shakespeare in bed. I had by now reached *Measure for Measure* when my father came in.

"Get out of bed, you lazy hound," he said. "What are you reading?" He took the book and started reading himself and was perhaps startled by Claudio's proposal.

"Poetry," he said. Then very seriously and quietly: "Do you really want to be a poet?"

"Yes I do."

He went red with temper. "If that's what you want," he shouted, "I have nothing more to say to you. I won't allow it. Get that idea out of your head at once."

Why my father raged against my literary tastes I never really knew. He had been very poor, of course, and really feared I would "starve in a garret." He wanted—in fancy only—to found a dynasty in business; and he heard no word of money in writing poetry. At this time he had many anxieties, and the family, from my mother down, exasperated and tormented him. He was a perfectionist. He was also an egotist who had identified himself—as indeed I was doing—with an ideal state of things. And then there comes a time when a man of strong vitality finds it hard to bear the physical sight of his growing sons. He found it harder and harder; and he was to be even more severe with my brothers and my sister, especially Cyril, who adored him. We were at the beginning of a very long war; these were the first rumblings. One by one, we fell into secrecy. In self-preservation we told him lies.

He was behaving exactly to us as his own father had behaved to him; there was a strain of gritty, North Country contempt and sarcasm in all of us.

7

One thing is now clear that was not clear when I was twelve. My mother came to collect us from school one day. She scarcely ever did this. She walked along in her raincoat and felt hat muttering to herself and worried. The Business—that shadow—was on her mind. She had come out to calm herself. For my father, in his hotheaded way, had brought a legal action against his landlord in the City, had won it, but had lost it on appeal. It had cost him £800, an enormous sum for him.

"You can never win against Property in the City," he said.

"He's a fighter," she said with pride, but also in terror.

There were often noisy scenes in our house. Money was one trouble; Mother could not get it out of him. The Business made him neglect her. He went off at seven or half past in the morning and returned at eight in the evening; on Saturdays he came home at seven. They had no pleasures; my mother did all the household work herself. He did not buy clothes for her. He hated her talking to the neighbors and perhaps feared her careless tongue; was she telling them about his bankruptcies?

"Other men take their wives out."

"I am not 'other men,' as you are pleased to phrase it."

"Mr. Carter does, so does Mr. O'Dwyer." (They were our neighbors.)

"Civil servants!" said my father. "They're living off me. And let me give you a thought there. I don't want neighbors. God is my only neighbor."

"The boys ought to have friends."

"Their father is their friend. They will realize it one day." The dispute would soon get out of hand; the two began shouting. There were knocks on the wall from the Carters next-door. Father, in a temper, knocked back with the poker. "Perhaps that will shut them up."

The Carters and the O'Dwyers were so unlike us, their lives—to our minds, so normal—that we felt we must be foreigners. Mr. Carter, aged forty-five, was a doggish, gray-haired clerk, married to a much younger wife. They sang for the local choral society and were Fabian socialists. Mr. Carter had a complete set of classics and I tried to read Thucydides in his house: there they were, another thirty volumes, exposing the fact that I had a mountain before me. Would I "catch up"—my mania?

Mr. and Mrs. Carter wished to civilize us. I had made a toy theater, a rocky construction in cardboard which kept falling to pieces, for I was not a very practical child: the Carters saw it and at once put it to rights and made me give a performance of *Aladdin* to some guests in their sitting room. These guests paid sixpence. The performance was in aid of Jim Larkins' dock strikers in Dublin. I had mixed feelings about my theater being taken over by people cleverer than myself; I had simply wanted to muddle away with it in my own way—a feeling I still have about writing. I still feel this jealous fear when I hear that someone has read what I have written—No (I think), this is a private thing. I do not want it to be seen. Or not yet.

One evening Mr. and Mrs. Carter knocked at the door while one of our rows was building up. They were civilizing again.

"We *heard* you were at home," they said darkly, in refined voices, "and came to apologize if our singing practice disturbs you. The walls are very thin."

They indeed drove my father to anger by their scales.

"Ah ah ah ah ah; ah, ah, ah, ah ah," went Mrs. Carter's soprano; then, at the breaking point, intolerably down the scale, Mr. Carter would join her. Mother was excited by these allies. She often spoke over the garden wall to them. She spied on them. She was flushed with merriment when she found out they lay down on their bed together on Saturday afternoons.

"We often have a word, don't we?" she said flirtatiously to Mr. Carter.

"This very morning, in fact, Mrs. P," said Mr. Carter waggishly.

"Oh," said my mother, beginning to blush and laugh and covering her face with her hands. "I was hanging out my . . ."

"Something long, I was too polite to mention it," said Mr. Carter. "Made of wool. Tubular."

"Combs. Two pairs," said my mother, giving a scream.

"I didn't like to mention them, but since *you* have, Mrs. P, I noticed the articles in question," agreed the lewd Mr. Carter.

"And *his* long underpants too," screamed my mother.

Father looked very shocked.

"You work too hard, Mrs. Pritchett. Why don't you get out? You never go out, do you?" said Mrs. Carter.

"Only once to Brixton a year ago. Meat is cheaper there," said Mother, disloyal and defiant. "Because of the Business."

My father intervened here, the tone of conversation rose. Mr. Carter was in favor of Cooperatives. He asked ironically if London Bridge "paid." My father was opposed to this. Cooperatives were the enemy of the small man. He'd seen enough of that in Yorkshire. An argument about capitalism began, the cash nexus and the profit basis—all news to me— but Father ended in astonishing Mr. Carter by telling him that he, Father, did not run his business, but God did. Ah ha, we thought, admiring our father—Mr. Carter had never thought of that. Hence Father was not going to have a lot of socialists running it.

Afterwards Father said: "I put that old fool in his place." We agreed.

The Carter children went to the grammar school. The youngest, aged eight, said that he knew how babies were got and born. I did not believe him. His sister, a romping, red-headed girl with freckles, joined in and snubbed me.

"Our parents told us," she said gravely. "It's true. You can ask them. Haven't your parents told you? I expect not. They're religious, aren't they? We are rationalists."

"I don't believe you," I said.

"You go into your outside lav, I'll undress and I'll show you," she said. "Go on now. I'll be there in a minute."

I went to our lavatory and waited, but she did not come back.

"Oh, I changed my mind," she said next day and laughed at me and said, "Let's go up the garden and talk about torture and cruel things." We sat by her fence and talked about torture. Mr. Carter, who was pruning his roses on the other side of the fence, put his head over and said: "I've heard everything you said. I have never heard such disgusting children. Talk about something interesting."

The Carters held high-class badminton parties on Saturdays. The voices of schoolmasters and dons came over the fence.

"Look at Mrs. Carter," cried my mother, excitedly peeping from behind our curtains. "You can see right up her . . ."

If the Carters were clever, advanced people, the O'Dwyers were negligent and cheerful. Mrs. O'Dwyer was French.

"Oh Mrs. Preech," she called over the wall. She would be standing on a beer crate and would put her fat, wild face over the wall, looking like an untidy sorceress. "Vere is that clever son? I want to have a conversation with him about Racine."

"Racing?" said my mother.

I went into a dirty sitting room, where the ashes of a week's fires were all over the grate, reviews and books were thrown about on tables and chairs among beer bottles and glasses. Mrs. O'Dwyer was only half-dressed, greasy-looking and bearded. She looked at me with merry, gloating eyes and kissed and tickled me, then talked to me about France.

"Vat are you reading? Wordsworth. I don't like him. I'll read Racine to you. I will teach you French if you want. You want? I'll give you another kiss."

Mrs. O'Dwyer's enormous breasts nearly knocked me over. She declaimed some Racine to me. Oh God! The Carters with the classics, now the O'Dwyers with Racine: the road lengthened every day. She had been a singer, she said, in Paris—not like those snobbish little Carters who tra-la-la'd in the ridiculous local choral society and spent their summer holidays in Ventnor. *La belle France* for her!

Mrs. O'Dwyer had two sons of about fifteen and seventeen with whom she boxed in the garden. She put up a rope ring and trained them to fight till her blouse was half off and her hair down. Often a light blow knocked her over, for her fat body wobbled on her heels and she went down on her bottom, calling out "Bring me a glass of beer." Then she drove them indoors to their studies. She stood over her sons while they worked, brought them beer and made cold compresses to put on the clever one's head as he read for his university exams. The sons often chased her round her house with a broom. One day she peeped out of her bathroom window and saw one of the boys climbing the drainpipe towards her. She got a pail of water and emptied it on him. These youths adored this fat and merry mother. She helped the one who was a naturalist to skin his guinea pig and mount the skeleton. Beer crates clattered in the yard and she would sometimes shout over the fence: "Mrs. Preech, vy don't you educate yourself? Give up the vashing. I'm reading a book, vat are you doing? Read. Improve your mind."

Our dog Jim and the O'Dwyers' dog got on well. They used to rush up and down, each on its side of the fence, barking at each other and tearing at the palings. Jim had caught our family hysteria. He frothed at the mouth and licked and slobbered over the palings in his frenzy. When a paling fell down, loud laughter came from Mrs. O'Dwyer's kitchen. Like ourselves, the O'Dwyers were garden wreckers. On summer evenings Mr. O'Dwyer, austerely silent, sat in the wreckage of his garden, smoking his pipe and drinking a glass of whiskey.

Mother had her own amusement. Mrs. O'Dwyer might box, Mrs. Carter might play badminton, Mother's sport was moving furniture. She would be sitting in the dining room when, without warning, she would say: "I can't stand that old piano over there. Help me move it, you boys." But the room was so crowded that you could not move one thing without moving the rest. We would all lift the table first.

"From me to you. From you to me. Lower a bit. Tip it," my brother would say, mocking the many removal men we had seen at work. This brought all those removals to Mother's mind and she would drop her end of the table or piano, whatever it was, and start on the tale. Soon the room was in confusion.

"Don't be a cure, Cyril," Mother screamed.

In an hour everything was in a new place and we stopped for breath.

"No," she would say. "I don't like it. Get it all back as it was."

"Back with it!" we shouted. We started shoving and lifting. The piano chimed.

"Bang goes the 'Maiden's Prayer,' " said Cyril.

We always said these words.

She would sit down and say: "I get sick of these things stuck in the same place. You've only got one life."

Down at Rosendale Road we talked of football, "Jocks" and sex. "Jocks" were members of a small secret society who talked in a peculiar baby language they had invented or picked up from one of the comics. I longed to be a Jock but was shut out. The anti-Bartlett campaign succeeded: the progressive movement was defeated and we were moved en bloc to a more conventional class, even more crowded. Mr. Williams, the geography master, taught the geography of India and told me I was Welsh: my name derived from Ap-Richard. I denied that I was Welsh. Boys who had lovingly called me Pritch, Prick or even Shit, now called me Taffy. There was an effusive cockney music master, all roar and spit, who taught us to sing a song of Pope's. He sang out the words:

> "Where e'er you walk
> Cool Giles shall fan the glide"

in a fine voice. I at once took to reading Pope's *Essay on Man* during algebra.

The worst thing was that our new teacher was a woman. All the boys in the class hated her. Her figure was ridiculously beautiful, going in and out from bosom to waist and hips like a bottle; to walk behind her and see her lovely bottom sway made us giggle. One of the masters, a gingery, hairy, curly fellow like a barber, was courting her. We decided that she was "hot" and that he "had it up" with her. I felt the desire to kick her. This woman had a high-class voice and finished herself for me by telling us that Bartlett was an out-of-date Impressionist in painting. I did a picture of Tower Bridge and she told me it was a mess. I told her I was not trying to put in every brick but that I was trying to get the "effect" of the bridge, not a copy. What exactly, she asked, did I mean by "effect"?

"Well 'effect,' " I said.

"You have been badly taught," she said.

"Volume" and "shading" were what we had to aim for. Imagine: a whole hour drawing a pudding basin in pencil and then shading it. But Dexter, the draftsman's son who sat next to me in this class, told me his father said she was right and that Bartlett was a slapdash old fool. A painting I had done of a Yorkshire moor in a storm was removed from the place of honor on the wall.

Holidays were getting near. The teacher said they were an opportunity to see unusual things. She would give a prize to the value of five shillings to the child who brought back a drawing of the most unusual thing he had seen. Five shillings! But how, since we never went away for holidays, would we see anything unusual? Five shillings—the books one could buy for that! I was nearly mad with determination to get it. I had a brilliant idea which I am afraid exposes the dirty cunning—the "deediness" as Mother called it—and flightiness of my priggish character. I decided that museums were a store of unusual things. I dragged my younger brother and sister for a couple of miles across Dulwich Park because I had to look after the children—stopped them from playing on the way, with bribes of ginger beer, and got to Horniman's Museum. Oh sacred and blessed spot, oh temple of knowl-

edge, oh secret Bore. I dragged the kids round the cases.
Mr. Bartlett had been keen on stone arrowheads and flints,
Uncle Arthur had gone in for fossils and quartz—I had
bought a book on geology and had tried to memorize the
names of rocks: the craze lasted a week or two—but what
was unusual about them? And, in any case, how difficult for
an "effect" artist like myself to draw things like these. I
searched for something foreign, exotic and simple. I found
it. There was a collection of amulets from India. Quickly I
drew the childishly simple shapes and noted the colors. I took
the other children back home, got out my paints and did a
full page of amulets, inventing some extra ones as I went
along. Some I called Indian; at a venture, I lied and called
some African. The whole swindle in yellows and purples
looked pretty and salable. I longed for the holidays to be over.
I had turned my mother's talent with curtains and her husband's trousers into something approaching an aesthetic.

My culture-snobbery and faking were successful. Most of
the boys and girls in the class had forgotten to go in for the
prize. Howard had spent his time selling newspapers; Nott
had been to Somerset and had seen stalactites in caves, but
could not draw. Those self-indulgent rivals had been caught
napping. They were not obsessional boys. I won the prize,
the only one of my school life.

"And what would you like for your five shillings?" the
teacher said.

"A book."

"That's good. Which book would you like? Henty? Conan
Doyle?"

"No, Ruskin."

"What?" said the teacher. "He wrote a great many books."
I did not know the titles of any of Ruskin's books.

"Any one. Some."

"You realize he was a social reformer and art critic?"

"On art," I said blindly, sucking up to her love of volume and shading, remembering Aunt Ada and Barlow Woods.

The woman with the ludicrously beautiful figure whom we mocked and whom I had wanted to kick, presented me a few weeks later with eight volumes of Ruskin, *Modern Painters, The Seven Lamps of Architecture, The Stones of Venice* and —most enlightening of all—an Index. I had blotted out the *Gem* and *Magnet* fiasco.

I went home and opened the first volume of *Modern Painters*. The title startled me. This surely could not have been the writer Grandfather admired. It contained nothing about social justice. I was faced by an utterly strange subject: art and the criticism of art. Those pictures I had admired for their silence and their peace, even their self-satisfaction as images, were not—it seemed—at peace at all. I struggled to understand the unusual words and nearly gave up; but I was kept going by Ruskin's bad temper, his rage against Claude and Poussin—whoever they might be—and his exaltation of Turner. Ruskin was in a passion. Until now I had never been inside Dulwich Gallery, but now I went. And there I stood in those empty, polished rooms that sometimes smelled of the oil paint of a copyist who had left his picture on its easel, in Ruskin's world. Here were the Dutch, the Italians. Here was Rubens. Here was Mrs. Siddons as the Tragic Muse. I was happier than I had ever been in my life; I was also oppressed. It was the old story. I was self-burdened. There was too much to know. I discovered that Ruskin was not so very many years older than I was when he wrote that book.

It took me a year to get through the first volume of *Modern Painters*. The second I skipped. The third bored me until I got to the chapter on the Pathetic Fallacy. This I read easily: in the conflict between painting and literature, literature always conquered. I was shocked to see Pope attacked. I was shamed to see that I was on the side of the Pathetic Fallacy. I had not realized that there was unrest in literature, too, and that one was allowed to attack "the great." Seeing that Homer was praised, I bought Chapman's Homer from the second-hand box. How could Keats have been bowled over by it? Why no "wild surmise" for me? All the great poets had praised the *Iliad*. I was bored by it. Slowly Coleridge and Wordsworth drifted away into regions that were, evidently, unattainable.

There was presently talk at home of my sitting for a scholarship for a place at the Strand School, a secondary school at Streatham. (Many a time I had walked over to Streatham Common in the belief that it was an approach to the Sussex Downs where Mr. Bartlett had found coltsfoot. There were only dandelions on Streatham Common.) Miss H had been nagging my father about scholarships; and because of the Ruskin "prize" he was impressed and I was in a state of euphoric self-confidence.

Soon Father and I were on the bus to Streatham. I was going to sit for the examination. I was impressed by being at a school where there was a dining hall and where boys could buy buns, chocolate and drink cocoa in the break. They also wore long trousers. There was a touch of Greyfriars in this. I was sick with fright and had had diarrhea, of course, but I felt I could rely on my genius. But when I sat down to the examination papers I found that my genius was not being called upon. The effect of Mr. Bartlett's system was that I was totally unprepared and ignorant—even in English. I could answer scarcely any of the questions and I could hope only to get by in Scripture. There was a question about Noah and the Ark—something about the numbers of people aboard, size and location of the Ark, the duration of the Flood, and how many times the dove flew in and out and with what in its beak? I had inherited my father's dislike of a fact. I ignored the question and wrote at full-speed a dramatic eyewitness account of the Flood, ending with that favorite device—a lament. I made the drowning millions lament. A month later

I heard the inevitable news: the genius, the inhabitant of a higher plane, had failed to win a scholarship.

I did not know how to bear the shame of this. It was made worse by hearing that I was older than all the other boys that were sitting. I could never sit again. I found it hard to face my brother. He who hated school, and except in carpentry always did badly—Cyril welcomed me to the brotherhood of failures. He had had a worse humiliation. A school inspector had come to the school and Mr. Timms, to show off his efficiency, had sounded the fire alarm for fire drill. Everyone appeared except my brother, who didn't hear the alarm. He was hauled up to the platform in the school hall, where Mr. Timms made a speech saying that all had obeyed the call of duty, that call irresistible to the heart of every true Englishman, except this miserable specimen beside him—my brother. He had disgraced the whole school, and what was more, before a representative of the London County Council.

Failure to win a scholarship was a blow to vanity and to hopes. For me it would be decisive. In those puzzled hours at the desk my future was settled. How often my grandfather and my father had urged me on with the joke "Victor— always victorious." I wasn't and I began to be cowed by my morally pretentious Christian name and to hate it. I was never good at examinations and was never near the top of the class in spite of all my efforts. In English I was always near the bottom of the list. My memory was poor. Mr. Bartlett had scorned to teach English grammar and I knew nothing of it until I learned French and German. I was bad at spelling and had a bad handwriting. The most serious result of this failure was that it was now certain—although I did not realize this —that I would never go to the University. If I had passed I would have stayed at school until I was eighteen and would surely have got another scholarship to London University; probably I would have become a teacher or an academic. I had had a narrow escape. But I would have had friends whom

I would have met again and again in life, and in university days they would have helped as much as my tutors to put some order and direction into a drifting and chaotic mind.

So farewell to Greyfriars, for the moment; back to Rosendale Road. A gang of us used to go to Brockwell Park, put down our coats for goal posts and play football on Saturday afternoons in the autumn and winter, tagging on to the brother of Fatty Page who had a job and who treated us to American gums and ice cream sodas made of R. White's ginger beer. My brother and I were well-equipped for football; we wore football boots to school every day, blackened over, for we had no others. Ford cars were coming in and we went home shouting down the street:

> Old iron never rust,
> Solid tires never bust.

The school was beaten by Effra Road Higher Grade—boys stayed until fifteen there and were heavier than we were—on a frosty morning, near the railway arches, one to nil. It was a desperate game. The assistant teacher came with us and sang the school song on the touchline, in his weak, cockney voice. Roses was pronounced "Rowsis."

> Roses on the ball, Roses on the ball,
> Never mind the halfback line
> The Roses beat them every time.
> Give the ball a swing
> Right over to the wing,
> Roses, Roses, Roses on the ba-a-ll.

His eldest son, who had left school a couple of years before, came to visit it. A few of us gathered in the school lavatory with this hero who knew the outside world, to hear about life and his experiences. We asked him what his work was. He said—to our amazement—that he hadn't decided on anything yet. But he was not going to settle into some dull nine-to-six office job. He was determined to travel, take some job that would get him out of the country, be a reporter, on "some rotten paper," edit "a cheap magazine." I pricked up my ears. If he thought it was possible to write and to begin on a rotten paper, it must be; one could postpone being poet laureate for a year or two until one found one's feet.

He was an expert on sex too. He told us what went on in the bushes on the allotments opposite the school. All of us talked about sex at school but few knew the facts of life; he told us. As far as I was concerned, a god suddenly fell. I did not believe a word of what he told us. I had not believed the Carter child either.

"Not the King and Queen too," I said scornfully.

"Of course, he screws her," he swanked.

"Liar," I said. And walked home indignantly and troubled, presently remembering Aristotle's masterpiece behind the chamberpot in my parents' bedroom.

We looked at the girls and the girls pouted and put out their tongues and giggled and their warm eyes winked at us. Their dresses, pinafores, jerseys, their tapes and buttons and ribbons fascinated me. A rough-tongued girl called Kate sat next to me in class, pushing, snubbing and wheedling. The descendant of Sir Francis Drake wrote romantic notes in medieval handwriting to one of the beauties. Asked by Kate which girl I liked best in the class, I dreaded that she expected me to choose her, but was wise enough to conceal from her the name of the child I admired, the little oval-faced Portuguese who sat behind me, who scarcely spoke and had a neat handwriting. I dissembled and chose a tall blond creature called Gladys who wore glasses and who gave herself queenly airs. Her gold glasses attracted me. They magnified her blue eyes. I told this choice to Kate in secrecy and she let it out at once: a lesson there. Gladys walked giggling near me for a yard or two, looking me up and down as if I were a meal. We dropped each other at once. Our sizes were incompatible.

There was a large, sallow, sulking Jewish girl with big breasts called Sadie who—we all knew—had started her "monthlies." This led one of our biggest louts to snatch a Bunsen burner off the master's desk and make it protrude erect from his fly buttons and walk up and down, to the laughter of the class, when the master was out of the room. But the German boys and girls were the licentious ones. They lived up our way. The youngest, a child of seven, had found her father's contraceptives, and blowing one out, chased her sisters and brother round their garden with it.

The year before the 1914 war, and especially in the spring and summer before it started, my brother and I were great friends with the German boys and girls. A straggling gang of us used to go to the beautiful park in Dulwich, and we learned to say, *"Liebst du mich? Ich liebe dich"* over and over again, when we had nothing else to say. We played cricket or rounders. If we had enough money we rowed on the lake, which in honor of Wordsworth I tried to think was Ullswater and in honor of Scott, Loch Lomond. I saw Alan Breck land on its concrete banks under the bushes.

But we talked all the time of who had "had it up" with whom. These innocent erotic fantasies were exquisite to us. There were three sisters: a clinging romantic Lolita of about eight, a freckled tomboy of twelve, and a very pretty older and petulant one of fifteen called Greta, a girl with black curls, long eyelashes and blue speckled eyes like a blackbird's egg who was already coquetting with the youths of the neighborhood. We all used sometimes to go into a vacant patch of building ground, a place of long grass and trees, hidden by the railway bank, and there we would light a fire and kiss and bicker. To show off to her, I climbed the embankment and put a halfpenny on the railway line and waited for two trains to pass over it—for it was a busy suburban line. Two trains could flatten a ha'penny and spread it to the size of a penny.

Then you slipped along to West Dulwich Station and got chocolate out of the slot machine with it.

I could not take my eyes off the enticing Greta. One day I jumped on her and wrestled with her. I was instantly in love. This was different from my other childish loves because her beauty made me afraid. I expected a slap but I was astonished to see she was pleased; now her glances confirmed me. I could not believe that a girl as sought after as Greta should look at me. What about my jersey with the holes in it and my made-up trousers? Compared with us, the Germans were what we called rich. They lived in a bigger house than we did. I felt that I was in flames when she asked me to tea with her. We sat at a table in her garden and ate strawberries. She had her exercise book with her. This was the first shock. Her handwriting was childish and her mind was feeble. I told her about Coleridge and others. She gaped at me and said, offensively, that I was "funny," and "What's clever in that?" I went home, still alight, and rejecting the help of the Lake Poets, I copied out a love poem from the *Windsor* magazine, a poem which ran:

> *Stars of the heavens I love her*
> *Spread the glad news afar.*

I put it in her letterbox that evening, lay awake all night, and at seven in the morning slipped out to walk up and down outside her house, wondering which room was hers. Back and forth I went to her house, maddened by the hours. At last she and the freckled tomboy came out. They stared and then giggled together; she laughed a laugh I shall not forget, a high, chilling laugh of mockery, and put her tongue out. They both put their tongues out and walked away. After a yard or two she turned round and screamed: "I hate you."

I stood there, choking with sudden tears. At home I was sick and could not eat. Only the words from *Sartor Resartus* are turgid enough to describe my state: "Thick curtains of night rushed over his soul." And I had lowered myself to sending a poem from the *Windsor* magazine. Grief changed to anger. The wound to pride was real. It was many years before I could speak to a girl and even longer before I could —as I was prone to—fall in love. And I avoided the pretty ones. But I kept up with the dreamy Lolita, the youngest of the German sisters. An errandboy followed us down the street one morning and kept shouting, "Fancy a kid like you having a little tart."

My mother used to say of us: "It's all life and death and hammer and tongs with you. It worries me. You don't seem balanced, not in your right minds half the time."

I liked the German boys. They had a freer life than we had. They talked about Germany and they boasted about the greatness of their country in military science and in music. We used to think that it was for them the German band would come trumpeting with its brass instruments up at the corner of their street. For ourselves, we had to put up with the lavender sellers, the last of the London criers, singing "Will you buy my own sweet lavender? I will give you—sixteen branches for one pe-e-enny"; the singing beggars who always walked in the middle of the road on Sunday afternoons, bawling with their right hands held to their jaws and over their ears. Once a year the man selling almanacs, sang out: "Penny Old Moore, date of the War," and Mother, eager for prophecy, made us run for a copy of the paper. The muffin man rang his bell on Sundays. The "window bang" seller came on windy days, calling out "Bangs for your windows, buy a window bang." Newsboys went by calling "Stop press" late at night. Tramps came for a slice of bread and butter, an incident which always made us recite a joke from one of our comics. A young man is cuddling a girl while another tramp pops his head over a hedge and dangles a pair of his dirty socks in their faces.

"Your golden locks!" says the young man.

"My stripey socks!" says the spoilsport tramp.

They were our favorite lines of English dialogue and often brought back peace to family life.

These were ballooning days. Suddenly, low over the house-tops and looking at first like the bald heads of spying old men, would rise a group of enormous balloons sent up from the Crystal Palace and we would see the aeronaut empty out sand and the wind creasing the skin of the great ball.

We had a struggle to keep our dog Jim from the fighting terrier of the street, a bloodstained murderer with torn ears and a drunken walk. I bowled my young brother's hoop under the legs of a butcher's horse and Jim got his foot run over and ran yelping mad and we had a job catching him. And there were the London thunderstorms, worse in the South, my mother said, than in Finsbury Park; she was frightened of them and ran crying to hide herself in her bed-room cupboard and sometimes put her head under the sofa cushions downstairs, clinging hysterically to my hand and moaning: "Is it getting any lighter?" "Artful Art," one of the boys we played with, had his house flooded two feet deep in one of these storms; we envied him.

On Saturdays we went up to the Norwood Cinema, sat in the front row, cheered the Westerns, saw Bunny, the fat man, and Charlie Chaplin and came back wagging our shoulders in the swanking walk of the cowboys; but we did not tell our father.

The spell of the German boys still held, but their tempers were touchy. One fierce Saxon with wheat-white cropped hair, a budding young Fritz of the caricatures, carried a pair of scissors to defend himself against the Fräulein who looked after him. He had got a razor hidden under his mattresses, ready for her, he said. Another set about trying to hang himself in the bushes of Dulwich Park after being given "out" at one of our cricket matches. One day I saw an older girl cousin of the Germans with a quarreling party in a boat on the lake. Her name was Else and the Germans were always talking about her. If anyone had for certain "had it up," it was Else. She had been expelled from school because of her love affairs with two teachers. I gazed at this wicked girl with consternation. She was a tall creature with reddish hair and fine gray eyes and a wide, warm mouth. Soon, as I was watching the boatload from the path, she stood up and, shouting an insult at her party, calmly stepped into the water waist deep in the middle of the lake, and waded across to me. I gave her a pull in and she stood grinning and dripping beside me.

"I've heard all about you," she said in a friendly way. "I've got a brother who wants to be a writer. Are you going to be a poet?" I was overwhelmed that such a wicked girl should talk to me.

"Look at me. Help me get my skirt off and wring it out. Will you show me your poems? They're stupid people here."

I stared at her sunburned legs and she was pleased.

"Could you write something about me and show it to me? I'm sure you could."

And then she gave a loud, jolly German laugh and went off home. But before she went, she shook hands. I felt her wide eyes and woman's body drawing me to her in friendship with an amused, helpless intelligence of their own. I felt I had grown a year older. I never saw her again. For the 1914 war started a month or two later and she and the other Germans were interned.

A bad thing occurred at Dulwich Park Lake in November of that year. One morning, at breakfast, just as we were putting the milk on our porridge, my father and mother had a terrible quarrel. We were used to these rows, but there had never been one in the morning before. We were scared. My mother pulled me by the arm, just as I was dipping my spoon in my plate, and shouted: "I'm taking my son and leaving you. Come on."

We usually grinned at these rows, but now she pulled off her apron, got her hat and coat, made me put on mine and pulled me with her to the front door.

My father was very pale and looked silently at her and mockingly at me. I looked appealingly at him to try to convince him that all this was against my will. I was frightened.

"I shall kill myself. I shall drown myself in the lake," she cried out.

Her grip on my wrist was hard. She raced down the street with me and nothing I said could stop her. So we went on in the morning fog and got to the park—I was surprised she knew the way—and made for the lake. I was old enough to know my mother's tantrums would not last. The only thing I could do was to take her the long way round the railings to the boathouse gate, which I guessed would be closed at this hour. So round and round the lake we walked until she calmed down. Gradually I edged her towards home. Tactfully my father had left the front door open. She went up to her room, locked herself in and came down later with her bag packed.

"I'm going to my sister," she said calmly. And she did go there.

We felt she had betrayed us all and now turned to our father. He became unexpectedly kind. He explained to me how I must get the lunch for everyone and that he would be back soon in the afternoon, for he had to go to his office. He kept his word and appeared with a large quantity of plaice. He put on his apron, cracked eggs, got breadcrumbs and soon fried one of his wonderful fish suppers. The house filled with blue smoke, the delicious fish was golden on the plate.

"Your mother isn't getting fish like this at the Buggs's tonight," he said. "A bit of cold mutton it'll be, I expect."

What a fool she was; how genial he was, we thought. A big

fry of fish was always the solution to his emotional problems.

What the quarrel was about we did not know. In two days Mother came back. Mr. and Mrs. Bugg bored her with all their "Yes, dear," and "No, dear," she said. "Silly old infatuated fool. Ada's spoiled."

European War! Another case of "Prepare to Receive Cavalry." This was good news for us, I thought, because it looked as though the war and worry of our household had spread beyond our garden fence and that our neighbors and the world in general had been infected by our example. Wasn't Mother always saying life was a fight? Until then we had seemed to be the only fighters. We were now the norm. Uhlans! German batteries on the Crystal Palace Parade: our personal boredom vanished. Father had customers in Frankfurt and said you could never trust Germans. One had "gone down on his knees"—as people often did with Father—and had cried, in order to persuade him to knock a few shillings off his prices. We felt proud. Father was fighting for the Business. And as for myself, the *douceur de vivre* and the high bourgeois culture was at an end. Of course I had no idea that either of these amenities existed. In many ways, for us, this most shocking of wars, a cattle slaughter, was a liberation. A hungry generation pressed forward over the graves of the dead; great states and great families decayed and their certainties with them.

We knew nothing about the forces controlling us and Father was too concerned with his trade to think about them or talk about them. Mother, in her simple, practical, backward-looking way, was more aware of what was happening. Her first thought was for the royal family. What would happen to poor Princess This and poor Queen So-and-so? Fancy, too—all that boasting of the Bugg family that they had once let one of their houses to the Kaiser; a smack in the eye for the Ipswich lot. I went out to find one of the German boys down the street. I found him outside an ironmonger's where he had just bought a wash-leather, and shouting "Dirty German," I hit him, without more warning. He was a tall, handsome and scornful boy, Greta's brother, and would not deign to fight first of all; but I wouldn't let him alone. I wanted to knock the Rhineland or Hamburg out of him. Soon we were on the ground and I was getting the worst of it. Unlike Father's customer he did not go down on his knees and cry. An old gentleman separated us with his walking stick, as if we were dogs, and said he would report us to the College. We slunk off together, sneering back at the old gentleman. I put my fingers to my nose: "We don't go to the College." The old gentleman caught me and cuffed me. He was scarlet with anger.

Mrs. O'Dwyer put her head over the fence and told Mother about the superiority of French culture. Mother nodded; she always nodded when people spoke to her. She had learned that in the millinery and the wily doorways of Kentish Town.

"When your dad and I went over their house, Vic," (My father and mother were supposed to keep an eye on it while the O'Dwyers were away, and had the key) "we looked under the beds and the po's had not been emptied."

Mr. Carter was upset by the lack of unity among European socialists and took up rifle shooting.

Mother groaned and said Father would be ruined and was, for once, sorry for him—and so he was, but not in the way she expected. Father considered the prospect of disaster but brushed it aside. He took a chance, and characteristically, moved his business. He took larger premises. Mother cringed at this recklessness and prayed for him to get a safe job like everyone else—Mr. Carter or Mr. O'Dwyer. Going into the butcher's shop she always opened her purse, put the money she had decided to spend on the counter, and told the butcher to cut accordingly. The new factory was a three- or four-story building in Middle Street off Cloth Fair, close to the meat market which Father loved; indeed, he was a "follower" of old London institutions. In a glow of civic pride he even became a sidesman at St. Bartholomew's nearby, though he disliked the Anglican religion.

In the evenings he showed us the plans of his factory and talked about them for hours. Every now and then Mother pointed one of her fingers in a random way at the plans and said: "Walt, what's this 'ere?"

"Showroom."

"No, these."

"Fittings."

"Oh," she groaned. She was thinking of those disastrous fittings in the stationer's shop when I was born.

He invited her to come and see the building. She refused. She wanted to have nothing to do with the new venture. All she said was: "As long as it's straight. Credit, debit, I don't understand it." But we were excited and mocked her.

One morning my brother and I were taken to see Father's new place. We saw the dirty Thames crawling under the girders of the bridge near St. Paul's and got out, with thousands of office workers, at Holborn and felt once more the dulling blow of the Central London headache. Father whisked like a fly through the traffic.

Father's showroom was a large, white-walled place, newly furnished with counters and cabinets with sliding doors. Miss H, tall, accomplished and gay, came rubbing her hands together. I knew it was disloyal, but I admired her. She wore her white blouse, gray skirt, black stockings and serviceable shoes. She had a touch of scent. On the counters of the showroom were displayed pretty tea cozies, in all colors and designs, cretonne-colored boxes, delicate, voluptuous cushions of the best down, silk handbags, scented sachets, embroidered, worked teacloths. The large room smelled of heliotrope and lavender and lily of the valley. The air was pure and luxurious, the place spotless, and my father himself was fastidious as he walked quietly among his goods, in a white starched dustcoat and a bowler hat. He had the air of a priest. The machines hummed on the floor above as he told us that his goods were the most expensive and the most luxurious in the trade; only customers willing to pay high prices were tolerated. He preferred a few customers only. Once or twice a year he would go to Glasgow, Edinburgh, Perth or Exeter and Torquay and get large orders; outside of this he condescended to sell only to Harrod's or Liberty's, but Toronto was "on its hands and knees." His customers were the wealthy and overfed Edwardians who were just about to be impoverished by the war—their very houses looked overfed with hangings, bric-à-brac and cushions— who lived cholerically and almost untaxed, on their means. They were, above all, a race who draped themselves.

I was puzzled when I saw the Sunday processions of unemployed marching with their banners and when I thought of my father's struggles in his trade; and now when I read books of nostalgia about Edwardian times, I find I remember nothing but the English meanness.

Miss H, whose accent was more precise and grammatical than Mother's North London cockney, told us we should be proud of our father and understand that his eye for color and original design and his gifts as a salesman were the foundation of his success.

Mother said of this: "He gets it from his mother— thoroughness. The old b—— always said she must have the best. He's got taste. He always had."

Father might scowl at home but here we saw a new being, the artist-priest, a pleasant mixture of the active, the fussing, addicted draftsman and perfectionist. A tiny defect in workmanship would send him up the stone stairs to his workroom to start a row with the girls, and we soon realized that at home he treated us as "hands" also. His manner to them was censorious and sarcastic. The girls chattered and sang as their machines hummed, but when the door opened and he stood there, silently, in his starched white coat, they stopped at once. His presence silenced them as he silenced us.

Until now we had had no idea that our father was an artist. We had often grinned at the number of times he washed his hands and had feared him when he passed his fingers over the edge of a table. We had been told often that many things, such as carpets, the upholstery on our chairs and the sofa— which had a violent design of peonies and parrots—were not actually ours, but belonged to the Business and might have to go back. This was true enough of the things he had bought on "appro" or had not paid for; but the deeper explanation of his habit was that he hated things to be used or touched by anyone but himself, just as a painter will be distressed if anyone touches his painting. He saw in every room a personal dream. And when he was an old man he told me he kept his hands soft and clean because by keeping his skin in a sensitive condition, he was able to tell the qualities of silks and cloths; and his underlip would pout with pleasure. This possessiveness of things was also feminine. I gradually grew into a hatred of his love of Things and my mother had a recurring nightmare about it. She would dream of going into three rooms: the first, full of valuable and beautiful china and furniture; the second, even more beautiful; the third, full of stench and decay.

He himself was awed by his creation and lowered his voice when he spoke in the showroom. But when we went there, he was always irritated and Miss H had to placate him and quietly take our side. It was obvious at once to us that his factory and office were another home—and perhaps his real one. His office was more like a pleasant studio than an office. It had his secret collection of clocks, many articles of silver and china, far superior to those we had in our house. He and Miss H were on terms of pleasant, teasing friendship. At eleven in the morning, when the machines stopped in the workroom above, a girl would bring in coffee and he would put a record on his gramophone. He would play "Where My Caravan Has Rested" and also a song by his favorite singer, Clara Butt. A powerful, ox-like rumble came from this woman as she sang:

> "If all the ships I had at sea
> Should come a-sailing home to me."

(It was feared, in the last verse, that one of these might fail to return, which in Father's case was prophetic. It sank overloaded.)

His eyes moistened with emotion as he listened to the booming, curdling voice of this man-woman: Mrs. Eddy, Miss H, Clara Butt—three women in his life! He was very happy. But at ten minutes past eleven he looked at one of his watches—he had two—checked them with each other, then with the clocks, and said sharply: "The machines aren't on yet. The second time this week."

"Sit down, Father," said Miss H. "I don't want you making trouble with the girls."

Father sat down: imagine that—Father doing what a woman told him. We were amazed. The machines started up. Miss H was a miracle worker: their life was, in these days, a business idyll.

Better things followed. We had been brought up to London in order to get a new suit each at Swan and Edgar's, in Nash's Quadrant. Miss H came with us and easily calmed Father down, for his temper was dangerous in shops. Then he took us all to Eustace Miles's New Food Restaurant, where we ate energized bread and hygienic omelettes, for Father was now a follower of the fashionable food reformer and had a large photograph of this fat man in his office. The playing of a lady violinist and a pianist helped to waltz the reformed food down our throats. Afterwards Miss H told us, in a very serious way, that we were going to be sent to a grammar school at a great sacrifice on our father's part. Not until twenty years later did we discover that, in fact, Miss H paid for our education, indeed, I believe for the education of the younger children too: Mother told us. I think Miss H was in love with Father and he had skillfully turned this into a love for his family.

My brother and I went back home by bus.

"What was Miss H wearing? Did she say anything?" said Mother, searching our faces suspiciously.

All we could remember was what Father had said. We decided to say no more.

Father was severe about our new school. We would have to reform our characters, he said, stop being round-shouldered to begin with. Boots cleaned, care with clothes, not playing with every Tom, Dick and Harry, and so on. A total change—or he would alter his plans. Greyfriars at last! We went home and told the Carters and O'Dwyers, who were relieved, welcoming us to civilization. But we had to earn it, Father said. Jim had to be chained up so as to stop him tearing down the garden fence. So he went mad and bit his kennel. He was very like us. We had to clear up the worn-out grass, hoe the path, dig the flower beds, weed. In the next few weeks Father himself joined in and conducted his favorite war. He hated trees. He cut them down, chopped a branch off the laburnum, killed the lilac, destroyed a pergola and soon reduced the garden to a place without vegetation. He drew a plan of a new garden. This preparation for secondary education was fierce and it left me with a lifelong hatred of gardening.

Our first day at Alleyn's School in Dulwich began with the sort of shame we were used to. Our new clothes were stiff, Father was late and in a temper. It was a two-mile walk, past the old College and Art Gallery, through Dulwich Village and up the hill beyond it, to the group of high red brick buildings. He was a brisk walker in spite of his weight; he had his father's soldierly carriage and the print of insult on his face. He had the art of turning any occasion like this into something like the sacrifice of Isaac. When we sighted the school, we exclaimed at the fine trees and large playing fields. He blew up and said he wasn't sending us to this school to waste our time and his money playing games. We feared he would insult someone at the school. For, as usual, we were not being taken on the first day of term: it had begun two or three weeks before, Father pointing out that his time was more valuable than any schoolmaster's.

We got through the main gate of the school without trouble. There was an awkward quarter of an hour in a corridor while the Headmaster kept us waiting; Father was beginning to pace. We peeped into the high school hall and saw a row of large portraits of Charles I and Henrietta Maria staring at us; we were to be Cavaliers here, not puritanic Cromwellians, as at Rosendale Road—a rise in the world. And then came the alarming encounter. Alarming, because we knew from talks with the Carters and O'Dwyers who went to the same school that in spite of Swan and Edgar's we were incorrectly dressed. It had been laid down firmly that we must wear black jackets, striped long trousers and black shoes. Father had said he was not going to allow any tuppenny-ha'penny schoolmaster to dictate to him! We were pushed before him into the Headmaster's study, my brother wearing a very loud yellow tweed knickerbocker suit and myself a slightly less savage brown one. We wore painfully banana-colored shoes as well. The Headmaster of Alleyn's School was a tall and leathery retired Colonel, an Anglo-Indian, whose large nose stood out with a naked look. It had faced tigers. He was a terse man who looked stonily at Father. The Colonel was used to giving abrupt orders and sinking into long silences.

"You'll have to do something about those," he nodded drily at our suits.

Father was bland. He wasn't a salesman for nothing. He quietly pointed out, with a commercial charm, that our suits were made of the best West-of-England tweed from one of the finest mills in the country, its products sold all over the world—foreigners on their hands and knees for them—hard-wearing, and in fact, our colors were the new season's line, as he knew well from his own tailor in Savile Row. Father said he was sure the Colonel must be aware of these facts. The Colonel said that nevertheless the school regulations were what they were, and then went dumb. Father supposed that the World War might have changed people's ideas and that as the Managing Director of a high-class business, he knew that *his* ideas had, at any rate. What was more, he said, he couldn't afford it. And whenever he said he couldn't afford anything a spacious, even wealthy look came on his face and his tone was grand. Moreover, since we were three weeks late, he imagined that a wealthy foundation like Alleyn's would make a discount. The Colonel sympathized but said decidedly, "No reduction" and would Father be so kind as to see to the clothes promptly? Anyway the war, once the Russian steamroller got to work, would be over by Christmas. My father said his time was money and he had a train to catch.

My brother and I made a striking pair at our Greyfriars that term: Father did not buy us new suits. I wore mine the whole two and a half years that remained of my school life. I was led into the Fourth Form just as Dr. Ludwig Hirsch of Bonn, never interned, enormous in his black gown, his mortarboard tilted over his pale, offended face, was starting his German hour.

"*Der Knabe:* the boy; *Die Knaben:* the boys" and with a carnivorous and rich German laugh: "*Mit den Knaben,* de latest news from the front, de dative plural always ends in '*n*'."

Alleyn's School (of God's Gift) is one of the many good London grammar schools. There were 700 boys. Locally we were known as "God's Gifts." It was well-endowed by the Alleyn Estate, which had founded Alleyn's College in the seventeenth century out of the fortune of Shakespeare's actor-manager. But our school was really founded as a result of the Education Act of the seventies, which aimed at educating the lower-middle classes and was separated from the College. The school fees were very small: a large number of the boys came up on scholarships from the elementary schools and we were intended to become the trusted clerks of lawyers, insurance companies and bankers, cashiers to the future executives who, at this moment, were going to the Public Schools. The school claimed to be a Public School and was run very much on those lines, but we were all "day" boys and in the social hierarchy we were a cut below the College boys; still our masters, we were proud to see, were almost all from Oxford and Cambridge. We had everything the College had, except the architecture—and no swimming bath—and we were taught only two languages instead of three, until we got to the Sixth Form; then Greek or Spanish was added. The

College, when it condescended to play cricket or football with us, usually sent us their second team and beat our first; the College could pay for better coaches. The College produced many famous men—Shackleton, P. G. Wodehouse for example—but, except for one freak Colonial Governor and some top boys in the civil service, Alleyn's School had not achieved much beyond that in my time; the English social system, being what it was then, made this unlikely. In my youngest brother's time the school standards were higher.

We were snobbish, of course; snobbery is one of the romantic aggressions of schoolboys. If the College snubbed us, we snubbed the rest. We had two advantages over the boarders at the College—freedom of the streets and a wider mixture of classes. We were not homesick or lonely. It was very possibly a loss, but I never heard of homosexual crushes —nor indeed of homosexuality—till I was well into my twenties, when a Frenchman assured me that all Englishmen were homosexual. I must have been innocent. One thing separates us grammar school boys from those who have gone to Public Schools—we are not traumatically fixed on our schoolboy life and friendships. I have only once met a boy from Alleyn's School since I left it fifty years ago.

Father decided that since he intended me for a business career, I should go on the Modern side and take French and German instead of Latin and French: French would be useful in the silk business, German in the handbag trade. I hated this decision. Wordsworth and Coleridge both knew Latin and Greek—so did Grandfather. Then, I was backward; a large number of the boys had already done a year or two of Latin and French at prep schools; and at nearly fourteen, I was a year older than the rest of my form.

There was no saluting of the Union Jack as at Rosendale Road. Here we began with prayers, the Collect for the day and prayers for the soul of Edward Alleyn, our founder and benefactor. This was the first time I learned of Anglican practices. They seemed chilly. The Colonel barked out the Lord's Prayer and two or three times a week would forget the line after "As we forgive them that trespass against us." The pause would be long and a very audible drawling reminder came from the assistant headmaster, who had a High Church accent. At lunchtime we assembled for a large meal of roast beef or mutton, very good stuff, in the dining hall, while the masters drank their beer at the high table at the end. We were fed as well as we were fed on Sundays at home. Grace was said by the school captain. In the afternoons we played games three or four days a week, or sat about in the very good library.

In the next few months I gave up literature, in fact I now concealed my desire to be a writer by saying that I wanted to be a schoolmaster. Father said I'd soon get over that and was relieved. I had never succeeded in English, but it turned out that I was good at languages. We were taught French and German every day; I learned fast and was usually far ahead of my form. Also, I secretly relearned shorthand and could soon write sixty words a minute. Little Froggie Reydams and the Herr Doktor from Bonn were jokes to most of the boys, but not to me. Someone set fire to the Herr Doktor's gown that first winter, someone else tied a rope to the leg of Froggie's chair and pulled it off the platform just as he was going to sit on it. Froggie, a little man with a thick accent, enjoyed being ragged, but the large Herr Doktor would make sounds like a boiler bursting; then he quieted down and shook his head sadly and said we'd never beat the "Chermans" if we didn't study like the "Cherman" boys did. This caused loud jeers about the Germans never getting to Paris. They had just been driven from the Marne. In the end, the Herr Doktor had to call on the form captain, a New Zealander, to bring us to order.

Dr. Hirsch resembled Emil Jannings in *The Blue Angel*: his big flaccid head lolled sadly and he looked like a condemned capon. He smiled slowly at our larks and was sometimes charmingly interested in them. He was fascinated when he found that several of us had put lighted candles in our desks and were boiling our ink.

"Vat are you doing?"

"I am boiling my ink, sir."

"In English boys, scientific curiosity, a new thing!" he mocked us, turning his eyes to the ceiling.

The hullabaloo did not prevent the Herr Doktor from being a good crammer. He ground German grammar into me so that I can never forget it. The discovery of other languages had an intoxicating effect on me.

I was not happy at home. Suburban life bored me. When I looked at the streets and houses around us, the unending stretches of London villas, the great buildings, the town halls, my spirits fell. I had been born into a family that was isolated —it seemed to me—from all the amenities that I had read of in English literature. There was no bridge between us and the rest of English life. Boys went to the sea for their holidays; a few had been abroad; country boys had horses, town boys went to pantomimes and theaters; they owned bicycles, went to parties, had sporting fathers, went swimming, played tennis; we did none of these things, partly because our parents were locked in their own drama, partly because theaters, bicycles and holidays were too expensive and also partly because—despite appearances—my parents really belonged to a timid generation. My father's grand air was a little man's fantasy. My mother, who had a terror of water, would not allow us to swim, saying she could not afford to buy us swimming suits out of the housekeeping money, and I did not learn until I was in my middle twenties: I became as frightened of water as she was. My father, very moved and almost in tears, would often exclaim when we were restive: "I don't want you boys to grow up. I want you to keep your innocence." We were a mixture of intense emotionalism and pusillanimity.

After a few months at Alleyn's School, and although I worked with a Puritan's fervor, I understood that I was backward and would never pass crucial examinations. One by one, masters gave up teaching me mathematics and geometry; history was a muddle; in chemistry and physics I was at the bottom. My memory—being of an associative kind—was bad. Continuous failures in English were humiliating. So words had to rescue me: not English words, but French and German words. I now dreamed of leaving the tedious city life of England. I could become a Frenchman—even a German when the war was over. I had liked the German boys and girls. As I walked home from school, I walked along the Rhine, through France, crossed the Alps with Shelley and Byron; or, because I had read Thackeray's *The Virginians,* I could see myself on the Potomac. I saw myself as an explorer.

All the signs of commercial life—I suppose because of my early years in the Yorkshire fells and moors—depressed me; and I was sad, uncomprehending and scornful when I heard my school friends talk eagerly of getting into banks and insurance offices. At Rosendale Road we had had our Bartlett phase; at Alleyn's School there was no one to talk to about art and writing. This was natural, for we were being introduced to that accomplished philistinism which was the tone set by our betters. It was a relief to have a better accent and to be almost a little gentleman, but I was also disillusioned. I had felt deprived of education, but—outside of French and German—look at it! Nor was I a "healthy-minded boy." I liked games, but only in an undisciplined way—unable to keep my place in the field. I hated the popular adventure books. The librarian caught me reading *Bacon Is Shakespeare,* which instantly converted me. I was told not to be a prig and to read John Buchan. I found his thrillers unreadable. The characters were not like human be-ings. The library did provide one real drama: two prefects had a very ungentlemanly and savage fight, attacking each other with chairs. It was about a girl. The school in general was mad about "birds," who had now become known as "flappers." This was stimulated by a new gay French master, a wounded air force pilot, who kept us delighted by pictures of his mistresses and of French brothels.

As the war went on masters left for the Army and tired-out, old masters took their place. There was one tragic figure when we got into the Fifth. He was a Shakespeare scholar of sorts, a man with slipping glasses and a weary, breathless, cultivated manner and almost blind. He had a distraught and noble face. He was the victim of crescendos of boot shuffling, dart throwing, desk-lid banging:

> *"We are the boys who make no noise*
> *Um ha! Um ha ha."*

His chair was chalked. The desks were barricaded so that he could not get at them. He would gaze at us helplessly like some contemptuous saint.

"Wretched little boors," he used to say to us.

"And cads!" one day he said, drawn by a boy's tears. They came from an elderly-looking, pimpled orphan of loving and trusting nature, down whose neck we used to stuff decay-ing sausage, because the little swine came to school in a celluloid collar.

"He stinks," several of us protested.

He loved us too much. His spotted face, his doleful large eyes, craved our good will; and he was kind enough to smile pacifically as he let us stuff more food down his neck.

The view was that a boy who dared to come from an orphanage in what were obviously orphanage clothes and who already shaved and had bleeding pimples was a swine. When these attacks were over, he pulled the mess out of his collar and all he said was: "Oh flick!" A vulgar expression! One day he gave a roar and fell shouting on the floor: he was an epileptic.

The war became serious. Having moved his workrooms, Father celebrated the worsening times by moving house again, this time a few miles further out, to Bromley, which was half country town and half suburb. There were no cabs, hymns and tears this time; in this removal we left Dulwich almost in triumph for the country.

We found ourselves in a small semidetached late-Victorian villa with a large garden facing open fields. The air was purer, Father said. It was a pity, he later said, the water wasn't soft. All his life he longed for the soft water of his Yorkshire childhood. Already having got his desire, he was dissatisfied.

"Listen to the thrush singing," he said. Every evening, in the spring and summer, a thrush sang in our fir tree, but as it sang in the quiet summer evenings we heard a monotonously repeated bumping sound from the south. It was the sound of the guns in the Battle of the Somme.

Battle! Father cut down fifty yards of hedge on the road-front and replaced it with expensive laurels. He also bought 500 rosebushes and made me catalogue them and plant them. Food became scarce; we went in for rabbit breeding, but there were scenes about killing the pets, so he turned to chickens. First he moved the furniture out of the back room and put in three incubators, but something went wrong: none of the eggs hatched; they were fried, and left a rotten smell. We imported day-old chicks, moved them about in batteries, and then transferred them to a scientific chicken house, known as the Paradise House, which had arrived in sections. At first Father bolted the wrong walls together, then in a rage rushed off to church and left the task to my practical brother. Mother screamed when pieces fell; cats brought dying pullets, with their entrails hanging out, into the kitchen.

Father was thirty-eight or thirty-nine and he was called up to join the Army. He decided on the Navy. His fancy had been taken by the sausage-like balloons that swung over the Crystal Palace, and he applied to be a naval balloon observer and bought binoculars. He was annoyed when he was rejected because of his enormous weight.

Mother said: "Two balloons in the air."

But some months later, as the demand for more soldiers came in, he faced a crisis. He was ordered to leave the Business and go to work in an aircraft factory. The order appalled him.

"I've had a blow, Beat," he said to Mother.

Mother said to us: "It seems a fate. He tries and tries and something always hits him. But your dad never gives in, I'll say that for him."

Our dog Jim's emotional life had been too much for him. One morning we found him stiff in his kennel. So Father bought a bulldog, a sloppy bitch, to guard us while he was away, but Mother was angry: one more female to contend with—Mrs. Eddy, Miss H, Clara Butt and now this animal. When it was in heat, she screamed: "Not in front of me, with those boys here. Walt, how dare you!"

But Father went off to Hertfordshire to the aircraft factory and left Miss H to run his business. She was a shrewd and economical woman.

In the next few months my desire to be a writer returned. It arose out of an air raid on the town. The difficulty I was in is the general one: one may love the arts, but how does one know whether one has any talent? The doubt tortures and depresses; one can only try. But how? To find a subject is bad enough. It was baffling to me that Howard and Nott could dash off a thriller easily—and they were out of my life now— and that I could not come near to their facility.

But now the autumn had come, the moon grew large and

the Zeppelins could see their way to London. They would come, as all raiders of England have done since the days of the Danes, up the Thames estuary. Owing to the winding of the river, Southeast London was vulnerable. A lost Zeppelin would often drop a bomb or two in Bromley Recreation Ground and smash a few windows thereabouts. The air-raid warning was given by a maroon which made a sharp cracking noise like a rocket. One of these went off at eight o'clock one night after Father left us, and very soon the gunfire started. My poor mother was frightened and became hysterical. She sent my brother and me to get the young children down from their bedroom, but we stayed up there to get a good view of the raid. Someone seemed to be driving nails into the sky with a hammer and knocking sparks off it; and now and then a lorry with a gun on it started rapid fire, just over the fence by our silver-birch trees. Mother screamed. So we all came downstairs and she grabbed us in her fierce arms and moaned, dragging us round and round in a circle with her, while we twisted our necks and struggled to get away in order to see the gun flashes and to hear the shrapnel coming down (we hoped) on our garden path. What we were really waiting and longing for was to hear the great naval gun go off at Pickhurst Green, across the fields, for the flash of this superb gun lit up the country for miles and the majestic detonation shook the whole town. Now, it fired and fired again, as we rocked together in my mother's grip, so that we were like some moaning animal with five heads and ten legs struggling with itself.

Next-door to us lived a shaggy and freckled music teacher and church organist, a young man in poor health, not long married: Mother giggled at the way this couple cuddled and kissed in the garden. Father said the man looked like a weak fellow—fancy playing the organ; ridiculous. And he needed a haircut! When an air-raid alarm went off, this young neighbor knocked on the wall with a poker, and then struck up loudly on his piano which we could easily hear through the thin walls of the dining room. He played Sibelius to begin with and made enough noise in the louder parts of *Finlandia* to drown the sound of the artillery. He did this to comfort my mother, and in other raids went on to Brahms and Rachmaninoff's Prelude in C Sharp minor. So, for the first time, I heard classical music. One night during a raid we all went to his house, but Mother did not like this because she noticed that his wife had been cooking tripe and onions on the sitting-room fire and that the saucepan had burned. "You could see she's not been married long," Mother complained. For other raids, we kept to our own house.

We had no telephone, so after a few raids Father came to see us. He chased a chicken to kill it for supper and made a mess of it; he wrung its neck clean off by mistake and was sick. Mother stewed rhubarb leaves, having read in the paper that it was as good as spinach. It did us no harm but we soon learned from the papers that it was poisonous.

"Well, you see," Father said when he recovered from beheading the chicken, "Father comes home and everything's quiet."

He was in a good mood. He had arrived with a case full of letter files which belonged to a new filing system that was installed in the aircraft factory and explained it all to us. He worked, for two pounds a week, in the Central Registry of the large organization, and he was enchanted by dreams of office organization. You could file tens of thousands of letters and papers a day with it, he said. He was going to introduce it into his business.

"But you only get a dozen letters a day," Mother said. "And no one writes to me, except Ada."

"We don't want to bring Ada into this," Father said. And went on all evening.

We went to bed. About two or three in the morning, my brother woke me up and said: "Man, man, listen."

A light flashed in the room. We heard guns. There was a raid.

"Shall we tell them?"

"Wait."

We went to the window. There was no sound from our parents. We watched the beams of the searchlights cutting up the sky like scissors and then suddenly the beams stood still; four or five of them converged and tented their light. At the apex was a silver Zeppelin, but silver for only a few seconds; suddenly it became vermilion and the whole of London's sky was lit by this red light. Our own faces were reddened by it. The Zeppelin was on fire; it became a red cigar and then it buckled, broke in two and fell in two torches beyond the roofs. And then came the sound of cheering, taken up from street to street, across the city: the airship came down thirty miles away. We did not wake our parents. We wanted this show for ourselves.

At Alleyn's School the next day everyone was excited. Two or three masters said we were savage little beasts. Had we no thought for the wretches burning alive in the sky? Another master, a cynical-seeming young man who smelled horribly of stale cigarette tobacco, told us to "get it out of our systems" and write an account of an air raid. What a chance! But what a problem! I knew what Howard and Nott would have done. "Bang! Boom!" I began and could go no farther. I was said never to stop talking and was as bad as my mother for my exaggerations and mimicries; I knew I was muddleheaded and given to showing off. But rocking with my mother, my brothers and sister, in that room, had moved me; and being "the man" of the house at that time, I was sorry for her. I was suddenly released by recovering an emotion; I hit by this accident on the first duty of the novelist —to become someone else. I pretended to be my mother, and in her person, told what she felt as she called her children down and hysterically thought of her husband. And the old theme from my absurd Alhambra novel was a help: the lament of the women. The story was a lament. I think most of my stories have been laments.

The daring of this idea scared me. Obviously the story was a lie; obviously to write from the point of weakness and in the voice of a woman would make the toughies of the Fifth Form double up with laughter. I handed the story in. The next thing I knew was that the story was a success. It was read aloud in the masters' common room and to the upper forms of the school. I was treated as a young marvel.

Fame is like fire. Baker, the photographer's son, and Hillyard, the "knut" who oiled his hair and brushed it straight back, said Pritch had genius: Baker borrowed the thing and showed it to his sister, a typist, who confirmed it. "Ma soeur says it's clever." Jackson, who sat next to me and who had persecuted me because I would not join the masturbation gang who met in the lavatories, left me alone at last, with a final sneer. Fatty Foley, whose father had a small newsagents business, stopped his punch-ups and made flattering jokes. "Look at old Prick! Look at old Prick!" he kept saying in wonder. Wizam, the Indian, paid me an obscure compliment. He said that I had pretended to be a woman because I never left the girls alone and had tried to seduce his sister, a child of seven, who lived near us. He shouted this in the schoolyard —which the romantic Hillyard called the Quad; he was our chief Greyfriars addict—and Wizam and I started a fight, which drew a good crowd until a prefect separated us. Bailey, one of the "train boys" who traveled to Penge, invited me to a new sensation. The tunnel between Sydenham and Penge is very long and he allowed me into his compartment where we opened the door and rode through the tunnel terrifying ourselves with the door open. But fame fades away. It also corrupts. I sat down a month or two later to write an account of my emotional sensations while listening to our neighbor playing Sibelius. It was a disaster. Callaghan, the frightening master of Remove B, my next form, covered it with insulting marks, gave me zero for it and scribbled "Cribbed from Ruskin and badly assimilated." In fact it was pure Corelli again.

I was rushing downstairs at school because I was late for the parade of the Cadet Corps which I hated, when one of my puttees came undone. I tripped and fell down the full flight of stairs. A hot pain shot into my foot and I fainted. A master came to help me and told me it was nothing; my ankle was not broken, but I had sprained it badly. A boy wheeled me on the crossbar of his bike to West Dulwich Station and then took me home. I bathed the foot and Mother put a cold compress on it, and I lay aching but happy in the thought of a week or so's holiday from Mr. Callaghan.

My father was home on one of his visits that evening and called me into his study. I said I could not get upstairs. "You can get up easily," he said. I put on a great act in getting up the stairs.

We rarely went into his study, for it was uninteresting. We were used to the small bookcase, the sacred gate-legged table with the art needlework runner on it, the engraving of Daniel in the Lions' Den, and a fading photograph of the Mother Church of the Christian Scientists in Boston. There were piles of unopened American periodicals on the table and a small collection of morocco-bound books. Father rarely used the room himself.

"Now," he said. "I want you to understand there are no accidents in God's kingdom. You think you have sprained your ankle, but it says in the Bible that we are all the children of God, made in His image and likeness. How can you believe that a good, omnipotent God would let one of His children sprain his ankle?"

The argument floored me.

"I suppose not," I said. "But . . ."

"I have purposely not told you anything about this, but I expect you have heard I am a Christian Scientist. I have no wish to force my religion on you and perhaps you prefer to believe what your mother believes, but I will tell you about it and then you can make your mind up. Christian Science can heal your so-called sprained ankle this very moment. In fact it is healed now, for nothing has happened to it. That is simply a mistake."

My father then explained to me the doctrine of Christian Science. If I agreed that God was Good and Infinite and Omnipotent and had created Man in His image and likeness, then there was no place where evil could possibly exist. Evil was an illusion, generated by the five senses. They were unreliable.

"Your eyes tell you that railway lines meet in the distance, but that is an illusion; they do not meet. You believe you can see a swollen ankle, but God can't see a swollen ankle, and nor can you, in reality, for since you are made in His image and likeness, you can only see what He sees."

My father said that if I wished, he would demonstrate this to me by treating me in the Christian Science way, at once. I agreed. He closed his eyes and began the process I afterwards understood as "knowing the Truth" about me.

I was very moved. I had often hated my father, but this first moment of intimacy with him was good. I felt that I was going to be cut off from him no longer. And that there would be other good results. If what he said was true, the quarrels would stop in the house, we would see more of him, he would take us to his Christian Science church, we would have some friends, for we were not allowed to have friends to the house. Anyway, in Bromley, we knew no one except the organist next-door.

His eyes opened. He said: "You are healed. I want you to walk to school tomorrow. You'll find in the morning that you can."

And then he slipped one of the periodicals on his desk out of its wrapper and said I could read it. It was the *Christian Science Sentinel* and it contained not only articles, but a number of testimonies of healing of all kinds of diseases. He opened another wrapper. It contained a newspaper, the *Christian Science Monitor*. I discovered it had a literary page. I resented being sent back to school but I was impressed by being taken into my father's confidence and of hearing about his religion properly—for until then we had no real notion of what it was and why he made the startling statements he often shouted in our home.

I woke up next morning and my ankle was still bad. He made me walk to the station and then walk to school from West Dulwich. I was in great pain. In a few days it gradually got better, which is not surprising, for doctors recommend walking on a sprained foot. At the end of the week my father said I had had a startling proof of the truth of Christian Science teaching. I did not think I had, but I set about reading the works of Mrs. Eddy. There was a great deal I could not understand, but the fundamental teaching was that life was a dream—how many writers had said that! The novelty, the dramatic and beneficent nature of the doctrine, exalted me, the hatred, sins and defeats of my life seemed to melt before my eyes.

"You believe what your father does?" my mother asked, peering suspiciously at me.

"I do," I said and explained to her. She had lost an ally.

"I can't fathom it," said my mother. "I keep on having these whitlows. It's cruel. Look at it." She held up her poisoned thumb.

Underlying my conversion to Christian Science was a desire for friends, and the fact that this church had a Sunday School to which one could go until the age of twenty was a strong attraction. The Sunday School met in a pretty house, the church services were held in a light and pleasant hall. The sect was cheerful and business-like: the notion of original sin had vanished, so had guilt. We were all good. It is true that evil was said to be an illusion caused by malicious animal magnetism, a mysterious yet unreal force that did its best to influence the mind and particularly "worked through sex"— whatever that meant. But the evil was not in ourselves. One became as guiltless as any atheist, and I have never since been able to regard the doctrine of original sin as anything more than an intellectual convenience, though it is more than forty years since I last went into a Christian Science church.

It is natural to have religious emotions in adolescence, and —except for the very few who have a religious vocation—it is well for these emotions to be short-lived. The influence of Christian Science on my father's life and upon us was eventually dulling and even tragic; for although doctors now speak with mild tolerance of the usefulness of its belief in the influence of the mind upon the body and are amiably amused by their patients who dabble with both medicine and faith in order to be on the safe side, the occasional healings or even the many tragic failures to heal are not the important aspects of this religion. The real objection is to the impoverishment of mind, the fear of knowledge and living that Christian Science continuously insinuates: the futility of its total argument and its complacency. It operates like a leucotomy that puts the patient into an amiable stupor. A debased form of New England Transcendentalism, Christian Science spread easily in New England in the general pessimism that followed the Civil War; it was one of the symptoms of the decay of the vigorous New England culture. William James treated it gently in his *Varieties of Religious Experience* because of his psychological curiosity; but he understood it was an enfeebled form of Emersonian metaphysics; and, in fact, my interest in it was sustained by the discovery of Emerson's writings. How clearly now one sees the sage, drifting as he grows older, in two directions at once; up into the thin upper air of a beautiful but nebulous metaphysical persuasion and down into the cult of success. The heirs of the Transcendentalists were businessmen; they blandly denied the reality of matter in order to justify themselves in raking in more and more of it.

To England, Christian Science was brought by one or two aristocratic ladies, heirs of that small evangelical movement which had caught the consciences of the upper classes in the eighteenth century. The new religion was a resource for those who could not face late-Victorian doubts: the mixture of religion (without theology) and of supposed science smoothed over the troubles caused by Darwin and Huxley; its optimism accorded with the continuously growing wealth in England. The religion appealed to the ambitious lower-middle class and also to the insensitive and organizational among the blander uppers. It solved so many problems of public conscience: there were nice women who would go down to the slums, watch a hospital train packed with wounded go by at Bromley Station, look at processions of unemployed, close their eyes, "Know the Truth" and go away convinced that they had helped to "heal" the situation. Their complacency was naïve and sentimental; they were indignant if you suggested that they had closed their minds to reality, for they regarded themselves as true revolutionaries, and indeed had to put up with a lot of ridicule and attack. This stimulated them. Most of them had belonged to the traditional churches and were glad to be free of the tragic implication of the Christian myth and its cult of suffering. There was something Quakerish about them. It is characteristic that they had a daily newspaper which reported no crime, no accounts of disaster (though the war was a problem), in which the general tone was liberal and which for years had some of the best foreign correspondents in daily journalism; its literary pages were unadventurous, but many good English and American writers contributed to them. The gap between the tone of this paper and the material of their purely religious journals was great: the difference between literacy and amateur moralizing.

Most of all, I was attracted by their newspaper: to one as little educated as I was, it was a popular educator, for it expressed that unembarrassed seriousness about learning things which gives American life its tedium but also a moral warmth. In Europe the standards have been high for the few, the path of education made severe. If we learn, if we express ourselves in the arts, we are expected to be trained by obstruction and to emerge on our own and to be as exclusive, in our turn, as our mentors; willingness and general good will are—or have been until very lately—despised. There were, in fact, better popular educators in England than in America, but a paper like the *Monitor* made my interests sound easier. In reality the gaps in the *Monitor*—as I came to know when later on I wrote for it—were preposterous. It was good about foreign politics because no Christian Scientist and no American— at that time—was very interested in them.

I thought of Christian Scientists as living in a dramatic and liberating illumination. It was natural that I should be affected by this religion. Its idealism and novelty appealed to one who had scarcely ever been to church but had lived in a house filled with religious echoes and disputes. I had been brought up as a Christian without being taught very much of what Christianity was. It was nothing but words. This new religion was *taught* to me. Father had a natural attraction to all quacks and to any crank—outside the political—who was mellifluous.

But how was it that I, with all my literary pretensions, did not see that Mrs. Eddy was a loose thinker and a very bad writer; that scarcely one of her sentences followed from its predecessor; that when in doubt she blocked in long strings of big words like Soul, Principle, Substance, God, Good; that her books were a rambling collection of assertions and jumbled quotations from the Bible? How was it—after all the jokes at school about "artful alliteration's awful aid,"— I could stand a phrase like "Meekly our Master met the mockery . . ." and many more like it? Or not laugh out loud at "Thou art right, oh immortal Shakespeare," whom she showed no signs of having read except in a book of quotations? It is astonishing how faith makes one shut one's eyes; or how willingly the intelligence takes a holiday from intelligence. Why, at least, did the language of the King James Bible not preserve me? The answer to that is simple: *that* language appeared to me not of this world, a spiritual utterance and not a language at all. After all, why had I swallowed the Bible and believed that the Israelites were superior in spirit, history and culture to the Greeks, the Medes and Persians, peoples far more gifted and enlightened?

Fortunately, nature asserted itself. I was soon leading a double life. I believed, yet did not believe, very comfortably, at the same time. The believing part of me was the simple idealist; also the insubordinate youth was vain of belonging to a sect that was often ridiculed. It appealed to my vanity to belong to a peculiar minority and I did not notice that we were a mild and tepid group who had cut off our noses to spite our faces. More than the nose: I was to discover among my co-religionaries that we had become as mild as eunuchs.

What began to save us was our family egotism. From our mother we had inherited an eye and ear for comedy; from our grandfather and father, a gift for irony and sarcasm.

All sects have their jargon, and Father, eager as an advertising man is for slogans, had picked them all up and lived by them. We soon saw that we were supposed to go through the fundamental process of "knowing the Truth" about this or that person or situation. For example, the truth about a burglar was that he was not a burglar but a child of God, who had seemingly taken to burglary because he had failed to see that he had "abundance" already, for did not the Scriptures say that "Day by day, the manna fell"? Or, rather, a hymn said that. A phrase that infuriated Mother. If I "knew the Truth" about Mr. Callaghan, that child of God, he would stop insulting my English; or if I knew the Truth about my father's violent opposition to our inviting friends to the house, or to my desire to be a writer, he would stop these tyrannies. I tried it, but was haunted by the danger that I was transforming Mr. Callaghan and my father, without their permission. Suppose they, or indeed I, became transfigured; would it not be unnerving? I was handing out dangerous halos. It seemed far too risky to know the Truth about oneself. But many of the good people—though mostly the bossy ones—in the church that met at the town hall were knowing the Truth about one another right and left. And even more, they were enjoined to "voice" it when it was opportune; it was constantly opportune and rarely complimentary.

Not to know the Truth was a certain way of "letting Error into consciousness." I have since discovered that this, like the word "problem," is a common Americanism: perhaps, after all, Christian Science is a normal product of the middle-class American ethos. One of the ways of "letting Error in" was to "outline" the desire we were "working," i.e., praying for. It was right to "work," say, for a better job; but it was "outlining" to say what precise job you wanted. Father never outlined that he wanted fifteen pounds to pay the quarter's rent and stop a writ being served: he worked for "Supply," i.e., the infinitude of God's blessings, a fatal thing for his character; he would always have been better off with the Finite. Instead of outlining you let God's will "unfold." Hence the delays in sending us to school, the refusal to take a family holiday: and eventually, Father took to allowing his manufacturing and sales to "unfold" and sat in his office, gazing at estate agents' offers in a dream that at last became stagnant, then corrupting and finally pernicious. Still, when something did "unfold" one had "made one's demonstration," i.e., demonstrated the truth of Christian Science. If anything went wrong in the lives of any of the church members— Mr. X was still stone deaf, Mr. Y losing his job, Mrs. X still walking on a clubfoot—Father would snort that they "had not made their demonstration." We had a sad example in our own home: Mother, in refusing to have anything to do with this religion, and becoming more and more a worn-out, nervous wreck, was obviously not going to make her demonstration. But what could you do? Father would ask. It's no good casting your pearls before swine. We let a great deal of Error in, in our home.

Sunday was the worst day for Error. It began early with my brother and me standing in the scullery and cleaning the boots and shoes of the family. We did the younger children's first, then our own and then moved on to a long display of Father's. This was an anxious task, for when the boots were done, we would have to take them up to his bedroom where he examined them, pair by pair, and often sent us back to do them again. He was vigilant for specks of cunningly disguised mud; and he always turned the boots over to see if we had blackened and polished the instep between heel and sole.

This was a preparation for his rising and dressing, a long business. Once or twice he was asked to take the collection at the church and then he was in a state only to be compared with that of an actor on a first night. His lotions and perfumes made the air heady, as he changed from shirt to shirt and went through his collars minutely examining them. Mother would send us up to spy, to see "how your father's getting on." At last, on these occasions, he appeared downstairs, in a tail coat, a waistcoat discreetly outlined by a white, piqué underwaistcoat, and a pair of trousers of astounding and tigerish stripes. He wore a winged collar, a silk stock, a pearl tiepin, and a buttonhole. On his feet were spats.

"Beat," he would call, in the voice of one getting ready for sacrifice, "Brush me."

Mother, dressed anyhow, came out of the kitchen, and going down on her knees would brush him, working upwards to the summit. He stood there like some exotic tropical plant that perhaps needed watering.

It was our duty to go to church with him and not to the Sunday School on these special Sundays. On the way, except to mutter words like "Keep your feet up" once or twice, he scarcely spoke, from fear of spoiling his entrance at our tabernacle. He so outshone the other sidesmen that they backed away and he walked up and down the aisle between the chairs with all the polish and savoir-faire of the perfect shopwalker. Sniggers—we were annoyed to hear—came from one or two of our friends, and ladies nodded ironically to each other.

"The guv'nor," Cyril muttered, "has overdone it."

He had. Yet, if anyone of that crowd appeared to be the image and likeness of the Divine Mind, we felt that man was our father. We kept our eye on him, our excess of glory, as

Mrs. Norman (the First Reader) read out the first words of the King James Bible and the Second Reader (Mr. Gordon) responded with what were called the "correlative passages" from Mrs. Eddy, which had little or no relation to the Biblical passage, and which were of impenetrable verbosity. They held our attention for a while because, I now suppose, they appealed to that self-satisfaction which is born out of straining to find meaning in the meaningless. Our minds were in the Information Office that directs one to the Absolute.

After the service everyone chatted happily. Father stood apart as a rule, on the lookout for Error, and as the congregation was mostly female, there was a good deal of it about, from his point of view; but generally his view, and mine, was that we had had a refreshing contact with the Absolute. We walked home but the voyage down from the Absolute to the Relative is tricky. Mother would be in her usual state of fighting with the kitchen stove.

"Walt, look at this brute. Look at the smoke."

"Letting Error in," muttered Cyril.

Mother spoke of the stove as of a horse kicking up its legs.

"Push the damper in," said Father.

"You expect me to slave . . ." Mother began. She was a talented wrecker of Sundays. Father changed his clothes, and from this moment the day went to pieces.

Why, I asked, did this happen? Why did Eternal Harmony vanish so quickly? Mrs. Norman and others would have said we were being "handled" by malicious animal magnetism; others, "higher up in the movement," would have said we were being "handled by Rome," for it was well known to advanced students that the Roman Catholic priesthood sent out spells of witchcraft, especially upon Christian Scientists; many a "problem" was made difficult because the jealous Jesuits—highly trained in these things—were sending out antiprayers to frustrate us. Having escaped from the dead hand of theology, we found ourselves eager for magic and superstition. This disturbed me, but Mrs. Norman told me not to worry about that now and asked me kindly how "the writing was getting on."

The words "Desire is prayer" on the first page of Mrs. Eddy's *Science and Health with Key to the Scriptures*. I was nearing my sixteenth birthday: I was desire in person, frantic, stiff with it. To sit in our Sunday School faced by several pretty girls was an ordeal. I could not take my eyes off the breasts of Mrs. Murstein, our teacher, a Rubens-like woman who wore her blouses so low, in the fashion of the time, that the tops of those rumbustious globes were easily seen, indeed positively offered. Her rich lips, her faint mustache, her forty-year-old but innocent doll-like eyes destroyed me as she explained to us that the true meaning of "to commit adultery" was the "mixing of incompatible elements"—an example was adulterated food. I had read, fortunately, a popular book that told me masturbation would *not* affect my health or drive me mad; but my burdened state was too much for my modesty. At Alleyn's, someone would pass the word along that "old Johnson" was playing pocket billiards and so was Fatty Brown; the whole of Remove B was as stiff as monkeys. Cook, the new French master, made jokes about it, which was a relief. But, at that age, one cannot get it out of one's head that one is, if not unique, at least visible in this villainous and muscle-bound state. I hated to go into shops where girls were working because of it; yet I could not stop myself trying to catch up with girls in the street. In Sunday School I sublimated.

"Still, still with Thee when purple morning breaketh," we sang the hymn, but as fast as I sublimated, so the sublimation increased the desire, and as I sang I was in bed with holy Eileen or Doris or Isabel singing in the row in front. I dared not look up from my hymnbook at the pretty girls and my eyes sought out the plain and ugly ones; but the disadvantage

of this was that the pretty girls looked coldly innocent and
the plain ones were more eager to respond. One could only
cling to Mrs. Eddy's mixture of sentimentality about "tryst-
ing" and her severe teaching—and St. Paul's—that sexual
intercourse was something to "overcome" in the interests of
something higher. One clung. One believed. Yet every in-
stinct told one that the doctrine was ludicrous; and the result
of it was that my desires were perverted in their fantasy.
Dreams of sadism, of terrible sexual sacrifices on altars, of
torture by machines haunted my pious head; so that, when
I hear of some maniac tried for crimes of sexual perversion,
I think: There, but for the Grace of God, go I. But it is not
by the Grace of the Christian Science God or any other that
I have escaped.

Certainly fear of scandal or disease were responsible for
my chastity for many years. I might dream otherwise, but
chastity was a pride. The possibility of becoming an artist of
some kind seemed small, but on chastity it seemed to depend.
I should lose command of my whole self if I lost it, and that
would be the end of the force that made me want to be an
artist. At school, when the boys said they had girls, I knew
they wanted to settle down in little villas where they lived,
in jobs like their fathers' jobs, marry, have children. The
thought repelled me. To go from family life into family life
again seemed to me tragic; for myself, a death. To be alone—
I told my mother—was the ideal; to be unhappy was inevitable. But there was one infallible resource: literature and
art.

Mother looked mockingly at me; I could see the alarm
and the humor move over her face, and then her expression
settle into something stonily accusing.

"I never heard anything like it in me natural. You are
going to be a very wicked man," she said. And covered it
up with: "I can't make head or tail of any of you."

I found many things to interest me in Christian Science.

It introduced me to Emerson, Thoreau, Hawthorne. I was rather snobbishly shocked to see Mrs. Eddy had admired Whittier, a namby-pamby poet. To keep me occupied the following year, Father made me translate a Christian Science pamphlet from the German: the smattering of German metaphysical terms interested me. The religion sounded better in German. I had a bad month with the origin of evil, because, to my dismay, I defeated several older members of our church in my inquiries and arguments. There was alarm about my doubts: I was handed on from eminence to eminence, and eventually to a visiting Christian Science lecturer. The young are surprisingly decent and tactful; I agreed with what was said, but I did not believe a word of it.

A more serious concern for me was the attitude of my coreligionaries to literature and the arts. Clearly art prolonged the errors of the senses; the greater the art, the greater the error. The word "death," for example, was never used by Christian Scientists; one "passed on," for one never, in fact, died. Similarly, descriptions of battle, illness, "inharmony," etc., were banned or had, at any rate, to be so framed in "Suffer it to be so now's" as to be emasculated. Insofar as Shakespeare or Homer approached Christian Science beliefs they were considered good, yet sadly lacking. It was disappointing to see that Christian Scientists were quick to "give up" things. They gave up drink, tobacco, tea, coffee—dangerous drugs —they gave up sex, and wrecked their marriages on this account, and it was notoriously a menopause religion; they gave up politics, they gave up art, but, oddly, they did not give up business.

Mr. Graves gave up music; he looked back lingeringly at his passion for Beethoven. He would play a little but reflect that it was hard to see which part of the music came from the Divine Mind and which from Mortal Mind. Mr. Hotchkiss, the lawyer with big feet, occasionally took a glass of wine, but he had given up reading Russian novels: there was something fleshly in Tolstoy. A Miss Humphrey had given up the National Gallery, for though the pictures (she said) were works of genius, it was a waste of time now to consider anything but the images in the mind of God. There was almost unanimous feeling against a couple called Fitzgerald who had not yet given up socialism. Many sympathized with a Mrs. Merton, a lady of a large, low duck-like breast which she bore before her like a personal tragedy: her husband played in amateur theatricals and wanted to leave the bank where he worked and go on the stage. So far nothing had "unfolded" and Mrs. Merton conveyed to her friends the reason for this. So did he to me: he was one of those lost middle-aged men who confide in everyone. "Victor, I know what's holding me up. I'm carnal." Also he was a chain-smoker. Everyone was sorry for Mrs. Merton because she had a carnal husband.

It seemed to me that if I approached the Divine Mind on the subject of literature, I would have to give it up or—and this is what generally happened in our religion—I would be allowed to start and then I would find I had risen above it and leave it. However, Father came down from London one day and said that in Hollywood many actresses were Christian Scientists. That was a long way off; in England people took a less cheery attitude to the religion.

Such was my state of confusion in the autumn of 1916. I went to my room at the top of the house in the evenings to read Macaulay and to see if I could get a sight of the large lady lodger in the house opposite, undressing. I gazed at my own naked body in a mirror and could, at mere thought, make my organ stand upright; how surprising I looked. What was the Divine Mind going to do with this? I tried to write but could think of no subject. I sat in the laburnum tree at the bottom of the garden, feeling the lift of its boughs in the wind, imagining I was flying or sailing. More than once in that tree I shut my eyes and tried to divest myself of my mortal senses and mind, and in a few empty seconds, waited to be filled with the Divine as the mystics, I discovered years afterwards, tried to experience a unity with God. Sometimes I seemed on the point of this union, when a car hooted or my mother called and I came sulkily down. I did not know then that my methods were dubious: I ought to have felt conviction of sin, I ought to have mortified my body; alas, I liked my body. But one afternoon in the laburnum tree, where I had taken Molière's *L'Avare* to read, I *did* have a convincing experience. The pleasure of finding that French was getting easier to read, the pleasure in the sparkle of words in that comedy, suddenly made me hear a voice. The voice said, "You are a skeptic." It was my own voice, but speaking as I had never heard it before. I closed the book, climbed down the tree and stood on the lawn, longing for the sensation to remain, for someone to tell it to. Even as I longed, the beautiful sensation faded; but I had had it and I felt older.

An event—innocent in appearance—soon showed that I had been "letting Error in" on a serious scale. It was announced that my grandfather and grandmother Pritchett were coming down from Yorkshire to stay. Mother set about cleaning the house from top to bottom, for she knew the old lady would open every cupboard in it. The larder was cleared, for Grandma would bring two large boxes, one containing a week's baking of her best bread, cakes and pastries; the other, a couple of geese from Appleton. Mother prepared two stewed rabbits—no other meat being available in wartime— and my brother betted that he would be given the heads, because Grandma disliked him. So prepared, we waited for the three-o'clock train, when my father (who had slipped away from his aircraft factory) would bring his parents down. They did not arrive. Nor at four. Nor at five. We had no telephone and could not ring up my father to ask for news. Not until eight o'clock did they arrive. Into the house

walked Grandmother, white-faced, in pain, holding one hand
to her chest, and leaning on my father's arm. After her came
Grandfather, his hand and his right arm in a sling and his
head bandaged, his eye blackened. Once a soldier, he now
marched in wounded like a true soldier. The train they had
traveled in from Manchester had come off the rails and their
coach had struck a bridge. They were scarcely in the house
before a reporter came to interview them. The next day we
were proud to see for the first time Granda's name in the
papers:

MANCHESTER EXPRESS DERAILED; MINISTER INJURED

It is to misunderstand our family to think that this drama
passed off entirely in anxious questions, affection and con-
dolences; within half an hour Grandmother, Grandfather
and Father were shouting in angry argument across the
table, about God and "that Eddy woman." Grandma, for
once, was on her daughter-in-law's side and said she doubted
but what Father wouldn't drive Beatie "to go elsewhere."
She was appeased by serving the rabbit. "Eh Cyril, ah'd forgotten you," she said, when we were all served except him.
And she gave him the head of one of the rabbits.

After the meal talk became serious, about trade, the war,
and so on, while Grandmother told how Father had given
her the best handbag in his showroom and asked my mother,
"Has he given you one?" "Yes," said my mother and went to
get it and showed her. The old lady was upset.

"Eh Walter, you gave Beatie a better handbag than you
gave your own mother."

"Here, take it," said Mother.

"Eh, ah think ah will," said the old lady. And did so.

Grandfather said: "How old's Victor? Fifteen? And still
at school?" I gazed expectantly at the man who I thought
was a friend to my hopes.

"Put him to work," said my grandfather.

So one is betrayed. I could not believe it. Everything I

hoped for collapsed in that minute. Tears came to my eyes.

"There's three more mouths to feed," my grandfather said. "You must start earning."

How was I to face the boys I knew, boys to whom I had boasted and before whom I had unwisely glittered? How was I to face Mr. Callaghan? Where was the school prize for French? To despair was now added shame. If Ginger Reed could have seen me then, what a triumph for him.

In fact, at school, everyone envied me and Callaghan said: "Just as well. You haven't done much good here. What are you going into?"

"The leather trade." For so it had been decided.

Callaghan gave one of his delighted sniffs. "Nothing like leather," he said over his shoulder, as he waltzed out of the room under his rusty gown.

My boyhood was over.

10

Why the leather trade? Father had met a man who belonged to the Chamber of Commerce and who had said he knew a firm of leather factors that had an opening for an office boy. Begin (he said) at the bottom of the ladder, like Henry Ford. I shall not forget that spiritless January morning when Father took me to a place in the Bermondsey District of London. The one pleasant but intimidating thing was that for the first time I sat with Father in a corner seat of a first-class compartment of the train on the old South Eastern and Chatham Railway. I was wearing a new suit, a stiff collar that choked me, a bowler hat which bit hard into my forehead and kept slipping over my ears. I felt sick. There were two or three City gentlemen in the compartment, smoking pipes; my father presented me with a copy of the *Christian Science*

Sentinel and told me to read it, while he closed his eyes and prayed for me. I closed my eyes: I disliked being seen with this paper. He prayed as far as Hither Green—I opened my eyes for a glance at a house which had been torn in half by a bomb in the autumn raids—and then he leaned across to me and, not as quietly as I would have liked, for the City gentlemen were staring at us, reminded me of the story of the infant Samuel. Father was becoming emotional. To me the situation was once more like the sacrifice of Isaac.

"When he heard the voice of God calling Samuel, he answered, 'Speak Lord, thy servant heareth.' When the manager sends for you, I want you to remember that. Say to yourself 'Speak Lord . . .' as Samuel did and go at once. It's just an idea. You will find it helpful. I always do that when I go to see the buyer at Harrod's."

I had thought of myself as growing up fast at school. Now, under my bowler hat, I felt I was sinking back into infancy. At London Bridge, where we got out, a yellow fog was coating the rain as we went down the long flights of sour stone stairs into the malodorous yet lively air peculiar to the river level of Bermondsey. We passed the long road tunnels under the railway tracks, tunnels which are used as vaults and warehouses convenient to the Port of London. There was always fog hanging like sour breath in these tunnels. There was a daylight gloom in this district of London. One breathed the heavy, drugging, beer smell of hops and there was another smell of boots and dog dung: this came from the leather which had indeed steeped a month in puer or dog dung before the process of tanning. There was also—I seemed to be haunted by it at the critical moments of my childhood—the stinging smell of vinegar from a pickle factory; and smoke blew down from an emery mill. Weston Street was a street of leather and hide merchants, leather dressers and fellmongers. Out of each brass-plated doorway came either that oppressive odor of new boots, or, from the occasional little slum houses, the sharp stink of London poverty. It was impossible to talk for the noise of dray horses striking the cobbles.

We arrived at a large old-fashioned building and walked into a big office where the clerks sat on high stools at tilted desks. The green-shaded lamps were lit. A hard bell struck over an inner door. "Speak Lord," I instantly murmured— and a smart office boy who had given a wisp of vaseline to his forelock took us to the office of the head of the firm.

This ancient gentleman was like God himself—Grandfather and all Victorians would have recognized him. He was a tall, massive, hump-shouldered man in his late seventies, with a waving mat of long thick white hair which had a yellow streak in it, and a white beard. He had pale blue eyes, very sharp, a wily smile and an alert but quavering voice. He was the complete City gentleman of the old school. My father and he were courtly with each other; the old man was soon on to the slump of the 1870's, when his uncle had sent him to Vienna for the firm and where (he slyly said) he had got the better of a competitor because of his knowledge of German. He said he was glad to hear I was a churchgoer, for he himself held a Bible class every Sunday; and his secretary, an old woman like my grandmother, taught in Sunday School too. He mentioned his eleven children, four of the sons being in the business. My father said I was good at French. The old gentleman suddenly snapped at me: "*Assez pour tirer d'affaires?*"

I was bowled out and could not speak. The old gentleman grinned kindly. We were interrupted by a sugary, languid tinkle on the old-fashioned telephone that stood in the middle of his large desk. It was really two desks joined; it had spawned some odd side tables and was covered with papers, letters and periodicals. I watched the bent knees of the old man rise, then his back heave up, then the hump elongate itself and finally a long arm with a powerful and shaking hand on it stretched across the wide desk and reached the telephone. The quavering voice changed now to a virile, barking note; the mild blue eyes became avid, the teeth were the teeth of a lynx. His talk was brisk and commanding: when it was over he sank back in his chair and gazed at us as if he had never seen us before, and panting a little, said: "The *Arabic* has docked with four thousand bales." His knees went up and down under his desk, feeling for a concealed bell, and the office boy came pelting in.

The room, I saw, was like a studio under a dirty glass roof, and was supported by iron pillars here and there. In two corners of it were two more crowded desks and against one of the walls was a large Victorian fireplace. The smoke of the coal fire mingled with the fog that had entered the room.

I worked for four years—until I was nearly twenty—at the leather factors, starting at twelve shillings and sixpence a week and finishing at eighteen shillings and sixpence. The firm was one of the most important factors in the trade. Other factors, it was said, were merchants on the side, a lack of probity which the firm denounced: we—as I quickly learned to say—sold on commission only. We—it turned out—were the agents of a very large number of English tanners and fellmongers, also of large sheepskin tanners in Australia, of hide merchants in general, and dealt also in dry-salted South American hides. More rarely, and reluctantly, we dealt in Morocco and India dressed leather and wooled sheepskins. There was more money in the raw material. A large part of this stock was stored in the warehouse attached to the office, but also in the docks, in the wharves of the Port of London and in the cold storages. The firm also dealt in tanning materials: oak bark, shumac, myrabolams and tanning extracts. The correspondence came from all over the world and was heavy; the size of the checks the firm paid out astonished me; they ran often into the thousands, all of them bearing the large, spidery, childishly clear signature of the old gentleman.

It was incredible that a firm in such shabby, old-fashioned offices should be so rich.

The premises were opened at seven thirty in the morning by an old clerk called Hazlitt who wobbled in fast, lame and gouty, but always wearing a flower in his buttonhole. He was one of those gardeners of *The Waste Land*. He was satin-y pink, fat and very bald and went about singing bits of music-hall songs or making up words. He then went over to let the workmen into the warehouse. One of these, a young, feeble-minded man, cross-eyed and strong, would lumber down to the safes and carry up a load of heavy ledgers which he set out on the various desks. Dust flew out of them. His name was Paul—he, like one of the carmen, who was known as Ninety because it was the number of the house where he lived —had no surname. Paul lived with his mother and was very religious. When he had put down his ledgers, Paul would advance upon Mr. Hazlitt and say his usual morning greeting in a toneless voice and unsmiling: "Well, my venereal friend."

To this the gay old Mr. Hazlitt would reply: "Good morrow, good morrow, good morrow." And add one of his made up words, "Hyjorico," and shake with laughter. Paul, who wore a heavy leather apron, lowered his head and looked murder at Mr. Hazlitt, and went off on his bandy legs, waving his clenched fists dangerously.

At eight we office boys arrived and often saw this scene. The other office boy, whose name was Les Daulton, had to teach me my job. He was a weak-voiced, fair creature, as simple as Paul and also famous for his comic mispronunciations. Offices—like my mother's shop in Kentish Town of the earlier generation—depend for their life on repeated jokes. Goods were often collected from Thamesside quays: Daulton always called them "kways" and the clerks concentrated on getting him to say it. Daulton gave a simple smile. He knew he was a success. Once we had arrived, Mr. Hazlitt went to the w.c. in the basement where he sat smoking his first cigar and reading the paper; Daulton and I followed him down, taking with us the packs of rubber sheets which were used in the copying of letters in the letter presses, and soaked them in the washbasins. This done, the boy took me out with the local letters that had to be delivered by hand. We went down to the Hide Market, to the tanners and leather-dressing firms and then came back to our main job: answering the Chairman's bell (he was known as Mr. Kenneth). This bell was fixed outside Mr. Kenneth's door, in the main office, and snapped in startling, rusty and panicky agitation.

"Boy! Bell!" Mr. Hazlitt would call out in panic, too.

"Speak Lord, Thy servant heareth," I murmured. One of us would jump off his stool and go in to see what the old gentleman wanted. Sometimes he handed us an urgent letter which had to be copied, but often his knee had pressed the bell by mistake; or he had forgotten he had called us and he gazed at us blankly with the lost, otherworldly eyes of an old man.

Occasionally the bell was rung from another desk in Mr. Kenneth's office. This was the desk of another old man, Mr. James, Mr. Kenneth's brother, well-known to be the fool of the business and never trusted with any serious matters. He wandered in to "work" at eleven or so, wrote a private letter to Lord This or Lady That—for he was vain of aristocratic acquaintance—and would then shuffle out into the main office, calling out "I'm going to get me hair cut" in a foggy, husky voice. Sometimes he would wander into the warehouse and watch the bales of leather swinging on the crane.

"Coming in or going out?" he would ask, putting on as much of a commanding air as he could manage, considering his voice and the absurd angle of his pince nez glasses which were held lop-sided on his nose by a piece of black ribbon.

Under his foolishness Mr. James concealed the character of an old Victorian rip and he was terrified of his pious brother Kenneth. Mr. James's only work was to hand us our wages every Saturday in a sealed envelope. I was warned that he would slyly pay me too much the first time—another Victorian trick—to test my honesty. Sure enough he did; he gave me fifteen shillings instead of the agreed 12/6d. and I had to go through the farce of explaining there had been a mistake. The expression on his face was one of immense self-congratulation at his cleverness.

We liked Mr. James because his daily hair cut took place at a smart Bar near London Bridge. Everyone envied his life of sin.

We also indexed the letter books, putting the number of the previous letter written to the firm at the top of the flimsy page in blue chalk. This indexing took us a large part of the day, for we, as well, had to see the customers at the counter, answer the bell and begin copying the next crop of outgoing letters. Late in the morning, Mr. Hazlitt, our boss, would go off on a round of messages in the City, carrying shipping documents, contracts, checks and so on, and would return about three thirty, rosy in the face, smelling of cigars and scent.

"Where's he been, the dirty old man? Up Leicester Square. Lounging in the Leicester Lounge," the other clerks would greet him enviously.

Les and I, in the meantime, went out to lunch together into the Boro' to someone's Dining Rooms, a good pull-up for carmen, near the Hop Exchange. Upstairs we ate the same food for the next year, every day: either steak and kidney pudding followed by date or fig pudding, or steak and kidney pie followed by the same. The helpings were heavy; the whole cost eightpence, but went up to tenpence the following year. I was afraid of London and especially of the price of things and it was pretty well a year before I had the courage to go into the Express Dairy Café under the arches at London Bridge Station.

We walked back to the office, past Guy's Hospital. The clock crawled from 2:00 to 2:05, from 2:05 to 2:10 on the tedious afternoon. At four we had a quarter of an hour's break for tea up in the housekeeper's kitchen, I having been sent across to a little cake and tobacco shop for sugared buns. Relays of clerks came up for tea. We sat at a kitchen table, looked after by a cross woman called Mrs. Dunkley, or—as she sometimes wrote it—Mrs. Dunkerley. The clerks munched their buns and made remarks about how much she stole, about her corset, her bottom, what she did with her lodger, and built up fantasies about her sexual life. She (like Daulton) could be cornered into saying one of her classic sentences such as the one made to Mr. Elkins, the dispatch clerk: "Ho, Mr. *Helkins,* I dropped the *heggs.*"

Among the clerks there was the weedy, lewd and sarcastic Mr. Drake, a sandy-haired man who invented the day's dirty jokes and backed horses. At a desk under the long iron-barred windows sat a respectable, puffing, middle-aged man with a dirty collar: the shipping clerk, his desk a confusion of bills of lading, delivery orders, weight slips. An inaccurate and overworked man, he was always losing important documents and was often blown up by one of the angry partners, the sons of Mr. Kenneth. There was Mr. Clark, a dark, drawling, defiant figure who looked like a boxer. He was the invoice clerk. He would stand warming himself by the fire, unmoving, even if the Head Cashier arrived, until the clock struck nine. If the Cashier glared at him, Mr. Clark stood his ground and said: "Nine o'clock is my time."

The arrival of the Head Cashier set the office in motion and something like a chapel service began. He was a tall, grizzled, melancholy man who stood at his desk calling over figures to an assistant, like a preacher at a burial. He was famous for his sigh. It was a dull noise coming from low down in his body. "Um, ha, ha," he said. And sometimes he would call to an idling clerk: "Press on, Mr. Drake."

"Press on what," Mr. Drake would mutter.

"Your old woman," from Mr. Clark.

"I did that last night," sniggered Mr. Drake. "The air raid upset her."

"Sit on her head," called Mr. Clark.

Conversations that were carried across the office in penetrating mutters.

The Head Cashier's stomach noise pleased everyone. If he left the office for a moment, it was ten to one that Mr. Hazlitt would mimic it and bang his desk lid up and down, like a schoolboy.

About nine arrived the only two women employed in the main office—there were five sacred typists upstairs. These two women were quarreling sisters. Women were in the post-corset, pre-brassiere period and it was the joy of the office to exclaim at the jumpings, bobbings and swingings of a pair of breasts. One lady combined a heavy white blouse-ful with an air of swan-like disdain.

"Things are swinging free this morning, do you not observe, Mr. Clark?" Drake would say.

"Do you fancy fish for lunch?" Mr. Clark would reply, nodding to the prettier sister.

The elder girl raised her nose, the pretty one shrugged her shoulders and pouted.

Hour after hour, the Cashier and the swan carried on their duet.

"Feb. 2 By Goods. Cash £ 872. 11. 4."

And the swan answered: " £ 872. 11. 4."

"Comm. and dis. £ 97. 16. 2," intoned the Cashier. "Um, ha, ha."

The mournful singsong enchanted us.

At nine thirty the "lady secretaries" arrived. They were the secretaries of the partners, their little breasts jumping, too, and their high heels clattering. These girls were always late.

"The troops stay so late," sniggered Mr. Drake. "How can a working girl get to work?"

As the day's work went on, the foremen in their leather aprons would come over to the office from the warehouse. They were responsible for different kinds of leather and they usually came over to settle matters arising from the chief problem of the leather trade. Most of it is sold by weight, but leather can gain or lose weight, depending upon the season and the weather. The men in the warehouse despised the "shiny-arsed clerks with their four ten a week."

Sometimes Bermondsey life would break in on us. The kids would climb up the wall, and hanging on to the bars of the office windows, would jeer at us. A clerk would be sent to drive them off, but they picked up stones and threw them at him or spattered our windows with horse manure. But often the clerk could not get out because they had tied up the door with rope. If a boy was caught and got his ears boxed, the mother would be round in a minute, standing in the office and shouting she wanted "the bleeding bugger" who had hit her Ernie. The mothers were often hanging about in the pub next-door, feeding their babies stout or a drop of port to keep them sleepy.

We worked until seven in the evening. On Saturdays we left between two and four, this depending on the mail. In the evenings I went home from London Bridge Station. In *The Waste Land,* T. S. Eliot wrote of the strange morning and evening sight of those thousands of men, all wearing bowlers and carrying umbrellas, crossing London Bridge in long, dull regiments and pouring into that ugly, but to me most affecting, railway station which for years I used. I was captivated by it as I suppose every office worker is by the station in the great city that rules his life. Penn Station in New York, St. Lazare in Paris, Waterloo, Paddington and Liverpool Street are printed on the pages of a lifetime's grind at the office desk. Each is a quotidian frontier, splitting a life, a temple of the inexorable. The distinction of London Bridge Station, on the Chatham side, is that it is not a terminus but a junction where lives begin to fade and then blossom again as they swap trains in the rush hours and make for all the regions of South London and the towns of Kent. The trains come in and go out over those miles of rolling brick arches that run across South London like a massive Roman wall. There were no indicators on the platforms in my day and the confusion had to be sorted out by stentorian porters who called out the long litanies of stations in a hoarse London bawl and with a style of their own. They stood on the crowded platform edge, detected the identifying lights on the incoming engine and then sang out.

To myself, at that age, all places I did not know seemed romantic and the list of names was, if not Miltonic, at any rate as evocative as those names with which the Georgian poets filled up their lines. I would stare admiringly, even enviously, at the porter who would have to chant the long line to Bexley Heath; or the man who, beginning with the blunt and challenging football names of Charlton and Wool-wich, would go on to comic Plumstead and then flow forward over his long list till his voice fell to the finality of Greenhythe, Northfleet and Gravesend; or the softer tones of St. John's, Lewisham and Blackheath. And to stir us up were the power-ful trains—traveling to distances that seemed as remote as Istanbul to me—expresses that went to Margate, Herne Bay, Rochester and Chatham. I saw nothing dingy in this. The pleasure of my life as an office boy lay in being one of the London crowd and I actually enjoyed standing in a compart-ment packed with fifteen people on my way to Bromley North. How pleasant it was, in the war years, to stop dead outside Tower Bridge and to see a maroon go off in an air-raid warning, and even better, for a sentimentalist, to be stuck in one of those curry-powder fogs that came up from the river and squashed London flat in its windless marsh. One listened to the fog signals and saw the fires of the watchmen; there was a sinister quiet as the train stood outside the Surrey Docks. And when, very late, the train got to Bromley North and one groped one's way home, seeing the conductors with flares in their hands walking ahead of the buses, or cars lost and askew on the wrong side of the road, and heard footsteps but saw no person until he was upon you and asking where he was, one swanked to oneself that at last one had had a load of the traditional muck on one's chest.

The thing I liked best was being sent on errands in Bermondsey. They became explorations that I made every excuse to lengthen. I pushed down south to the Dun Cow in the Old Kent Road, eastward by side streets and alleyways to Tower Bridge. I had a special pleasure in the rank places like those tunnels and vaults under the railway: the smells above all made me feel importantly a part of this working London. Names like Wilde's Rents, Cherry Garden Street, Jamaica Road, Dockhead and Pickle Herring Street excited, and my journeys were not simply street journeys to me: they were like crossing the desert, finding the source of the Niger. London was not a city; it was a foreign country as strange as India and even though I knew the Thames is a small river compared with the great ones of the world, I would patriotically make it wider and wider in my mind. I liked the Hide Market where groups of old women and children hung about the hidemen who would occasionally flick off a bit of flesh from the hides: the children, like little vultures, snatched at these bits and put them in their mothers' bags. We thought the children were going to eat these scraps, but in fact it is more likely—money being urgent to all Londoners—they were going to sell them to the glue merchants. The glue trade haunted many busy cockney minds. Owing to the loop of the river, Bermondsey has remained the most clannish and isolated part of London; people there were deeply native for generations. Their manner was unemotional, but behind the dryness, there was the suggestion of the cockney sob.

"What'll y'ave? Lovin' mem'ry or deepest sympathy?" the woman in the shop asked when I went to buy a mourning card for one of our office cleaners.

I would pass a pub called the Tanners Arms and wonder at the peculiar fact that the owner had a piece of tanned human skin "jes like pigskin." The evenings came on and a procession of women and children would be wheeling their mattresses up to the railway tunnels or the deep tube station to be safe from occasional raids. I would see other office boys wearing their bowler hats as I wore mine: we were a self-important, cracked-voice little race, sheepish yet cocky, regarding our firms with childish pride.

But my work was dull. The terrible thing was that it was simple and mechanical; far, far less difficult than work at school. This was a humiliation, and even now, the simplicity of most of the work in offices, factories and warehouses depresses me. It is also all such child's play and repetition and the correcting of an infinitude of silly mistakes, compared with the intellectual or professional labor. Most people seemed to me, then and even now, chained to a dulling routine of systematized and tolerated carelessness and error. Whatever was going to happen to me, I knew I must escape from this easy, unthinking world and I understood my father's dogged efforts to be on his own and his own master. In difficulty lay the only escape from what for me seemed to be deterioration of faculty.

The dullness, the long hours, the bad food, the low pay, the paring away of pleasure to a few hours late on Saturday afternoon, the tedious Sundays brightened only by that brief hour at the Sunday School—all these soon stunned and stunted me in my real life, however much they moved me to live in my imagination. I accepted, with the native London masochism, that these were hard times and that this could be my fate. London has always preferred experience to satisfaction. I saw myself a junior clerk turning into a senior clerk, comfortable in my train, enjoying the characters of my fellow travelers, talking sententiously of the state of affairs in France, Hong Kong and Singapore, and with profound judiciousness, of the government. Over the years one would know these season ticket holders—perhaps not speaking to them—as well as the characters in a novel. Sometimes there was an oddity—the man who read Virgil as he traveled up and down. And there was always, for diversity, the girls who knitted for the soldiers and read novels. There was also the pride I felt in being enslaved in a city so world-famous, in being submerged in its brick, in being smoked and kippered by it. There was the curious satisfaction, in those months, of a destiny and the feeling that here was good sense, and under the reserve, humor and decency.

But the office was brutalizing me. One morning I arrived and began teasing Daulton, the other office boy. He was slow and childish. I was trying to make him say Parson's *Kway*. He would take that from a clerk but not from an equal. He saw an enemy and flew at me. It was delightful; it was like being at school again. We were soon rolling on the floor and I was laughing, but he, I saw, was savage. Old Hazlitt, wobbling up from the w.c., found us disheveled in the dust. He put a stop to it and Daulton, trembling, began to cry. What had I done to him? He was afraid of getting the sack. Hazlitt took his side. So did the clerks. Daulton was their joke and treasure. I was spoiling it. When the Cashier came he called me over and I said we were only "having a game." "You have upset Daulton," the Cashier said gravely. "I am surprised at a boy like you wrestling with a boy of that type. You went to a better school than he did." And I who had thought that Daulton and I were fellow victims! Daulton gave me a look of pompous disapproval and wistful repoach after this. The matter went on being debated by the Cashier and the clerks, and I saw that I was in serious trouble. It was discussed with one of the partners. I became scared when he sent for me, and came away incredulous. I was to be promoted. I was to go into the warehouse and learn the trade.

My life became freer and more interesting at once and I scarcely spoke to Daulton after that.

His chauffeur brought the Chairman, Mr. Kenneth, up from the country at ten. Mr. Kenneth came in burdened like Abraham and went, knees bent, in a fast aged shuffle, like a man stalking, to his office, where he was soon ringing his bell. About the same time, his four sons arrived, four quarreling men between thirty-seven and fifty years old. The firm was a working model of that father-dominated life which has been typical of England since the Elizabethan age and perhaps always, for we must have got it from the Saxons and the Danes. In the Victorian age, with the great increase in wealth, the war between fathers and sons, between older brothers and younger, became violent, though rather fiercer in the middle class than among manual workers where the mother held the wage packet. Until 1918, England was a club of energetic and determined parricides; in the last generation the club appears to have vanished altogether. So, in their various ways, Mr. James, Mr. Frederick, Mr. William and Mr. John, active and enterprising City men, were at war with one another and attacking their father when one or other of them was in favor. Mr. John, the youngest and most genial, was the only one to regard the fray with grinning detachment. He sat on the opposite side of his father's desk, unperturbed.

Mr. James was the eldest, a precisionist and a cultivated and intelligent man; he dealt in heavy leather. Mr. Frederick, handsome, dashing and hot-tempered, whose eyes and teeth flashed operatically, was in foreign hides, a very speculative market; he lived in a fine house in Regent's Park; Mr. John drawled a shrewd and lazy life among fellmongers and raw pelts; Mr. William, to whom I fell, had an office on the warehouse floor and dealt in basils and skivers, i.e., tanned sheep-skins. On this subject, under his teaching, I was to become an expert.

The British merchant has the reputation of being a deep and reserved, untalkative fellow, slow to act until he is certain, not easily deceived and a shade lazy. The four brothers entirely contradicted this legend, except in one respect: they were not easily deceived. Reserve, they had none. They talked and shouted their heads off, they exposed their passions, they were headlong in action, as keen and excitable as flies and worked hard. Mr. William was the most emotionally self-exposing of the brothers. He was a sportsman who had played hockey for England, a rather too ardent and too reminiscent golfer and extrovert. Owing to a damaged knee, he was rejected for the Army during the war. His emotionalism annoyed his brothers. He would come into the office crying out: "Father hates me. James has been telling Fred . . ." and so on, a wounded and sulky man. What their differences were I don't know; but they were strong enough to break up the firm when the old man died.

I had often known the chapel-like groans of the main office to be interrupted by a pair of these storming brothers who pranced in a hot-tempered ballet. There had to be a peace-maker or catalyst, and there was.

When I described the arrivals at our office there was one figure I did not mention: a dandy called Hobbs. For some reason he was not called *Mr.* Hobbs and these were the days before people called anyone but a servant or a workman by Christian names or nicknames. The voice in which Hobbs was addressed was reverent; it might have been used to a duke who had, for some reason, condescended to slum with us all; it was a voice of intimacy, even of awe. He was on simple, equal terms with everyone, from the old gentleman down to the boys. One finds his type more often in the North of England than in the South, and indeed he came from Leeds and had a faint, flat, weary Yorkshire accent. His speech was plain but caressing. He had walked into the business, in his deceptively idle way, some years before and discreetly appointed himself to be the brains of the firm. To everybody, and to me especially, he was the only person I could talk to. He was a man of about thirty.

One saw him, a tall thin figure, a sort of bent straw, paddling down Weston Street early in the winter mornings, in his patent-leather shoes, his fur-lined overcoat reaching to his ankles, his bowler hat tipped back from a lined forehead and resting, because of the long shape of his head, upon a pair of the ugliest ears I have ever seen. His little remaining hair rose in carefully barbered streaks over the long egg-like head. A cigarette wagged in his mouth, his face was pale, seamed, ill and amused. Hobbs was a rake and his manner and appearance suggested days at the races and evenings at the stage door of the Gaiety, and the small hours at the card table. He looked as if he were dying—and he was—the skull grinned at one and the clothes fluttered about a walking skeleton.

Eyes bloodshot, breath still smoking the gin or whiskey of the night before, he arrived almost as early as the office boys, in order to get at the office mail before anyone else saw it. He memorized it; he was now equipped to deal with all the intrigue, quarrels and projects. By some nervous intimidation he knew whenever a girl came into the office and he smiled at them all and his large serious eyes put them into a state. To all, at some time or other, he said "Darling, I'd like to bite your pretty shoulders." Except to the Dragon, the old man's secretary, who often handed out religious tracts. She saw in Hobbs, no doubt, an opportunity for rescue and he deferred to her and started reading a line or two of the tracts at once while she was there and making expert comments on a passage in Exodus or Kings, so that the old lady began to blush victoriously. Girls liked to be caught in the warehouse lift with him, for he instantly kissed their necks and looked their clothes over. His good manners overwhelmed Mrs. Dunkley-Dunkerley in her kitchen. All office work stopped—even the Cashier stopped his callover of the accounts—when Hobbs went to the telephone, and smiling at it as if it were a very old raffish crony, ordered a chauffeur-driven Rolls to collect him in the evening and pick up one of his girls to take them to dinner at the Ritz. The partners listened to him in fright, wondering aloud about his debts, but would soon be confiding in him, as everyone else did, and angling for his advice.

"Look what Father has done. James has told Father that Fred . . ."

Hobbs, who always wore his bowler hat in the office and was the only one who was allowed to smoke, nodded and listened with religious attentiveness. The appearance of physical weakness and dissipation was a delusion. The firm chin, strong coarse mouth, the rapidity of mind were signs of great nervous strength. The partners were gentlemen of the cheerfully snobbish kind. Hobbs was an intellectual from a provincial university who had read a lot and was a dilettante. His brain was in a continuous and efficient fever. If trade was slack and he had no business or customers to deal with, he would go round the office, and with a smile that they could not resist, would take the clerks' pens from them with a "By your leave, laddie" and do all their accounts and calculations in a few minutes while they gaped at him. Their lives were ruled by having to work out exasperating sums as, for example, 3 cwt. 2 quarters 9 lbs. at 3/4½ d. per lb. less commission and discount of 3½ per cent. He could do scores of sums like these in a few minutes. Or, for amusement, he would tot up the Head Cashier's ledgers so fast that this sorrowing and pious man would look over his glasses, admiring, and momentarily forgive him his obvious debauches. With the workmen he was the same; he got them out of the laborious messes they made of their weighing slips, gave them racing tips, was knowing about prize fights and once in a while would buy them a drink in the pub next-door where he was well known. Where was he not well known!

"Out of the great kindness of your heart, duckie," I've heard him say to the barmaid of a discreet hideout near London Bridge, "would you give me a rather large gin and French?"

I had to work with Hobbs and soon, infatuated, I dressed exactly as he, in white coat and bowler hat, pushing it back over my ears in helpless admiration of him. I had to sit with him and keep the Epitome Book, a summary of the hundreds of letters that came in. I have always been prone to intellectual disaster. For years I thought this book was called the Opitomy Book, for I used to think of epitome as a three-syllable word.

I was enraptured by Hobbs. For a boy of sixteen is there anything like his first sight of a man of the world? I was enraptured by London Bridge, Bermondsey and the leather trade. I liked its pungent smell. I liked watching the sickly green pelts come slopping out of the pits at the leather dresser's down the street, I liked paddling among the rank and bloody hides of the market; I would cadge the job of cutting the maggots of the warble fly out of a hide in our hide shed. I liked the dirty jobs. I wanted to know everything I could about leather. Gradually, literature went out the window: to become a leather factor, or, better still, a country tanner was my dream. I spent my day on the seven floors of the warehouse, turning over dozens of calfskins with the men, measuring sheepskins and skivers and choking myself with the (to me) aromatic shumac dust. At home the family edged away from me: I stank of the trade. With my father and me it was a war between Araby and the tanpit.

The leather trade is an interesting trade, for skins and hides are as variable as nature. At certain seasons, in the breeding season, for example, the skin will be hard and "cockled"; heavily wooled sheep like the merinos drag the surface of the leather into ridges, so that the body of some old man seemed to lie under my measuring ruler. Some skins are unaccountably greasy and have to be degreased; others may have heated in the hold of a ship; yet others may have been oversalted by a tanner who perhaps hopes that when the temperature rises, they will pick up moisture and weight.

After a time one could tell from which town and county of England any skin came and from which tannery, for each tanner had his own methods, his peculiar waters and style. The names were cheerful: skivers and basils, shoulders, bellies, split-hide bellies and butts—the animals seemed to lie baaing and lowing, as one looked at the grain of the skins for their quality or their defects: to see which could be dyed in red or green, say, or which—owing to the flaws in the grain—would have to be dyed in the cheaper black. There was change in every bale that the crane lifted off the vans and heaved into the "gaps" where the men chalked the tally on the walls. And change in the human scene too.

On market days, many of the tanners came to the office. They came mainly from the small towns of England and the variety of character fascinated me. A brash, bearded fellow in a cowboy hat who came roaring in and shouting that we were "a lot of stuck-up London snobs" and his money was as good as ours; the trembling pair of elderly black-bearded brothers from Dorset who stood together, shoulders touching, like Siamese twins and had the suspicious and dour look of conspiring lay preachers; the flash Welshman; the famous sole-leather man from Cumberland; the sad country gentleman tanner from Suffolk; the devastating fashionable tycoon who was making a fortune, wore a monocle, was something to do with Covent Garden Opera and introduced me to the name of Flaubert.

In due time I was sent down to the wharves of Pickle Herring Street or the docks, to make reports on damaged

skins that had been dropped into the river, or on thousands
of bales which had come in from Australia. A literary job: as
the bales were opened for me in these warehouses that
smelled of camphor or the mutton-fat smell of wool or rancid
furs, I wrote in my large book, an estimate and a description.
It was curious to open a bale from the ship or barge alongside
and to see, as one got towards the center, that it was blacken-
ing with heat and at the center, charred and cindery. When I
grew up and read Defoe's *Complete English Tradesman* I
knew the pleasure he felt in the knowledge of a trade, its
persons and its ways. If I knew nothing else, at the end of
four years I was proud of my knowledge of leather. It was a
gratifying knowledge. During the last war I had to spend
some time in shipyards on the Tyne and on the Clyde and the
passionate interest in a craft came back to me; and although
I was then an established writer, I half wished I had spent
my life in an industry. The sight of skill and of traditional
expertness is irresistible to me.

My absorption in the leather trade went to comical lengths.
Father had bought a fat encyclopedia, secondhand, and
dated 1853; I discovered in it a full technical account of the
tanning process. I decided to tan a skin myself. I got a small
tank, brought home some shumac and then considered the
process. First I had to get an animal and then skin it: then,
either by pasting it on the flesh side with a depilatory, or
letting it heat to the point of decay that is not injurious to
the skin, I would have to scrape off the hair. There were
superficial skins to remove. I would then have to place it in
the proper liquids, having first transferred it for a time to a
tank of fermented dog dung in order to soften it. And so on.
The difficulty was to find an animal small enough. Our dog?
Our cat? One of our rabbits? The thought sickened me. A
mouse? There were plenty in the house. I set a trap and
caught one. But it was so pretty and the prospect of letting

its skin sweat and removing the fur with my fingers repelled me. I gave up the idea.

In my second year in the trade, in the summer holiday, I hired a bicycle and went up to Ipswich, stopping at a country tannery on the way. It belonged to the sad gentleman farmer. He gave me lunch and I showed off to his pretty daughter. After lunch he took me to the tannery. This was the life, I thought, as I walked round the pits: to be a country gentleman, marry this nice girl and become a tanner. There might be some interesting erotic social difficulties of the kind that occurred in *John Halifax, Gentleman,* by Mrs. Craik, a novel that fed my daydreams at this time. The pits were laid out like a checkerboard and we walked between them. I was in the midst of this daydream when I slipped and I fell up to the neck into the cold and filthy ooze of the pit. A workman hooked me out on his pit pole before I went under, for these pits are deep; I was rushed to a shed, stripped and hosed down. Stinking, I was taken back to the house, and dressed up in an assortment of clothes, including a shooting jacket much too large and a pair of football shorts belonging to the tanner's ten-year-old son. The nice girl had left to laugh in her room.

This was my baptism into the trade; now I think of it, the only baptism I have ever had.

I was happier in my hours in the leather trade than I was at home; and strangely, I believe, the encouragement to think again of being a writer came from people in the trade. One or two of the customers saw the books I was reading on my desk and I discovered that many of these businessmen knew far more about literature than I did. There was the tycoon with his Flaubert—whom I did not read for years—there was Beale, the leather dresser, who recited Shakespeare at length, as we went through the skivers on the top floor; there was Egan, our foreman, a middle-aged and gentle man with a soft voice who, in between calling orders to the men and going over his weighing slips, would chat to me about Dickens and Thackeray. Once a month he would get blind drunk for a few days and then return, otherworldly and innocent, to have a bookish talk. There was a leather-belting manufacturer who introduced me to literary criticism. They were amused by my naïveté; but when they got down to their business affairs with Mr. William and the watching of the market, I realized that although I knew a lot about leather, I knew nothing about trade and money, and that the ability or taste for making it was missing in me. Beale, the Shakespearean, showed that to me. He was a man of fifty who had inherited his business and was always in straits and was rather contemptuously treated in the trade because of his incompetence. He took me round his works and looked miserably at the rollers that came down from their arms, striking the skins, with a racket that he could not stand. "Keep out of it," he said. "Unless you know how to make money, it is no good."

Hobbs sat or dangled from his high stool and said, "Journalism's the life, laddie. You read too many classics. You ought to read modern stuff. Journalists are the bright lads. What about W. J. Locke?"

I saw at once when I read *The Beloved Vagabond, The Morals of Marcus Ordeyne* and *Septimus,* that Hobbs had modeled himself on Locke's gentlemanly, Frenchified Bohemianism. A bottle of wine, a French mistress was his ideal —often realized; at any rate he had soon established one of the new women who came to the firm, the widow of a French soldier, in his flat. There was Thomas Hardy, too, he said, and Arnold Bennett. So I threw up the classics and took to the open (French) road with Locke as a successor to Stevenson and a precursor to Belloc. I had discovered the writers I really admired: the travelers. I bought most of the books I read, and had done so at school, too, by spending my food money on them. I gave up the dining rooms and the Express

Dairy; instead in the lunch hour I bought a bar of chocolate or a packet of biscuits and a book for a few pence at a shop near the arches at the station, walked across London Bridge and went on lunch-hour tours of the Wren churches—to the organ recitals at St. Stephen's in Walbrook and St. Dunstan's in the East and to St. Magnus the Martyr in Billingsgate. I knew I should admire the Wren churches but they bored me. The classical Italian beauty of St. Stephen's in Walbrook seemed cold to the clerkly follower of Ruskin; cold and also —to a Dissenter—monied and even immoral. The elegant St. Mary Woolnoth and even St. Magnus the Martyr and its carving seemed to me as "worldly" as the board rooms of banks. And in Southwark Cathedral I had an experience of the "mechanical" worship of the Church of England. A young clergyman sitting at a harmonium in one of the aisles was teaching another the correct intonation of "The Lord be with you" and the response "And with Thy spirit," which they repeated dozens of times, trying to get it right. Now I could admire; then I scowled like a Bunyan at "vain repetitions."

The one real church, for me, was St. Bartholomew's.

I visited these churches as a stern cultural duty, but also out of a growing piety towards the London past. The pleasure was in the organ recitals held in the lunch hour. Lately introduced by our neighbor to Sibelius and Rachmaninoff, I now was entranced by Bach's fugues. This taste was literary and due to Browning; all my tastes were conventionally Victorian. The monocled tycoon who had revolutionized the tanning of sheepskins, heard with horror of my unfashionable notions. I seemed irredeemably backward and lower class and the cry of the autodidact and snob broke out in me in agony, "Shall I never catch up?"

I soon knew the alleyways of the City and successfully intrigued to be sent to Ministries in Westminster. I ventured into Fleet Street and stared longingly at newspaper offices.

Often I longed to be in love; but I was already in love with
London, and although too shy to go into pubs—and hating
anyway the taste of beer—I would listen to the rattle of
dominoes among the coffee tables of the Mecca as far north
as Moorgate, and obscurely feel my passion. I even walked
from Bermondsey to Westminster. To love, travel is almost
the complete alternative; it is lonely, it is exhausting, but one
has lived completely by one's eyes and ears and is immolated
in the world one is discovering. When, at last, I did find a
girl, all we did was dumbly walk and walk round London
streets till I dropped her at her office door. When I read books
of the glamour-of-London kind, I was disappointed with
myself and tried to whip myself up into a glamorized state,
for I could not see or know what the writer knew; but a
London of my own was seeping into me without my knowing
it and, of course, was despised because it was "everyday
experience."

One summer morning when I was on the heavy-leather
floor of our building, I heard the impudent whistle of Atter-
bury, the foreman of the floor. He was a cross-eyed, jeering
little man, known to everyone as Ankleberg. "I got a nice
birthday present this morning," he shouted. "My old woman
give it me. Somethink I coulda done without. Same as last
time, same as time afore that—nine bleeding times! Another
bleeding kid. And no lie either."

He had an accusing manner: "Know what the woman next
to her in hospital said to the doctor? 'E's never off me.'"

Ankleberg stared, and then he shouted with laughter and
went off looking like the devil. He was the man who let me
have a go at cutting maggots out of some cowhides in return
for loading a van with them.

"Here Ankle," said his mate, but coming over to me and
opening a wallet. "This is what you want." And showed him
a packet of French letters.

"Dirty bastard," said Ankleberg. "You'll get some poor girl into trouble."

Our talk was stopped by a curious sound of pumping and hammering going on in the sky and we went over to the gap. The sound was gunfire.

"Stone me, it's bleeding Fritz," said Ankleberg.

Up we went in the warehouse lift.

"Nine little hungry mouths," said Ankleberg on the way up. "What d'you make of that, son?"

We got onto the roof. Not far off, high in the sky over the Tower of London and coming westward, were a dozen German aircraft. They looked like summer gnats in the clear sky and around them hundreds of little cherub-like bursts of anti-aircraft fire were pocking the sky. Sudden bursts of bomb smoke came stepping down the Thames towards St. Paul's, where black and green smoke went up from the roofs: and then, down our way the aircraft came. In the street people were watching the planes; most of our staff were there and they ran indoors when a bomb fell—some said on a printing works in Newcomen Street nearby, or in the Boro'.

In a minute or two the raid was over. I was looking at the fires near St. Paul's. I tried to ring my father. There was no answer. I got permission to go and see if he was all right; but in fact I was longing to see the damage. It was, for those days, startling. A flight of aircraft had bombed London for the first time by day. Across London Bridge I went, down the steps by St. Magnus the Martyr, into Billingsgate, and saw the street walls of several houses and wharves had been stripped off, carts were overturned and horses lay dead among the crowds. The pubs in Bermondsey had filled with women pouring drink into themselves and their babies as I left; it was the same in Billingsgate. Outside a pub at The Monument, on the very spot where the old fire of London had started, one of those ragged and wild-looking women street singers, with enormous plumes in her coster hat, was skirling out a song, luscious with cockney sentiment and melodrama:

"Cit-ee of larfter,
Cit-ee of tears."

I kicked my way through little streets of broken glass in Little Britain, and passing the stink of burning chemical works, reached my father's office. The flames of the fire were so hot that he and I could not stay on his roof.

I went down to Alleyn's School one Saturday. The war became dispiriting, dragging and hungry. The casualty lists stretched halfway round the school hall. Appleyard, the captain and cross-country champion, was killed. Stevens with the strong glasses and the smutty mind had been washed off his ship in the Atlantic. Lake, our best cricketer, had lost an arm and would not bowl again; gentle Pace had been killed. Appleyard's death chilled me. For days I could think of nothing else. He had been so far above me, the hero: and yet, once seeing me across the street, he had waved to me.

Cycling on Saturdays in the country, I was obsessed by the trench war and I spun along, converting the countryside into a battlefield. Every hill, every bridge and road became part of an imaginary war game. On summer nights when the wind was blowing gently from the south, we would sit on our lawn listening, as I have already said, to the murmur of the barrage from across the Channel, hour after hour. Sometimes I went home by Charing Cross and would arrive at the station when a hospital train arrived and men unrecognizable and covered from head to foot in trench mud and weighed down with filthy kit got off it, while the bloodily-bandaged wounded were being hustled into scores of ambulances. The flower girls threw their flowers in after them. Romantically I saw myself going to the war and was depressed because I was too young, yet I was terrified too. It was all a daydream, of course, for if I had had more spirit and had been a less sickly-minded animal I might have got through by lying about my age. Many tough boys did. I was a small, thin, genteel and timid sentimentalist, dreaming the idea, afraid of the fact. By 1918 the reality came nearer. I got my father to apply for me to get into the Royal Flying Corps—it is strange that I did not apply myself, but it would not have occurred to me to do anything without my father's permission. I had no will except his; only my secret will. And anyway he told me—and I believed him—he would have to "see a man," it would require weeks of negotiation. I was not yet eighteen. There was also, he pointed out, the spiritual side of the matter. If the Divine Mind wanted me to go into the Flying Corps I would undoubtedly find myself in it. We must not "outline"; we must wait for a "demonstration." I must do my best by not letting "Error into consciousness." To that I must stop seeing "that girl" he had heard I'd been seen out with. I had met one of the Sunday School girls on the train and—with reckless daring—I had been to tea with her, and sung the wartime song while her sister played the piano:

> *"God send you back to me*
> *Over the rolling sea."*

Father was horrified to hear that I had a girl. "Soon," he said, "she'll be calling you 'her boy.' A man in my office has just had to pay out four hundred pounds because his young son got a girl in his office into trouble. I want you to know I haven't got four hundred pounds. I warn you. I made a great mistake myself. I married too young. A girl *has* to find a boy —that's, well, it's her trade, her living. I want you to stop that, at once, d'you hear. If you want to know about love, read what Mrs. Eddy says."

I was sunk in morbid thoughts and fancies, muddled by ambitions, sexual desire and boredom. Life at the leather warehouse was a relief, but my infatuation with the trade was fading. I bought a deep-winged stiff collar in order to look like Sir James Barrie, whose photograph I had seen in a magazine called *The Bookman;* the effect was spoiled by a large bleeding spot on my throat, a spot I picked away at, so that it lasted for most of a year; at times I thought I had caught anthrax from a cattle sore in the hide shed and saw an early death. As I have said, I had no interest in buying and selling, but I enjoyed the characters of the people in the trade. Story after story walked into the warehouse and I entertained my mother (and sometimes my father) with them when I got home. Occasionally in the relations of these people I saw analogies with the relations of my father and myself.

There was an old red-faced coster, an angry and effervescent little cockney who dealt in cheap loads of chamois skins, sometimes only two inches long, the torn-off pieces almost worthless, which he sold to the "sponge" trade. Men like him, who had begun life by pushing barrows, often made a tidy fortune, bought a slum house or two and became men of property. He lived in an alley called Wilde's Rents. He made state visits to us twice a year with his son, looking at every little piece and muttering: "What's the bloody use of this? Rubbish. Let's have a look at the other bale." And he would turn on his son and say, "What's the bleeding idea, bringing me down to look at this lot?"

The son, a weedy and pale, dressed-up young man of thirty-five, would cringe and wince and make a curious sound like "Tit-tit" with his teeth. After the father had denounced his son several times, he'd turn to me and say, admiring, "He's educated up like you, a proper little toff."

The next day the father would send the son on his own. He came sniffling and tit-titting, a young man, terrified of his father, who indeed looked as though he'd bite your leg like a dog. The son had literary pretensions, too, but of a political kind. He was a book-learned anarchist.

"The European bourgeoisie is destroying itself," he confided to me. "Did you ever read Kropotkin? Tit, tit, tit. The Russian?"

Oh, not another writer!

"Marx?" he said.

Well, I had read about the Russian Revolution in the papers.

"We've had nothing but propaganda for years," he said.

For ten days, first father and then son came in, until at last Mr. William would shout at the father: "Come on, you old rogue. What's the price? 4/6d?"

"Four and six, you're out of your bleeding mind—I wouldn't give a tanner. It's a waste of my time, isn't it Dick?"

"Tit. Tit. Tit. We'd never sell it, Father," said the obedient son.

"Sell it!" cried the old man. "Wouldn't get it home. Couldn't give it away. I try to teach this boy the business and what happens. Dresses hisself up like a toff, he doesn't know his arse from his elbow. Well, Dick, what d'you say? What is it worth?"

In the end a bargain was struck; the father blew his chest out and paid for tons of this stuff in dirty pound notes, with a last battle about how much off for cash.

"Never had a bank account, no, not me. Where would I be now if I'd had a bank account? I'll tell you. Down the drain! I seen it. What he calls"—pointing to his son—"bloody capitalism."

"That's it. Tit. Tit. Tit."

"See what I mean—doesn't know he's born. Come on, son, you let your old dad be twisted again. I'll never train the lad, he thinks he's bought the street."

The pair seemed to parody my life.

The war ground to a stop. On Armistice Day, people say, London went mad. I saw nothing of it. Some in Bermondsey didn't believe it and took their mattresses up to the tube or the arches, just in case. There was a bonfire in the yard at Guy's Hospital and a fireman's helmet was stuck on top of the statue there. We got off an hour earlier, but Mr. Kenneth worked late. Father was late home too. He had celebrated with Miss H at the Albert Hall, singing "Land of Hope and Glory," and he had had his wallet stolen. He was rather pleased, as if he had done an extra something for the country.

11

Now the war was over Father was exuberant. He had always had bounce: in the last two years he had bounced up high. Being away from us, in Hertfordshire, had freed and re-juvenated him. Mother said getting away from Miss H had done him good too.

We sat long after Sunday meals while he spoke to us about his new life. He had lodged in a pretty country inn. He told us, in a bashful, poetic way, what he had had for breakfast and for dinner and what fine houses there were in the country nearby—houses with barns and stabling, billiard rooms, a cottage for the staff: he wanted one. He had (he said, lower-ing his eyes modestly) joined a riding school. He had fallen in love again, this time with a couple in the handbag trade, real live wires. They drank this new drink: cocktails.

Did you have one, Dad? we asked. He may have had one, just out of politeness—Sportscar or Sidecar, oh yes, and a White Lady, too, he said. He did not drink alcohol—we never had even a bottle of beer in the house—but he did keep a bottle, he said, of "Chartroos" in his office, in case a customer came. Grandfather and Mrs. Eddy had kept him off drink; in fact he had drunk nothing since his twenties when he had had a calamitous bottle of Guinness on a rough sea on the way to Belfast. He was proud of this crime later on in his life when he gave us a glass of gin.

The war had changed everything. The stuffed, quilted and cushioned Edwardian age had gone; the age so soft for the bottoms of the comfortably off, so mean and bitterly exacting for the struggling, small man, so wretched for the poor. The old family and personal businesses were being shaken—the quarrels of those brothers in the leather trade were a symptom. The new order was appearing in the great organizations like the aircraft firm. At first when he went to work there, Father was a mere letter stamper in the Registry, which was in confusion. He could not bear disorder, so, always with an eye cocked for opportunity, he discreetly promoted himself. And then went on promoting himself. But he was not, by nature, an organizational man; he scorned the intrigues by which one gets a "title," creates a small empire, conquers other empires and is finally at the top of the organization, protected by secretarial outposts. Father's technique was different. He cultivated a look of owning the place, and sailed up alone to the position of general meddler. "I prefer to do things personally." His life as a salesman had taught him to start from the top.

The artist in him must have died at this time, and was succeeded by the impresario. From the way he told it, he seems to have converted himself into a Maskelyne and Devant —we had apparently often sent him, at our expense, too, to these magic shows and he gave us exciting accounts of them.

One had the impression that a curtain went up in the air-craft factory, that a soft explosion of pink flame and smoke was heard, and there stood Father, the magician, creating scores of new offices, typing pools, drawing offices, executive suites and board rooms; and, what was more important, ordering furniture on a lavish scale for them. Carpeting and linoleum he must have bought by the square mile. He was pursued by all the nabobs of the furniture trade. He purred from one to the other, in chauffeur-driven cars. There was always something of the Chairman and mine host about him—he had the proper waist measurements and courtliness —and he was soon dropping names so high-up in govern-ment and in aviation that Mother's underlip began to shake with fright, and the rest of us choked at the sound of them. He brought menus back from Claridge's and the Ritz and went over the dishes for our benefit. We were proud to have him eat on our behalf and admired the new, sad look of the gourmet under his eyes.

Our salesman had become one of the great buyers; and he did not forget us in this new occupation. There had been many periods in our lives when our various houses had no stair carpets and when neighbors complained of the clatter we made on our boards; wardrobes, cupboards and chests were unknown in our bedrooms. Now everything changed. Father was apt when buying something, to order two of it; so we now doubled up wardrobes and chests. We had two grandfather clocks for a while, also two pianos. From a local hotel which was getting rid of its out-of-date furniture cheaply, Father got an enormous sideboard from the main dining room. Our mahogany, walnut, rosewood and deal stood staring at one another in a state of orphaned acrimony. They obviously had been happier elsewhere and seemed to show it. We looked like a salesroom. New cleaners and polishers came in and a peculiar thing called an O'Cedar mop. This gift, Mother hid in a cupboard, going every now and then to look at it and swear at it, as if it were yet another woman in her life; and I think my brother Cyril, who was mechanically minded, thoughtfully broke it. Mother was one for mat, knees, a pail of water and a scrubbing brush.

It was only fair that Father should think of himself sometimes. He did not obtrude this upon us. Trips to Bond Street kept him supplied with pieces of old silver, bowls, salvers, cruets and engraved and crested objects, which he privately took up to his bedroom and modestly concealed among his pants and vests. Mother used to note this and go through his underclothes on the quiet to see what new treasure was there.

The words of the Christian Science hymn return to me:

Day by day the manna fell
Oh to learn that lesson well.

This was undoubtedly the lesson of the war. The Divine Mind had shown Father not to limit his thinking. The ominous words came out one day: "I can't breathe. I feel I can't breathe," and the expression on his dark face was so agonizingly sincere that we were all affected.

Now the war was over it was a shock for him to come back to work full time in a small business which had modestly survived. The busy and economical Miss H had seen to that: Mother wished Miss H had married. Father went pale with anxiety when she said that. It remained for him to take note of the changed times and demands and to go off and see his old customers. One of his first acts was to buy a large quantity of heavy brocades at a high price. Miss H became angry. The price fell at once and for the first time in its history, the firm showed a loss.

"Accountants can prove anything with figures," Father said and dismissed the matter.

Father considered the new situation in his business. Miss H told him that they must have orders. Father said No. First principles first: he must have Right Ideas. One of these was a larger showroom and workrooms, large premises at a corner, where "the world" could see them. In the next few months, he brought home the plans of several likely places and we cleared the table quickly so that he could spread them out. In these schemes he was frustrated by the cautious Miss H, who was getting stricter with him. She reminded him that he was not manufacturing airplanes, but cushions and tea cozies and novelties. Father said that you could not limit the Infinite. He retreated all the same, and fell to designing a trademark or symbol for his products.

"We'll ask the Professor to design one, since he's always telling us what a brain he's got." (I was the Professor.)

He decided on one of his own designs: the simple letters S. P., after that the words "The sign of Quality." He walked about the room saying it aloud. It was poetry to him—but should the *S* be entwined with the *P?*

Frustrated in his desire for larger premises, Father moved to the dream of getting a larger house.

There was an urgent reason for buying a larger house. We were chocked with furniture and now, secretly—it took a couple of years for the secret to come out—he had bought a grand piano and it would have been impossible to get it into any of our crowded rooms. Yet, if the Divine Mind had manifested itself in the form of a piano, this Mind would inevitably supply a place for it to go into. He was obliged to store the piano until accommodation for it "unfolded." Often, when he sat studying our dining room, he must have been trying to fit this secret piano in; and, in fact, we were more often asked to help move the furniture round—Mother's pastime.

"That old sideboard is a devil, Walt," she would say—her only criticism of these games.

In his office, while Miss H did the daybook on the other side of the partner's desk and the typist clattered next-door, Father sat back, reading the estate advertisements in *The*

Times and *Country Life*—"getting ideas for the Christmas trade," postponing the annual trip to Glasgow until it was too late.

Brooding on this, Father said that my brother Cyril had better leave school, for it was now my sister's turn for secondary education. My brother, who hated school, loved my father even more for this gesture. It was a step to his ideal: to work in the Business. The eager boy who did not like Christian Science as much as I did was hurt to hear that the "Divine Mind has not yet shown the way."

But the Divine Mind did deliver a motorcar: a Sunbeam. My brother, who was a good mechanic, was appeased. It appeared at Christmas.

Mother threw the Appleton goose off its dish onto the dining-room floor this Christmas lunchtime, shouting: "There it is. Eat it," and, giving a hysterical scream, locked herself in her bedroom. The two youngest children cried. Three hours later, about four o'clock, when she was calmer, we all sat down and did eat it: Mother trembling in an armchair, while we, annoyed with her, began to jeer at her. She sent looks of fear and hatred at us. Eventually she grew happier and an atmosphere of exhausted melancholy and remorse softened the room; Father brought out Sir James Barrie's novel *The Little White Bird* and read it to us with feeling; tears appeared on his cheeks when he got to the sad parts about the lost woman, and he loved the pages about undoing the "little braces" of the strange boy and putting him to bed. After supper my brother and I played chess. We had a board but no chessmen; but we used nuts and bolts and cogwheels from a Meccano set instead.

We were a problem. I told lies about what I was doing. I was going to be a writer, but carefully said I was going to be a schoolmaster; I said I was reading when I was really writing. I said I was going out with my brother when I was really going to see a girl. Cyril and my sister were, by now, helpless stammerers. Only our youngest brother appeared to be frank and normal.

My stammering brother was denounced for being idle. He wanted to be a ship's artificer, then a civil engineer; Father blew up and said he could not afford the training, so the boy sneaked off and got a job in a garage. Father said it was all he was fit for, then made him leave the job. In the end my brother bought a very loud cap called a gor'blimey and went for secret joy rides on a friend's motorbicycle.

For some reason this was the only boy allowed into our home; in fact he could not be kept out of it. He arrived in the evenings and sat with us, nodding at us and staring at us and saying little, but occasionally murmuring private jokes with my brother. The boy was called "Curly." He was one of those youths with big heads and rusty voices who are born middle-aged and at sixteen look about fifty. He rarely shaved, his face was covered with eccentric, curly yellow bristles, often very long; and he had many bloody pimples. We gazed at Curly and he at us; he was covered all over, you could tell from his hands and face, with a dense golden fur and he smiled out of his personal, rather pubic forest, looking at us with wet eyes. He looked like an aging dog, perhaps an Airedale. He worked in a gasworks, which made Mother scream with laughter.

"What are your duties?" Father asked once.

"Let the kids smell the gas," said Curly. "When they've got colds. Their mothers bring them in and ask for a smell of it on the way to school."

Sentences like this were not brisk; they came out slowly a few syllables at a time and were broken by long elderly sighs and meditative intervals.

Curly became important to me later on: I wrote a portrait of him.

Now my father had a motorcar, my brother was very necessary to him, for Father could not bear a drip of oil or grease on his own hands; my brother liked oil. Father was, of course, a fanatical car polisher and washer; or rather, a supervisor of my brother's washing and cleaning. The car affected Father's temper and he needed someone near on whom to vent it. My brother enjoyed this.

Before Father got into the driver's seat, he did "his work" and "knew the Divine Mind or Love" was "the only driver." We soon saw that the gifts of the Divine Mind were purely metaphysical; the Divine Mind was the most dangerous driver I have ever known. It hit banks, tore off the sides of hedges, chased pedestrians, scattered people about to get on buses.

"Dad, careful, you nearly hit him."

"Don't look round," shouted Father.

He backed clean through the end of his garage and one day on the Dover Road caused a brakeload of ladies to tip into a ditch: they were sitting on chairs, the chairs slid down to the side of the vehicle and one or two somersaulted out. The angry outing stood and waved their fists at him.

"Stop! Stop! Someone may be hurt," my brother said.

"Don't look round. Don't look round. There's a law against charabancs with loose seating. I shall report them to the police," my father said.

The car had cost a good deal. He drove it to central London one morning, taking with him an elderly and important draper and my brother. Passing by way of Dulwich, at a pleasant speed, Father shot straight across a dangerous crossroad and was hit broadside on by a steam traction engine coming fast down the hill and was rammed into a fence. The Divine Mind, I must say, saw to it that no one was hurt—no one, that is, in the family—and out my father got and wanted to fight the driver of the traction engine.

Mother said in the evening: "Where's that car?"

"There's something wrong with the engine. I had it sent back to the works."

"Just like his mother, so particular, never satisfied," said Mother, for once deceived.

The wreck was replaced by a dark blue Daimler of archaic design; it rose, in steps from its bonnet, like a couple of boxes at the opera. So distinguished was it, that it was rarely driven more than the distance between the garage up the road and our house.

I used to sit up in our attic bedroom, looking down at the car and hating it. The white roads of England were vanishing: the suburbs were eating into the country. The stink of oil and petrol was already spreading. Lanes that were once deserted were now fouled by people and machines. My old complaint returned: why had I not been born in the days of Wordsworth or Coleridge? The England of the Georgian poets had gone. It had scarcely existed, but was a last-minute artifice created by them, in order to stave off the contemplation of what was really happening. I had bicycled out to country inns and had seen, for myself, that the Chesterton and Belloc pubs could not have existed for fifty years. Yet I willingly joined in the fantasy and began living the sentimentalist's double life. I never learned to drive a car—the refusal was neurotic and one of the many errors of my life.

Under the blurting excitability of adolescence was the sense of exhaustion, hopelessness and failure. I seemed to have no will and to be dragged down, as if by the reeds in a deadly green river, by dreams, and caught in the sexual miasma. The enforced chastity of youths was one of the poisons of that time; but, in fact, I supported it, for only by its curious ferocity could I concentrate on what I wanted to do. Suddenly I had an enormous success: so it seemed then, it now seems pathetic.

There are pretty public gardens of sunken walks and rockeries under tall trees, next to the public library in Bromley. Once or twice, on some holiday, I would sit there for a while, on a fine morning, listening to the chatter of old men sitting on the benches, or reading *Pitman's Shorthand Weekly*—for I believed all writers had to know shorthand—or looking at some potted article on French literature which told me who the Pléiade were, or explained the Three Unities, for France more and more seemed to me my salvation. In France I would make up for my lack of education.

"Tell me one thing that makes you think it would be a good thing to go to France," Father would ask kindly.

I could not say I wanted to be free. "It's different."

"What is different?"

"Well, a street is called a *rue*."

"Is that all?"

I could not explain what an immense, strange world lay in that word *rue* and that words in themselves meant so much to me. Like a small brush stroke among a million on a canvas, a word seemed to me more alive than anything living.

The beauty of the garden was a torture because I could not find the words in which to describe it; and I would get up impatiently from my seat and start walking about fast, trying with a word to catch what I saw, and in vain. I would be seized by a breathless sensation for a moment or two when something real—that is to say, some definable vision—would seem to be there, but the moment passed; I would fall into the dreamer's exhaustion and ennui and a feeling of meaninglessness. This has often dogged me in my life; only writing and sexual love have enabled me to stand it.

I left the gardens in this empty state and went to the library. I had read all the periodicals and so I stared at the notices. In panic I could feel the minutes passing away and then I saw the notice of a University Extension Lecture on Milton. Such are the dramas in the lives of young prigs—I was mad to go to it. It was agreed at home that I could go to it if my brother came with me.

We set off at the dangerous hour of seven thirty and parted

at the corner of the street, he to the garage where Curly's motorbike was, I to the lecture.

The desire for learning in Bromley was strong. There was a large audience. The lecturer was a young woman with rimless glasses, an icy, cutting and donnish voice, who looked pink, as if she had just got out of a cold bath. She sliced the air above her respectful audience, among whom, distantly, I saw Mr. Hotchkiss from our church, backsliding into Milton's theology. He was covertly letting Error in. At the end of the lecture, we were firmly told to submit papers on the conjunction of the Renaissance and the Reformation in Milton's art. A discussion would be held the following week, after the second lecture, on Spenser.

That week I wrote and posted my essay.

I do not remember what I said in that paper, but I do know that I had started to be interested in unusual words, in the search for the *mot juste*—as it was then called. I chose words for what I called their intensity. I wanted to be terse and exact. I wanted each word to burn into the page. My pen tortured the paper.

I went to the second lecture, a dreary affair. Since my brother and I were not allowed to go out separately in the evenings we had a system of covering for each other. The second evening, by arrangement, he crept into the public library to suffer the last five minutes of Spenser. At the end we heard the lecturer discuss the Milton papers; anxiously I hoped mine would be discussed. It was not. But suddenly I heard the lecturer say, "There is one paper in a class by itself, an outstanding piece of writing, obviously by a professional writer," and announced my name.

"Vic!" said my brother, giving me a punch that nearly knocked me off the seat.

"Me?" I thought I must be dreaming. I got the paper back. She had been talking about me. I took the paper home and read it and reread it until I knew it by heart.

Now there was no doubt. I could write. My brother announced the triumph at home. Mother looked terrified of me. Father said apologetically: "It's a great pity you had to leave school. I am sorry about it. You ought to go to evening classes. The way will be shown."

The effect on my life was immediate. I needn't go straight home from the office. I could go on to the Polytechnic in Regent Street. I was able to spend evenings alone in London. I walked from Bermondsey as a rule, over London Bridge and then by St. Paul's, Fleet Street and the Strand and Piccadilly to Oxford Circus. I ventured into Soho and thought, in my innocence, that there was something sinister in those restaurants where the curtains were always drawn. I got the *Artists and Writers Year Book* and sent my essay on Milton, in the course of the next months, to a large number of papers and reviews—even to the *Leather Sellers' Gazette,* announcing I was in the trade. Milton came back regularly, and getting filthier and filthier.

Father got impatient about this. He opened all letters that came to the house, read them and handed them to whom they belonged. In this way, he knew about my girl and had instantly forbidden me to see her or write to her again. This led me to pick out one of his, open it and read it. It turned out to be a threat of court action if some debt was not paid. I had expected a storm, but the revolt failed.

"Just another circular," Father said and threw it away and added: "I see you are sending articles to papers. You can't afford to waste money on stamps and envelopes like that. You'll have to learn to live within your income. How much do you earn? Eighteen and sixpence? If you can afford to spend all that on stamps, you can afford to pay your mother more toward your keep."

Now the current was in my favor. I had found one or two listeners in Bromley and, released from the need of silence and evasion at home, I must have amused them, but they were good enough not to show it. Mr. Hotchkiss, who had given up Tolstoy for Mrs. Eddy, drifted back to his Tolstoyan days, and considering my case, said that he too had had little education, but that there was an alternative: travel. He pointed that out to my father. Rich Mrs. Flaxman, an exalted Norwegian with beautiful eyes, spoke of "glorious Ibsen" and asked me to tea to meet her daughter. I tried to be in love with this dark, thin, nervous, lonely girl who snapped at me in a rich girl's way. I had a bad accent. I used to walk past her large house and past the house of another exquisite half-German girl on summer evenings, hoping to see them, but I never did. And there was Mrs. Norman, a busy and sprightly little woman, very outspoken, whom Father "had to put in her place" several times, especially once when she caught him with me on the steps of the church and called out dramatically, "Loose him and let him go." I was very attracted to Mrs. Norman, whose marriage was so happy that I half wanted to turn my parents out of the house and move Mr. and Mrs. Norman in. She used to wear a small white ermine necklet. Father's reply was the worst thing you could say to a Christian Scientist: "Be careful. You are being handled by Rome."

But I did not really want listeners. I needed the sight of a fellow recalcitrant and I found him. He had been living next door but one for years, without my knowing that he was exactly the friend I needed.

Any morning in the summer, people walking up the road would hear the sound of a piano being played. Ringing out and enchanting in its accomplishment, the sound went across the gardens, into the trees, over the road and into the fields. People opened their windows and stopped to listen. Often a delivery van would stop. Mother would stand on the kitchen doorstep. The notes of a Beethoven concerto would be struck with shameless authority and passed like a flight of crystals into the suburban air.

"That's Frank again. He's got the windows open," Mother said. He was a boy prodigy—it seemed—who had played in Vienna, Paris and Brussels since he was a young child. At seventeen he was a well-known professional pianist. He was French.

At home we had the impression that Father was ashamed of Mother; it may be that he was wrapped up in himself and his religion in these years, but he certainly kept his own friends from the house. "I don't want people to see how we live," he said. But if neighbors dropped in—which was very rarely—they were soon laughing their heads off with Mother. Frank and his French family, who were intellectuals, loved Mother's tales.

"This town stinks, Mrs. Pritchett," Frank said to her, and would start mimicking the local refined accent: "Oh Frank, you wicked boy."

I began to listen to Frank practicing in his room. He had a puddingy, pale face, strong short-fingered hands, and wore his hair on the long side and had a musician's fur-lined coat.

We took to going out on Saturday afternoons into the town.

"This place stinks. It has a horrible smell," he said. "Look at these people, how they smell. They make you sick," he called out as we went through the shopping crowds. "The whole of England makes you sick. I hate the English—low, ignorant people."

And he would stop and make loud vomiting sounds over the gutter.

On top of everything else the Bromley people were Protestants; he was a Catholic, the only religion that cared about art. One day he said, "You go to that church where they don't believe in the Devil. You are a fool."

"No. I don't believe in the Devil."

"I've seen him. He haunts this town. He's dressed in red. He's a living person. Let's go out and you'll see him."

We used to go on long hate-walks, looking for the Devil. We would give up.

"He's at Sundridge Park, I expect," he'd say, looking at his watch.

I was refreshed by a boy who lived in his imagination and by his arrogance. Once or twice we walked round the Bromley shops, Frank making belching sounds, especially in the music shop.

"They are all ignorant and stink. Listen to the voices of those terrible girls behind the counter. 'Ow nao we 'event got eet in stock'" he would call out as he went into the shop. "'Nao there's no call for Mowzart.'" And then he would start making his vomiting noise or stagger about saying "I'm going to faint, I'm going to faint" and we would leave. I sniggered and was shocked, but with every shock I felt a load being taken from me.

"In the war, when the air raids were on, I screamed all the time" he would say petulantly. "Didn't you hear me? I hate the Germans, I hate the English." We used to talk like this in his garden while he pushed his pretty little sister on the swing. His mother was kind and gave me courage to talk French at tea.

"Why wasn't I born into an intellectual family?" I used to think when I left him. Their affection for each other astonished me.

At last, I thought, I have seen genius. I knew I had none, but Frank said I must have, because I, too, knew this was a stinking town. He and I were alike; our kind of egotism had its rights. After I was twenty I never saw him again, for neither he nor I were much in England. He grew up to a distinguished career. Childish though he was, he seemed older and richer in experience than I; I saw why: he lived by the discipline of his art.

Another rebel was my cousin Hilda. She was many years older than I—born, my mother always mentioned with dreamy pride, on the same day as the Prince of Wales. Hilda, as I have told, was the daughter of my mother's sister in Ipswich. She loved my father and mother. She adored especially my father and teased him; my father's dignity went out the window.

At school Hilda fell in love with a learned girl called Violet. Hilda had a wild ugliness. Violet was rich, Violet was a beauty, Violet was a rebel. She cared for nobody, men were wild about her; and all that stuffy old Presbyterian, Hilda's stepfather, could think of was how to separate the two girls, chiefly because Violet had made Hilda High Church. The two girls were threatening to become Catholics.

"My dear Aunt—I'm intoxicated by incense."

Father's jollity went when he heard this.

Violet and Hilda had worshiped the suffragettes, of course, and had set fire to a pillar box at Felixstowe—so they said. Mr. Bugg was upset by this. He regarded himself as one of the City Fathers.

When the war came, Hilda and Violet went to work in a munitions factory and came down to see us. Violet was a dark beauty with a long sensuous mouth who astonished me by asking Hilda: "I suppose *nobody* lives here," referring contemptuously to Chislehurst, Bromley and Bickley. "All business, I expect."

I realized that not only ourselves but these large wealthy neighborhoods were beyond the pale to fashionable society and that Hilda and Violet belonged to some distant, unattainable social set. When they left, Father and Mother whispered about them; they were, we gathered, leading loose lives. Father said severely that it could lead to only one thing. It led to something else. Telegrams, doctors, a Swiss sanatorium: Hilda had a hemorrhage at her factory. She had inherited the disease that had killed her father.

She was sent home, but ran away to London. She was going to set up house with Violet again. She worked on my father to persuade him to battle with her stepfather. She wanted money. She arrived looking gay and fierce, her eyes hollowed, her skin reddened, laughing at us all.

"You must stop that smoking, Hilda."

"Why? I've still got one lung left."

"Oh Hilda, don't dear, don't."

It was a painful visit, but for me memorable. For years I had admired Hilda, but she had treated me as a child; now an unbelievable thing happened. I was allowed to go with her to a concert given by American Negroes who had come over to sing spirituals—it was their first visit to London. We had lunch at an Italian restaurant in Soho—until then I had had neither the courage nor the money to go into one—and we talked about the war poets. She and Violet knew Robert Nichols and Sassoon. Hilda, though surprisingly kind and making me feel grown up, evidently thought my literary daydreams were idle. She took me into Hachette's and bought me a selection of Victor Hugo's poems and inscribed it with this quotation: *Seul le silence est grand, tout le reste est faiblesse.*

A smack in the eye.

I worshiped Hilda after this. Compared with her, the Bromley girls were dull. I longed to talk to Hilda but she, I indignantly saw, was on my father's side. When I murmured about him she passed it off as if I were suffering from a well-known illness.

"I can make Uncle do anything I want," Hilda said. "He is a dear, jolly man. You're lucky to have such a father. I adore him. I love him more than any man I've ever seen, except my own father."

A strange remark: her father had died before she was born.

"Tilly is a famous name. My father came of a family of admirals who fought with Nelson. There was a famous Comte de Tilly who wrote Memoirs. I will get them for you."

She leapt into romance about the melancholy facts of her

father's life behind the counter at Daniels of Kentish Town. She appealed to my father on this point. She was a large young woman and flopped onto my father's knee and knocked the breath out of him.

"It is true, Uncle, isn't it?"

"You've got Beatie's imagination," he gasped.

"Aunt," she cried. "You're marvelous. What did my father call you? Ecirtaeb Nitram."

And they all laughed until Mother had to leave the room, crying, "Oh, it's like your father, poor Frank."

And then, the following year, a terrible thing happened. She came to see us again. She was now feverish and ill. It was in the winter. The fogs were gray.

"Open the window. Let me sit by the open window. No, I'm very well as long as I sit by the window."

She had run away from Ipswich after a violent quarrel with her stepfather. She had come to my parents for money and for help.

"You're ill," my mother said.

"Don't voice Error," said my father sternly. And to Hilda he said: "If you would know the Truth through Christian Science you would get your healing."

He was very severe and she was taken aback.

"Don't be cross with me."

"I am voicing the Truth," said my father.

"I am well now. There's nothing the matter with me if I sit near the window. I'm sorry if it lets in the fog. You see, I don't believe it's the Truth. Mrs. Eddy was a very ignorant woman; she took drugs herself. Why did she die?"

"That's what worries me, Walt," said my mother, taking courage.

"There you are, Uncle. Aunt can see it's a fraud. And so cruel."

My father became angry. "It is you who are showing your ignorance, Hilda," he said. "I won't have you deny the omnipotence of Divine Love in my house. You have been very wrong."

"Uncle darling, you have never talked like this to me before," she said.

"It is time you knew the Truth. Go back to your father."

"You want me to go back to Ipswich to that mean hypocrite. I came to you for help."

"I cannot help you, but God can," said my father.

Angry words were spoken by my father. Hilda had fits of coughing.

"Close the window," he said.

"No," shouted Hilda. "It will make me ill. Open it."

And then Hilda sat with my mother on the sofa and sobbed on Mother's shoulder. "Did you hear him? He has broken my heart. Why has Uncle changed? His religion is not Love, it is cruel, Aunt, cruel. I can't speak to him. Aunt, he was never like this when I was a little girl. Victor, you don't believe this, do you?"

I could not speak. I did not know what I believed, but I was afraid to speak before my father. And this was a "scene" among the elders and we had had so many in our house that I could not bear them. I longed for peace.

We all went to bed and the next morning Father went off early to his office. Hilda came down to look for him and to say Goodbye, but he had gone. She could not believe it.

"He will never see me again, Aunt," she said. "And he never said goodbye."

She was indeed heartbroken. She left us. In a month she died in her stepfather's home, defeated.

The choir of Negro singers we had been to hear were all lost at sea that year; their ship was one of the last to be torpedoed.

12

I come to my last eighteen months of the leather trade and my last years at home. The wounded soldiers dressed in bright blue hospital clothes were fewer now in the street. At one time they had often seemed to outnumber the civilians; at the office the demobilized men returned. There were gaps which Hobbs talked sadly of; but those who came back were sunburned, healthy looking and wore new clothes. They looked like a race different from ourselves. They did not fit easily into the office. One or two left very quickly. Their experience had set them apart and the effect was to make me feel naïve and cut off; this feeling lasted for many years. A youth needs the friendship of men a few years older than himself; they act as a buffer between himself and his elders. Many of the serious personal and public troubles that occurred in the next few years ended badly because of the slaughter of a generation.

In a few months after their return, the new men lost their sunburn, they got married, their clothes became shabby, their faces were thinner and more anxious until in the suburban trains they were indistinguishable from the crowd. It was not until the war books appeared eight or nine years later that young men like myself knew anything about these older ones.

But the end of the war started a number of erotic episodes in our office. Girls suddenly looked like posters, for they wore coats made of army blanketing, patterned with gaudy squares; and they showed their ankles. One afternoon Flo, one of the younger, bouncing and innocent secretaries, who was engaged to be married, talked in a low, excited voice—telling me to go away—to a big, red-faced dispatch clerk home from the Navy, a man as soft as a sweating Frankfurter. They were whispering about an Anglican pamphlet on sexual intercourse. He had the missionary temperament; he and his fiancée, I heard him say, undressed in his lodgings in Bromley on Sunday afternoons and lay naked and innocent beneath an army blanket, reading together what one of the bishops had said. His fiancée, who came to pick him up at the office one day, was a huge six-footer too,—a passive girl with a big milky face who seemed to low rather than speak.

Flo's large blue eyes shone and her blushes were deep. Hobbs came into the room and the dispatch clerk scurried out. Hobbs looked wearier in these days; the deep lines of his face gave it the set smile of the comic mask.

"Don't be selfish, duckie," he said, going up to Flo and adroitly pulling at the low neck of her blouse and looking inside. "Don't save it all for *him*."

Flo was by now a trained flouncer out of rooms. Hobbs hummed a tune. "You can have the Latin Quarter, laddie," he said to me with a sigh. "Give me Saturday night in Manchester. Ask your father to let me give you a night out up West. What are you reading? Maurice Hewlett—he has a richer style than Locke."

Hobbs did not take me up West; instead he took a temporary telephone girl, a pleasant married woman. She was the second to leave the firm to settle for a time in his flat in Parliament Hill. He arrived one morning early, and putting a stool near the counter, snapped his gold cigarette case at the staff, including the Cashier, as they came in, saying, "Got you."

The Cashier moaned and almost wept at the dissolution of Hobbs. An hour later, Hobbs went over and did the Cashier's books, chatting, as he added up, about his brother who was training for the ministry.

About this time, Mr. Clark, the sullen invoice clerk, took his pretty assistant up to the chamois room. It was a small warm room with a U-shaped alley between the bins of chamois leather that reached to the ceiling. The clerks were not supposed to leave the office for the warehouse without good reason. Clark, always defiant, before the amazed eyes of all the office, snapped his fingers at the girl and off they went, she pitter-pattering obediently along, up the stairs, into the wobbling lift and up to the room.

"I've got a query," he said as he left the office.

"Four skins short?" Mr. Drake, the lewd one, said.

Like the term "belly splits" or "let's have a look at the flesh side," this was a daily office joke.

"Hobbs, Hobbs," moaned the Cashier. "I don't like a young girl like that being in the warehouse . . ."

"Quite, sir, certainly, sir. I have to go up anyway."

In a few minutes he came back with the girl, who in a minute or two was followed by Mr. Clark. The girl was sent to work at another desk. And Hobbs and Clark sat opposite each other, staring into each other's eyes. I brought a stockbook to Hobbs in the middle of the stare.

"I've been in this trade twelve years and one thing I have learned is that chamois comes off on a girl's skirt," said Hobbs.

"You bastard," said Clark, with one of his rare smiles. "Just in the nick of time."

"Don't mention it. He saved others; himself he could not save. You owe me a drink."

The Cashier groaned his private gratitude to Hobbs and Hobbs, being a thorough man, took the older sister for a ride in the warehouse lift. A ride with Hobbs was always an experience and she came back with a dreamy look in her eyes. She said to the Cashier that she thought poor Mr. Hobbs worked too hard and sighed that she had told him he ought to have sea air. She said this in a loud dreamy voice.

"It is a shame," she said. "He can't get away because he has to nurse his mother. She is an invalid."

The quarreling sisters became reconciled after this.

I sometimes had to write a letter for Mr. James, Mr. Kenneth's eldest son and the most cultivated partner in the firm. He was married to a Frenchwoman and he recommended that I read Balzac and explained the French family system to me. He was a neat, silver-haired man, soft in voice, precise in speech. He really gave me these letters to write as an exercise. I worked most of one morning on one letter, and being known for bad handwriting, I rewrote it several times and took it to him. I stood waiting and looking at his new secretary. She had lovely dewy eyes and one of them quivered, almost with a wink, as she smiled with a terrible lack of innocence at me. She was very small. She leaned towards me for her pencil and as she did so I could see her breasts in her low blouse. I gazed helplessly at them and she, pleased by the effect she was having on me, looked up. In these few seconds Mr. James had taken out his pen which had green ink in it and was saying: "Why is it, I wonder, you never dot your *i*'s?" and was dotting them in green. He turned to look at me; I was startled by his voice. I couldn't speak. I began to sway, the room seemed to spin.

"He's fainting," said the girl archly. I was. I clutched at the desk. Mr. James jumped up and held me. Quickly the color came back to my face and I was stuttering and blushing.

"Have you been smoking?" said Mr. James to me with a sly glance at the girl.

"I don't smoke, sir," I said.

Mr. James let go of me, gave me back the letter and sent me away. A delightful laugh came from behind the frosted glass of his door after I had left.

In October, when I had my annual holiday for a fortnight, my brother and I hired bicycles and went up North to York. We were met at the station by Uncle Arthur, who had his bicycle with him. With his trousers bagging over his clips and his broad black beard brushing his handlebars, he raced us across the city, pausing for us to admire the sight of the Minster in the darkness and the blind gaze of the Apostles frozen in the great doors and the gargoyles looking as though they were going to spew down on us. Great-uncle Arthur's wife had come into a small sum of money and they now lived in a little suburban house, lined with gaudy carpets and smelling of new furniture. The famous toad had gone from the kitchen. His butterflies and insects had gone and so had his cabinets of birds' eggs. He himself still put on his white apron and kneepads and went about hammering, but he had retired and there was a change in him. His sons and their wives were kind and prosperous.

The miraculous cure of Cousin Dick by Christian Science had caused a split in the family, particularly among the sisters. The miracle was a victory for the Bibliolaters, which put Uncle Arthur in a bad position. It shook his atheism, and looking around for new ammunition, he drifted first into theosophy and then—or so it sounded—into spiritualism. He had done this under the influence of a friend called Evans, a signal-box man. Uncle Arthur had given his stuffed swan to him and he would slink off to this friend's house on Saturday evenings and do table-turning with him, the swan looking wretchedly on. This was a decline. Uncle Arthur read Burton no more, but he said he would get Evans to show me a bundle of Burton papers; he and Evans had got through to Burton, several times, "on the other side."

At home our own obsessions had changed. My brother was now the center of attack; my father was merely sarcastic to me, saying things like "How is Professor Know-All?" or "What is in the superior mind of my sentimental son?" His sarcasm was often, I think, a form of shyness. My brother was more vulnerable than I.

It has always been a puzzle to us, but Father and Mother had decided early on that my brother was backward, lazy, easily led astray, like my father's brother who had been sent to Canada and had become a feckless casualty. I was still Cain-ish; Cyril was still Abel-like and all heart. I see from photographs that I am thin, small, look ill and have a melancholy smile; my brother is stronger, taller, jaunty but wistful. He is wearing a gaudily striped cap with peak unclipped and is standing by a friend's motorbike—Curly's I expect. He is good-looking; his hair is carefully greased by a hair oil we have invented: a mixture of olive oil and eau de Cologne, so that we smell like two young scented salads. His heroes are people who have been in the war—ex-captains, ex-majors, delight him; they are the successors of the "knuts" of early boyhood, for these are "out" now. "Hellish lads" have come in and will lead on to "blokes" and "chappies"; the "birds" of three or four years back have given way to "flappers" and "little tarts." He is no good at school; his gifts are in his hands. He has my father's craftsman-like patience, mingled with a love of splash. It is he who has done all the practical work— such as putting up the ultramodern chicken house in the garden. And he will drop anything for the sake of my father. This love has been his trouble; he has been bullied and jeered at, and for years he has been a bad stammerer. The one thing he wants to do is to work with my father in his business. Father accuses him of being a rich young idler who thinks that all he has to do is to step into his father's shoes without working.

Naturally my brother decided to exploit his bad reputation. He said he wanted to go to sea. (This was a genuine ambition: after twenty years in business, my brother joined the Navy as an able seaman at thirty-eight years of age in the last war; he had carefully toughened himself for the job. It was a romantic fulfillment.) A common sailor! My father was indignant. "Poor Frank, buried in the South Atlantic," groaned Mother. No, said my brother, he wanted to be an artificer—an apprentice naval engineer. Father asked if we thought he was made of money. But the postman's son opposite had become an artificer. Well, said my father, if you prefer to be a postman's son, go and live with the postman. Father was in a fix but made a lucky discovery: my brother was now over the age when artificers began their training. Procrastination had paid off, for the moment. Now my brother said he'd be a civil engineer. After an angry argument about the cost of the engineering school at Finsbury, my brother was taken to sit for the examination. Since he was ignorant of mathematics and other necessary things, he failed. What was to be done? He went off and worked in a garage and came home smeared with oil. He moved to the loading bay of a motorworks and became a loader, but was sacked from that.

"Dad, what about my job?" he would say, hungry for affection.

The request ended in protests, speeches and "unfolding." There were violent scenes while Father was doing his income tax returns.

The miserable, stammering boy went off to the public library to read the Situations Vacant columns and came back with suggestions that led to more storms. Suddenly, no doubt to win my father's affection, he went after a job in Father's own trade, a silk firm. He got the job and Father was not very pleased: it looked like an outflanking movement. Within six months, the firm (which was French) sent my brother to Lyons to work in the factory and to learn the trade. Father could not believe the outrage: it was one of the best firms in the trade. To punish my brother he sent him off without money and for six months the boy half starved on the low wage and bad food of a poor apprentice. He came back after six months, happy, Frenchified and covered with adolescent spots. He arrived at the front gate on a Sunday morning, just after Father got back from church. Father stared at him in fury.

"Your train arrives at five."

"I came by the earlier one."

"You can't have done—that is for first-class passengers."

"I came first class."

"You traveled first class," cried Father. "What d'you mean by that? Where did you get the money?"

"The firm paid."

"You're not asking me to believe that one of the biggest firms in the trade allows its factory hands to travel first class?"

"The manager told me."

"He was joking."

"He came on the same train."

"You didn't have the impudence to travel with the manager?" shouted Father. Now they had advanced to the lawn, just inside the gate of the house.

Mother was standing at the door, listening to the rumpus. "Oh dear, what's he done?"

"Only from Calais. I met him in the lavatory on the boat. We came to London together."

"You used the same lavatory as the manager?" screamed Father.

"Walt, what is it?" cried Mother.

"Look at his face," said Father in disgust. "The filthy hound has been going with prostitutes," moaned Father. "He has got a disease."

We stood on the lawn gazing at the delinquent.

"You'd better get inside," said Father wretchedly.

The spots were the effect of poor food, but my brother had enjoyed himself. He was soon showing Father he knew more about silk than my father did and—height of social dreams—had lunched often on Sundays with the British vice-consul—a "hellish" lad my brother murmured to me. Father contained his jealousy: on the Monday my brother would be sacked for his presumption.

"I cannot understand your lack of judgment," Father said. "You go to the same lavatory and then—it's past belief—you travel in the same first-class compartment to London with him."

"He asked me to. He doesn't speak English."

"What! You little fool, every Frenchman speaks English!" On Monday morning my backward brother was promoted.

Father was sad. He could see what it was. His son, his own son, preferred to work for a Frenchman rather than for himself.

"I shall go and see him," said my father indignantly. "They are not paying you enough. You must give your notice."

His jealousy was violent and it was sad. He began tapping his fingers on the table and Mother watched those fingers.

"You see, dear," she said to my brother. "The Business couldn't afford to pay you what these French people pay. Dad has a difficult time."

Father lifted his hand to silence her.

Father's dislike of fact and love of drama was a misfortune, for it made him unjust to himself. He was a poor man, not as well-off as he pretended to be. At its most successful, his business had a very small turnover. Once more our Micawber had become a disarming borrower and was encumbered by debts. He loved saying sentences like "The loan has my personal guarantee" in a grand voice; and it must have seemed to him that the guarantee doubled the amount of money available.

Mother said loyally, "Dad never gives up." His dreams were his courage, even though, in the end, they totally perverted him. He was too proud to say that his income was small; also his eccentric interpretation of the Christian ethic made him increasingly believe that behind all the human sources of money, there was the great investment house of God pouring out wealth. He believed this was literally true; and he referred people who sought to get their money back from him to the divine source.

In these spruce and clean-shaven days, Father got up at six thirty when my mother brought tea to him. He dressed in dark clothes, gray or navy blue, wore a low stiff collar and a knitted silk tie. His shining black hair was going a trifle gray at the ears, his complexion was dark and fresh, he had a benign-looking double chin, his brown eyes were deep set. He smiled as he came towards you, but paused for a frown of quizzical rebuke when you spoke. He carried his great weight without effort. His sleep, he said, was dreamless; beyond a rare cold, he was never ill in his long life. He charmed. He was a being who could have been patented and was almost an ideal. It was a great pleasure to be with him in restaurants. And when, in years to come, humiliation and disaster fell upon him, he never admitted it. In his sixties, his seventies, even in his eighties, he was always planning to start up again and had indeed to be restrained from grandiose schemes. The solution was to take him out to an expensive lunch, and the pleasure he took in it made our hard hearts melt. It is true he would say afterwards that we were on the road to ruin; but his main criticism of me was that I "limited" myself and did not "think big." The odd thing is that he did not really do so either. When he left his dreams for the facts, he was small in mind and easily trapped by petty details.

Right up to the day of his death, in his eighties, none of us children could settle our view of him. It was simple to call him the late Victorian dominant male without whose orders no one could think or move. It was only partly true that he was a romantic procrastinator, egotist and dreamer, for he was a very calculating man. Sometimes we saw him as the un-changed country boy, given to local shrewdness and gossip. (He loved the malicious gossip of his church and his trade.) Sometimes we saw him as a pocket Napoleon, but he never even tried to obtain the wealth or power he often talked about. His mind was more critical than creative and he was appalled by criticism of himself. He would go pale, hold up his hand and say, "You must not criticize me." He sincerely meant he was beyond criticism and felt in himself a sort of sacredness.

A clue was given to us, too late, after his death, by Miss H, who had long ago broken with him, as people did. She knew our quarrels well. The central passion in his life, she said, was for his children. Yes—that, I now see, was true. He was in many ways far more female than he was male. He was one of those fathers who are really mothers; he had a mother's primitive, possessive and jealous love and, indeed, behaved as if he and not our mother—who was not possessive at all—had given birth to us. He wished to preserve us for himself. He could not bear us to be out of his sight.

From his own words about his childhood as a favorite child under a severe father, it was obvious that he lived in constant anxiety about food and money—he ate enormously, as if to make up for early hunger—and, as so often happens with anxious people, his anxiety led him to go for power wherever he could. He was a man of immovable self-will. He was female, again, in his long-headed disingenuousness in obtaining money. Both my brothers eventually worked for him for a while and both quarreled with him and left.

Before the final catastrophe Father bought a new house, quite a large one, and the secret grand piano came out of hiding. I saw my sister playing "The Moonlight Sonata" on it, while my youngest brother tried to drown the sound by playing a ukelele. But this was years ahead, when my nearest brother, the backward one, had become a startling success in the silk trade and was earning a large income, more than the whole family put together. Indeed, Father adroitly wheedled money out of him to pay for the grand piano.

Christmas, 1919, came and we had our annual reading of James Barrie, also of a satirical story about business called *Letters of a Self-Made Merchant to His Son,* by Pierpont Morgan, Junior. Mother called for the short stories of W. W. Jacobs which she loved and I read them. She thought Barrie sentimental, but a few lines of Jacobs would make her pull her skirts up to her knees as she sat in front of the fire and cover her face with her hands as she laughed.

"I say, old duck," Father often said, when she sat laughing like this, "we can see your bloomers."

For Mother there was no funnier word than "bloomers" in the English language and she was off again.

I looked in the library for more books by Barrie and made an important discovery. It was a novel about journalism called *When a Man's Single:* in it a clever journalist explains to another the art of writing short sketches. It was a simple revelation. Twenty years later when I read H. G. Wells's autobiography, I discovered that Barrie's book had taught Wells how to become a professional writer. It taught me instantly. Indeed the writers who really helped me to start as a writer were not the great; they were W. J. Locke, Du Maurier and Belloc, who whispered to me to go abroad: I saw myself as a mixture of those three, out on the open road with Stevenson's donkey, and Barrie, the shrewd Scot, telling me how to write about it.

The strain of the last few years, the stunned boredom and

torn emotions were too much for me. Coming home by slow train one evening and changing trains at Grove Park Junction, I was sick on the platform, got home somehow and collapsed. The postwar flu epidemic had caught me. I fell to the floor. My father was as frightened as I was and luckily a doctor was called. I scared everybody by saying I was a kipper being cut in half. (This was true. I had been smoked by London and was split in two by the family quarrels.) I do not know how long I was in bed, but one morning, thinking I was well, I got up and fell unconscious to the floor again.

The illness was a long one, and the end of it was that I did not go back to the leather trade. I spent a pleasant couple of months, sometimes bicycling in Kent, but often going on long country bus rides with my mother. We used to go to the inn at Westerham and eat chops and have a glass of shandy. We did not talk at all about her woes or the Business, but about her childhood or the people we saw about us. They were all funny to her. At home, my father regarded me with respect: the leather firm had paid my salary and given me ten pounds as a present. I had told them I was going to Paris. They said I could come back to them when I wanted. I heard something odd about myself at the leather factors. Apparently, when asked to do something, I always said "Just a sec" and went off to do something else. Now I had twenty pounds.

"If you're careful you could live for a month in Paris and then we'll see," Father said. I could not tell him or my mother that once I had gone I would never come back.

But now I stood on the platform beside the boat train at Victoria with my father. Portly and almost sumptuous, he had several times asked where I had distributed my money and my ticket and I was moved because I could see he was moved. We were distracted by two Italians as dark as earth, a gray-haired oldish man and another of about thirty. They were held, wrestling and swaying in each other's arms, and they were howling with grief; the tears drenched their faces as they rocked in shouting agony and sorrow, and if they paused, it was only to get breath to rush at each other again with cries that outdid the stamping and steaming of engines and the shouting of porters. Two large women in black stood by them silently approving the display of the two men. It has often struck me since, that it would have been better for my father and me, especially as we too felt strongly, to have purged ourselves of our anxieties, hatreds and conflicts in the manner of these two Italians: my father would have found it easier than I, but I, whose eyes were soon full of tears in those days when I tried to speak to him, would have fought for pride's sake against it.

On my side it would have been impossible to howl. I was happy. I was excited. I was setting myself free. After Paris I saw myself turning up, shabby, weather-beaten and speaking whatever patois was desired in remote inns, in remote countries, in remote mountains. I would have arrived, of course, on foot. As it was, on the Paris train I was wearing a boater with my school colors on it, a ginger-colored tweed jacket, flannel trousers and a classy pair of tony-red shoes— the latest color—bought wholesale in the trade.

The train to Paris moved off. There is a small white farm-house near Dunton Green in the Westerham Valley and now-adays when I come back from the Continent I look at it in-credulously. It and I are still in existence. For on this first Paris journey I remembered all the bicycling trips of the last months on which I had often passed this farm, and was so homesick that I wanted to go back; but once out of home country my mood changed. By Ashford, where dozens of locomotives sat smoking, I had forgotten; and at Dover the white-hot flash of the chalk cliff and the sight of the silky blue sea set me free. I got a smut in my eye early on the crossing, for I stood on the top deck, eager to get my first sight of the dunes of Calais, but this bad luck was cancelled by a heart-ening incident. A young man with flopping fair hair, with heavy shoulders and a broken nose was standing there too, looking for France. He stepped back and trod with all his weight on my foot. He murmured and went off. It was Carpentier, the famous French boxer. How right I had been: to know the great world one must go to France! On the French train I drank wine for the first time in my life: it was vinegarish I thought, but I was committed to liking it. It was disappointing that there were no Frenchmen in the compartment. There was an elderly Englishman. He asked if I was going to Monte Carlo. He was a clergyman. I was soon showing off about myself and telling him I was not at all the Monte Carlo type and how eager I was to see the spire of Amiens Cathedral. Ruskin, I pointed out, had written about it. The clergyman said Gothic inevitably appealed to the disorderly minds of the young, was ramshackle in comparison with classical architecture or with Italian Baroque and made some discreet religious inquiries. My careless answers puzzled him. He spoke of how one was baptized into Christ.

"I haven't been baptized," I boasted.

He was upset. "I beg you, I beg you, to get that put right. A small matter, easily attended to, but most important!" he said.

We stopped talking. He sat in silence. It was obvious that I was an uncouth and swollen-headed boy. After a while he spoke again. He asked my name and then hopefully put a question that bowled me out.

"Are you by any chance a connection of the Gloucestershire Pritchetts?"

I was affronted to hear that there were other families with our name and then I saw I was being introduced for the first time to one of the openings of the English class game. The failure to be a Gloucestershire Pritchett—evidently a remarkable clan—dogged me for several years. The clergyman's doubt increased. When he heard I had not been to a Public School or to the University he was lost and he fell into a self-congratulatory silence. A mystery had been solved. As for myself, my new life as a young man had begun.

I saw very little of England for seven years. I could not bear the sight of it. For two of these years I worked first in a photographer's shop off the Boulevard des Italiens. Then, starting off from the Square du Temple, I traipsed for a year from one paint shop to the next round Paris, selling glue, shellac and, for a hungry period, ostrich feathers and theater tickets. I became a foreigner. For myself that is what a writer is—a man living on the other side of a frontier.

ABOUT THE AUTHOR

V. S. PRITCHETT was born in England in 1900. He is a short-story writer, novelist, critic, and traveler. His short-story collections have appeared in the United States under the titles *The Sailor and the Saint* and *When My Girl Comes Home*. Among his novels are *Mr. Beluncle* and *Dead Man Leading*, and *The Key to My Heart*. *The Living Novel and Later Appreciations* is a collection of critical essays, most of which appeared originally in *The New Statesman*. He is now a director of this paper and has been a life-long contributor. He also contributes stories and articles to *The New Yorker, Encounter, Holiday*, and the *New York Review of Books*.

Mr. Pritchett's extensive sojourns in Europe, the Middle East and South America have lead to the writing of several books of travel, the most recent being *The Offensive Traveller*. His books *London Perceived* and *Dublin: A Portrait*, each with photographs by Evelyn Hofer, have been widely acclaimed on both sides of the Atlantic. Mr. Pritchett has also visited the United States, where he gave the Christian Gauss lectures at Princeton, and was recently Beckman Professor at the University of California in Berkeley and writer in residence at Smith College 1966–67.

Mr. Pritchett is married and lives in London.

VINTAGE CRITICISM,
LITERATURE, MUSIC, AND ART